GHOST

James Chambers

Jeff Young

David Sherman

Jody Lynn Nye

L. Jagi Lamplighter

Danielle Ackley-McPhail

David Lee Summers

Gail Z. Martin

Larry N. Martin

Michelle D. Sonnier

Jeffrey Lyman

Bernie Mojzes

Greg Schauer

Other Steampunk Offerings from eSpec Books

Gaslight & Grimm: Steampunk Faerie Tales

The Clockwork Witch by Michelle D. Sonnier

Spirit Seeker by Jeff Young

The Troll King by Jeffrey Lyman

The Fall of Autumn by Jeffrey Lyman

AfterPunk
Steampowered Tales of the Afterlife

Edited By:
Danielle Ackley-McPhail
Greg Schauer

eBooks
Pennsville, NJ

PUBLISHED BY
eSpec Books LLC
Danielle McPhail, Publisher
PO Box 242,
Pennsville, New Jersey 08070
www.especbooks.com

ISBN: 978-1-942990-80-2
ISBN (ebook): 978-1-942990-79-6

Interior Design: Danielle McPhail
Sidhe na Daire Multimedia
www.sidhenadaire.com

Cover Design: Mike McPhail, McP Digital Graphics
Interior border and illustrations © Ed Coutts

Art Credits - www.Shutterstock.com
Baron Samedi © By Kiselev Andrey Valerevich

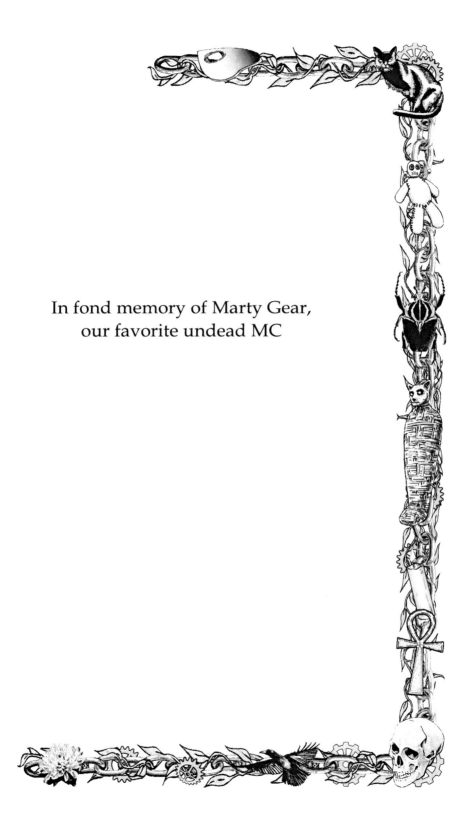

In fond memory of Marty Gear,
our favorite undead MC

Contents

A Feast for Dead Horses

James Chambers

MORRIS GARVEY CLUTCHED A CRUDE SACKCLOTH DOLL WITH A ropy tangle of black hair knotted around its neck and swayed as the steam trolley rocked toward Muhheakantuck Bay. He gripped the overhead strap and willed the machine to travel faster.

"Damn this slow-moving contraption," he said.

Detective Daniel Matheson squinted at his friend. "Trolley's the swiftest way across town this time of day. If'n you wanted real speed, we ought to have saddled up a couple horses."

"Is that how they do it in Texas? Should we gallop along the sidewalks, tramp through Plunkett Square Market, and lasso beggars from our path?"

"If that's what it took, you bet."

"Better New Alexandria should adopt my velocity regulator and double our trolley cars' speed. Some days it seems I've solved half the problems in this city, but the city council won't let me solve the other half."

"Think of the pedestrians trying to steer clear of your sped-up trolleys."

"The city could stand to lose some of its slower-moving populace."

"Morris…

"I'm joking, Dan." Garvey raised the odd doll. "If I'm right about this doll, its death I aim to thwart, which requires we reach the port before Anna Rigel does or at least before the *Port-Au-Prince* docks from Haiti."

"What's Ms. Rigel's beef with Haitians anyway?"

"With Haitians? Nothing at all. With one particular Haitian? Enough that she—as Queen of Witches—cursed him to death should he ever set foot in New Alexandria again. His last visit here had the three of us embroiled in an unfortunate matter of betrayal, involving a novitiate in Anna's coven. Not all his fault, but you know Madame Queen's temper. That he dares defy her means the rats have already nested beneath the cradle. This doll proves it. If I can explain that to Anna, she might stay her curse long enough for us to make sense of those twelve corpses your men found in Pluto's Kitchen."

"I'd be much obliged for that. Don't see what that raggedy doll we found there has to do with this muckety-muck from Haiti, though. I appreciate your aid, Morris, but I swear you take your damn sweet ornery time revealing your intentions."

"If I'm correct you'll know as much as I do soon enough. Are you familiar with the Afro-Carib religion of voodoo?"

"Voodoo, eh?" Matheson's squint deepened and his thick mustache wrinkled.

The trolley jolted and then trundled down Macedonia Hill toward the Muhheakantuck River, glittering in the late-day sun. Graceful sailing ships and powerful steamers traversed its waters. Between the river's bank and the trolley sprawled all lower west New Alexandria, its avenues bustling with raucous crowds, horse-drawn carriages, barking street vendors, and steam-driven trucks. Shadows licked its grimy buildings, a few of which rose higher than the others, fingers of a grasping hand from which the city spilled like a clutch of gravel and ants. White steam plumes and black smoke columns fed a haze that rendered the setting sun a blob of fire on the horizon, consuming the silhouetted hills and buildings of New Carthage across the water. Here and there, gaslights winked on, faint in the twilight, artificial fireflies at the command of the city's lamplighters.

"Well, I can't say I've come by my knowledge firsthand, but I understand voodoo's all about worshipping the *Legba*, bunch'a frightening gods who grant powers from the next world. Love spells, plaguing your enemies, making zombies, and hooey like that. That toy you're hugging is a voodoo doll?"

"A fetish doll, yes. I believe it's the key to your twelve dead men and women."

"How's that?"

The trolley bell clanged as the vehicle rolled into the port station.

"No time to explain now. We're here!"

Garvey leapt from the trolley before it stopped and raced for one of the piers. Detective Matheson followed close behind him, tamping his bowler hat down on his graying head of hair.

"Your hubris is unimaginable, Ricard LeFarge. You surpass even your own past pinnacle of narcissism. I've no idea how you defeated my curse upon you, nor do I care to allow you time to explain. I promised you death when you next set foot in New Alexandria. Now you shall learn I'm a woman who keeps her word."

From within the folds of her sea-green cloak, raven-haired Anna Rigel revealed a sheaf of holly twigs bound with braids of dried night-shade leaves. She shook the bouquet, sweeping air at the tall, lanky man she faced. His rich black skin peeked out from gaps in his leather vest, loose-fitting linen shirt and pants, and the black fur cloak draped from his shoulders. He wore sandals and carried a gnarled length of polished sandalwood as a walking stick. His burgundy panama hat, adorned with a clutch of colorful feathers, shaded his eyes, permitting only hints of white to define his irises.

Around the pair, the crew and passengers disembarking the *Port-Au-Prince* froze in place, fascinated by the confrontation, frightened to come too close, but trapped by Anna who blocked the only exit from the pier.

"Aw, goan now, Madame Queen. Cast your hinky woo-woo magic. You t'ink it can harm de likes of me? I go where I want when I want. Today, dis city is de where, and de when is now. You dare speak to me of death? I come on by de hand of Lord Cemeterie. You jes' forget dat dusty old promise I never took serious in de first place."

"I never forsake my promises, Ricard. More than anyone can say for you."

Anna traced intricate shapes in front of her with the holly branches. She curled her other hand, held it to her lips, and blew through it. Fire flashed out, licked the air, then extinguished, leaving a smoke cloud that gathered to the dried green leaves. Ghostly light crackled about it. Burning holly scent spread on the breeze.

Straightening to his full, intimidating height, LeFarge nudged his hat back and gazed into the cloud, seeking the nature of what magic Anna Rigel meant to unleash at him in such a public place. The Queen of Witches could take things only so far before compelling the city's world-renown constabulary to intercede. Even for one as influential, popular, and feared as Anna Rigel, murder — whether accomplished by means magic or mundane — hardly ever passed overlooked in New Alexandria.

A wisp of smoke tickled Ricard's face. He inhaled, sampling its aromas. His dark eyes widened, and he planted his feet, walking stick braced between them.

"You *are* serious, mon cher! How 'bout dat? Here I expected your intelligence to defeat your pride. Sad, sad, sad, but you goan an' do what you feel you must. I wait right here."

"No, Ricard, you'll die right there."

Waving the smoking holly, Anna initiated a chant. The rhythm quickened, became more strident. Haitian visitors to New Alexandria gaped and murmured. "De Minister of Hoodoo was on our ship?" they said. "Who knew?" "Not I!" "What he want in dis city?" "She goan kill de Minister?" "We must help him!" "Hush, you! De Minister don't need no help from de likes of us." "Dat woman goan be sorry she crossed Ricard LeFarge!" As Anna's spell intensified, the tenor of the crowd shifted from fear to anticipation.

Ricard's unworried expression only fueled her anger.

The holly smoke thickened and condensed, forming a shape, indistinct yet threatening — and then at the precise moment she stood poised to unleash the gathered energy, a voice shouted for her to stop — the voice of the only man she found more stubborn and frustrating than Ricard LeFarge. The smoke sputtered as she hesitated.

"I swear by Hecate, Morris, you better have the most perfect excuse in all the history of excuses for interrupting me, or I'll send you right out of this world with LeFarge."

"I do, Anna. See what I've brought here," Garvey said.

Anna glanced over her shoulder at Garvey and Matheson, both men winded from running. "What is that? A doll? You interrupted me… to show me a *rag doll*?"

"Not at all, Anna. I interrupted you to stop you destroying the one man who might spare New Alexandria the plague of death this doll represents."

"I'm unconvinced."

Anna paced the cellar of the Pluto's Kitchen brownstone at 55 East Major Street, scene of death for twelve men and women, all of whom looked to have died at precisely the same moment while taking part in an orgiastic celebration. Six male and six female, black, biracial, and a few white, all dressed in simple cotton tunics and trousers, bone carvings of horse skulls hanging from leather thongs around their necks. They wore more ornaments of death knotted in their hair. Rat and bird skulls. Cats' claws. Small bones. Bits of leathery flesh and insect husks. One clutched a brightly painted drum of leather decorated with black rooster feathers on his lap. They lay in a ring at the center of which rested a spilled iron pot beside a fire's cold remains. Rust-colored fluid from the pot stained the dirt floor. The odors of wet charcoal and burnt wood barely masked the charnel scent of a dozen bodies commencing decomposition. Further tainting the cellar atmosphere, each corpse bore odd smears of mashed habanero peppers and rum on its face and neck, and the scents of cigar smoke and apples lingered, incongruous and worrisome.

"De *Loa* were here, Madame Queen. No doubt about it. Dat rum-and-pepper mash on de dead one's faces is a ritual anointment. And I smell Papa Ghede's stogies in de air." Ricard stood outside the death circle with Garvey and Matheson, who had sent the police on watch to the first floor. "Papa was here, not for long, but I fear another came wid him, and dat one maybe not yet left us. Dat de one Papa bring me all de way to dis mad city to bother wid."

Anna sniffed. "Another of your endless panoply of saints and loa? I swear you concoct them as you go along."

"Show some respect, witch," said Ricard. "Dis no joke. De *Loa* haunted my dreams for weeks until I board de *Port-Au-Prince* and be on my way. Dey say bad t'ings coming to New Alexandria, t'ings only my eyes may recognize. I come here to help you."

"A self-fulfilling prophecy if you ask me," Anna said.

"What, you t'ink I come back to this forsaken nest of corruption if I had a choice?"

"Please!" said Garvey. "Save your bickering until after we've put the proverbial cat back in the bag. Is that too much to ask?"

"Far too much," Anna said. "But since it is *you* asking, Morris… very well. I'll grant you an opportunity to convince me your fears are justified."

"Much obliged, Madame Queen." Matheson removed his hat and smoothed his hair. "If you'll allow me, I can shed a bit of daylight on this here situation. 'Round midnight last my men got wind of disturbance here and found this lot of corpses. No signs of violence or other means of death…poison, asphyxiation, or whatnot. Appears they all simply dropped dead, like they were struck by a bolt out of the blue. I asked Mr. Garvey for his advice. He took a look at that doll we found and right off he sets to work his Sundry Troubleshooters. Those street urchins he employs like extra eyes and ears got us word of Mr. LeFarge's pending arrival. That fit some piece into a puzzle only Mr. Garvey can see, and without so much as a word of explanation, we hustled off to find you at the pier."

"I'm wearily familiar with Morris' penchant for playing his hand close to the vest, my dear Detective. Your explanation leaves nearly as much to the imagination," said Anna.

Garvey said, "I knew, Anna, that you would move heaven and earth to keep your word to LeFarge. But his arrival in the wake of these deaths couldn't be coincidence. We need him, and I wished to stay your vengeful hand. Trust me, though, when I say little in this situation is what it seems. We should be grateful for Ricard's help."

"What else could've struck these people dead so quickly but some kind of spirit?" said Matheson.

"*Loa*," LeFarge said.

"Excuse me?" said Matheson.

"One of de *Loa*, not a spirit. De *Loa* are more den spirits. To understand a t'ing, you need to know its proper name."

"Okay, then, one of the *Loa* killed these people."

"Since when, Detective Matheson, do you believe in such… ah, what have you called it in the past? Such 'superstitious claptrap,' I believe. Yes, exactly your words."

"Yes, well, Madame Queen, I've learned a lot since, seen some things, heard others. I'm smart enough to see the steer for the horns," said Matheson.

"Really, must we waste what time remains to spare thousands an ugly, premature death debating metaphysics?" Garvey shook his head. "The *Loa* couldn't care less if you believe in them, Anna."

"Oh, dey care, Mr. Garvey. Dey care very much," LeFarge said.

"My point is, we have bigger chimneys to sweep." Garvey gestured to the ring of corpses. "Mr. LeFarge, I wonder if you've noticed the same thing I have about this crime scene, the very thing that set me hurrying off to save you from Anna's wrath?"

"Didn't need saving by de likes of you. I had Madame Queen's attentions well in hand."

Garvey laughed. "I've thought the same many times only to learn otherwise. Now if you wouldn't mind sticking to the matter at hand, please?"

"Aye, I see." LeFarge pointed to more leather drums, black rooster feathers strung from their skins, in a corner, outside the circle, scattered where the drummer had dropped them. "Dey danced de *banda*, but where is de Bocor?"

"What's a 'bocor?'" said Matheson.

"A voodoo priest," Anna said.

"A priest turned to de dark forces of de *Loa*," said LeFarge. "I too am a priest, but I am *houngan*, not *bocor*. I serve my people and life, not me own self and death."

"The point is," Garvey said, "we're missing a bocor. The implication is clear."

"Maybe to you," Matheson said.

"To come into dis world, Detective, de *Loa* ride a body. Dis one, maybe he took de bocor and rode it right out into de madness you call a city."

"We have a death *Loa* loose in New Alexandria," said Garvey.

"How do we find him, or them, or whatever?" Matheson said.

"Only one way," LeFarge said. "We search."

Outside the brownstone, LeFarge produced a handful of bones from a pocket. He knelt on the corner, shook them in his closed hand, and then spilled them out onto the cobblestone. After several seconds spent studying how they fell, he scooped them up and repeated the action. He eyed them and shook his head. Once more he cast the bones, again producing only frustration.

"What dey say makes no sense," LeFarge said.

A horse whinnied. A second answered. The *clip-clop, clip-clop* of hooves echoed along the streets and alleys, their sound brittle and harsh in an abrupt silence that had fallen.

"Hey, now, what the devil?" said Matheson. "Where'd everybody go?"

They all looked up from LeFarge's bones. Not a soul in a sight anywhere, an unthinkable occurrence for evening in Pluto's Kitchen, when dive bars and cheap kitchens opened for brisk business and streetwalkers plied their trade to men returning home from a day's labor. Gone, the vendors and newsboys hawking evening editions. Absent, gangs of children hustling for food and pennies. Missing, the endless parade of stray cats and dogs begging for scraps, of rats and mice and pigeons, of flies that clouded above the stinking gutters, garbage piles, and drunks passed out in doorways.

"LeFarge, did you do this? Where did everyone go?" Anna's voice shed all its anger and obstinacy, adopting a new, serious tone. The horses neared, hooves knocking the cobblestones with a drum-like beat.

"Not me. And de people didn't go nowhere. We did," LeFarge said.

"What do you mean?" said Garvey.

In answer, LeFarge gestured at the mouth of an alley, where the shadows of two horses wavered in a growing fog creeping along the ground. The beasts themselves soon appeared. Both coal black with long, ragged manes and bodies far taller and more muscular than average horses, they paused in the street and snorted. Fog flowed from their nostrils and sank to the road. Their eyes glittered like embers. One chewed on a bloodied black arm as if it had torn the limb straight from its shoulder socket. The other gnawed on the gore-crusted neck of a black man missing that arm as well as both his legs. The first horse snapped its head, consuming flesh, crunching bone, and squirting blood as it chewed. After it swallowed, it neighed once then bit into the remaining arm on the torso clenched in its companion's mouth. The two horses tussled over the body until the arm ripped free, and then the horse devoured it like the first.

"Been around horses all my life," Matheson said. "Never seen the likes of that."

"Everyone back inside, now!" said Garvey.

He pushed the others ahead of him up the brownstone steps, but they found the front door locked tight. Matheson banged on it and shouted for his men to open up. No one answered. He cupped his hands over his eyes and peered in through a window beside the door.

"There's… no one there! My men are gone," he said.

"Dey all right where you left dem, Mister Detective," LeFarge said. "We de ones gone."

"*Where* have we gone, LeFarge?" said Garvey.

"No place good. Dose two horses, dey called Chenét and Zonbi, and dey forever hungry. Eat a dozen souls, it still not fill dem up. Soon's dey finish dat poor one, dey come after us."

"Let's go to my lab. We can figure this out there," Garvey said. "Anna, can you conceal us?"

"What *have* you gotten me into, Morris?" Anna said.

"A horse's belly, I fear, if we don't make a swift departure," said Garvey. "Maybe you should save your questions for later."

Anna sighed. She gesticulated above her head, whispering words so low no one but she understood them. When she finished, the horses interrupted their meal and gazed along the street, seeking the prey that had vanished from sight. They whinnied, stamped their hooves, and snorted streams of fog. Footsteps answered them. A third shadow joined them, the silhouette of a tall, gangly man with wiry, distended limbs, and a head much too large for his neck. The stink of cigar smoke — as if from cigars fashioned from hair, dead skin, and dung tobacco — filled the air. A sudden, basso laughter echoed among the dead buildings

"We must go!" LeFarge gripped Anna's arm, ignoring the expression of insulted disgust she flashed at his touch and guided her through an alley to a neighboring street. "Which way to Mr. Garvey's lab?"

Anna pointed even as Garvey and Matheson caught up, shouting "Follow us!"

They swept them into a race through the city and its shortcuts, thundering hoof beats hot on their trail.

"It makes my skin crawl to see your lab so quiet and dark, Morris," Anna said. "Not even your urchin mob of Troubleshooters running about."

Garvey cleared a worktable, pushing aside gears, nuts, bolts, screws, pins, wires, and an inscrutable, half-built, octagonal gadget with several glass bulbs affixed to it. The clang of metal sounded dull, as if heard through falling snow. Gaslights burned dim, their luminescence sapped, producing a thick gloom of flickering shadows in the enormous space that occupied the heart of the block-long Machinations Sundry building. Rows of worktables piled with machines, gauges, chemicals, meters, scales, burners, and tools stood abandoned. Garvey's researchers typically worked round the clock, tinkering and testing, lights burning bright and long, work unceasing. The uncanny absence of life here inspired unfamiliar sensations of dread in Garvey. A rational man, he liked rational situations with rational solutions. His current predicament, he feared, involved neither.

"What is dis place?" LeFarge said.

"This here's Morris' playground," said Matheson. "It's where he cobbles together bits of metal and steam into miracles — or menaces, depending on your perspective."

"This is the heart of Morris Garvey's Steam Sweeps and Machinations Sundry. It's where I invented the steampowered chimney sweeps that earned my first fortune, and where I continue to fabricate devices to improve life in New Alexandria. It's at the center of the city's most secure building. We ought to be safe long enough to sort out what's happened." Garvey placed the doll on the cleared worktable. "Mr. LeFarge, can you tell us who that was with the horses?"

LeFarge shrugged. He frowned at the voodoo doll and drew a penknife from his pocket. He stabbed the doll, startling the others, then cut the cloth from neck to crotch, leaving the hair tied round its neck intact. Parting the hole, he reached into the stuffing, a mix of dust, dirt, dried leaves, and rotted flesh scraps still bearing tufts of fur. His hand sank in deeper than the width of the doll, reaching past even the table upon which it lay, descending nearly up to his elbow. When he withdrew his hand, blood spurted from the opening. It coated LeFarge's fingers and wrist. In his cupped palm rested thirteen miniature, pulsing hearts, slicked red with blood. They squirmed like grubs unearthed in the sun. He showed them to the others and then spilled them back into the doll, which received them eagerly, sucking back all the blood, rendering LeFarge's hand dry.

"De *Loa* who claims Chenét and Zonbi, his heart brims wid hate for de living. He stalks de underworld wid his horses. Dere hunger never ends. De very moment dey fill dere bellies wid a soul, dey become ravenous for de next. Dis Loa did not ride de bocor to New Alexandria as I t'ought. It brought de bocor into de underworld. Dey left open de door to de next world, and we walked right t'rough into de land of de first man ever to commit murder, Baron Kriminel."

"Who?" Matheson said.

"One of de *Ghede*, de *Loa* of life and death. Papa Ghede, he de first man ever died, and he bring de dead into de underworld. De Baron be one of his, but he do de work of evil. Good people have no truck wid de Baron."

"What does he want from New Alexandria?" Garvey said.

"What de Baron always want: *death*. De dead in de circle sacrificed dere hearts to make de fetish doll and call him down. Dey tied dere own hairs around its neck, and when dere hearts stopped beating in de living world, de doll trapped dem in the next. Now de Baron wants back de doll you swiped from de house, Mr. Garvey, and when he feeds dose hearts to his horses, dey be set free in your city to run death rampant through its streets for as long as de hearts keep beating in dere bellies. When de living pass on, dey spend a year and a day in de underworld before finding final peace. De Baron wants as many dead as he can take to feed his hungry horses. A year and a day of horse food he means to take from New Alexandria."

Matheson removed his bowler, wiped his arm across his brow, and then replaced his hat with a firm tug. "Why would anyone perform such a ritual, Mr. LeFarge?"

"De Baron has his followers."

"You mean a cult? I *hate* cults. Why does every crackpot cult find its damn way to New Alexandria?"

"Baron Kriminel, his cult's don' last too long. He like to promise anyt'ing, everyt'ing you want, but he never means to deliver."

"As trustworthy as you, Ricard," said Anna.

"You really must learn to let the past go, Madame Queen," Garvey said.

"I prefer not to."

Matheson said, "Maybe the bocor who did this can undo it. Where do y'all think he's gone?

"I fear we already met him, in de horses' mouths, learning de hard way 'bout de Baron's treachery."

"Well, he's no help then," said Matheson. "Say we stop those hearts from beating. Can we prevent the horses getting loose?"

LeFarge shook his head. "We got no power to do dat here. In de living world, we could cut de hairs tied round the doll's neck and sever de t'ing dat links de dead hearts to de world. Dat would close de door. But de only way back is if Papa Ghede permits us to return."

Anna folded her arms across her chest. "Nonsense! I don't need permission to go where I wish, especially not in my city."

"What do you have in mind?" Garvey said.

"My own means of opening doors. We need to return to 55 Major Street. The Veil is still thin there."

Rumbling laughter reverberated through the lab before anyone could reply. A thunderous stamping followed in preface to a shower of wood and iron where the doors on the far side of the lab exploded. Horses neighed, and fog rolled in, crawling around the vacant lab tables.

"No time for dat! Dey found us already," LeFarge said. "Dere nowhere left to run."

Chenét and Zonbi strolled into the lab and whinnied, their cries anguished, needful, and burdened with hunger. Behind them came Baron Kriminel. He wore a rotting top hat with black feathers threaded into its band and puffed on a smoldering cigar. Shirtless, his deep black torso gleamed in the murk of smoke and fog, and displayed all manner of violent wounds from knife slashes to bullet holes to machete cuts and a slit across his throat from which smoke wafted. He grinned wide, and his chunky, white teeth shimmered in his skeletal face. His horses looked lost, still unable to see their prey guarded by Anna's spell, so hungry they took turns biting each other and swallowing chunks of their brother's flesh. The Baron looked straight across the lab, unbothered by the Queen of Witches' magic. He exhaled a cloud of smoke, tipped his hat, and laughed.

"We're not going to run," Garvey said. "We're going to ride."

Garvey's prototype high-speed trolley rolled out of the Machinations Sundry garage with Chenét and Zonbi in fevered pursuit. With Matheson's aid, Garvey piloted the machine along the ghostly trolley rails of New Alexandria's underworld analog. The velocity regulator raised the efficiency of the steam system to drive the car with several times more power than the standard engine. Despite the underworld's dampening effect, it exceeded three times the standard trolley speed. Garvey and Matheson wore goggles against the wind whipping through the cabin. Anna tugged her cloak's hood close to her face. Le-Farge hugged the fetish doll to his chest with one hand and kept the other pressed down on his Panama hat, its feathers fluttering. He stood in back of the car, watching the horses give chase.

"Chenét and Zonbi have our scent," he said. "Dey gaining ground."

"Don't worry yet." Garvey pointed to a control board near Matheson. "Flip that red lever and then twist the dial beside it to 13.5, would you, Dan?"

The trolley surged after Matheson completed the adjustments, rounding a curve so fast it teetered at the whim of gravity for several seconds before righting itself and clanking into Pluto's Kitchen. Chenét and Zonbi dropped behind then picked up their pace but soon fell out of sight in the neighborhood's labyrinthine streets.

"Now, Dan, now! Hit the brake," Garvey shouted.

Matheson yanked the tall brake handle. Steel wheels shrieked and spit up sparks from the track. Garvey's virtuoso fingers played the velocity regulator's master control board. The trolley ground to a shuddering halt a few blocks from 55 Major Street.

"God in heaven, Morris! You want to unleash that kind of reckless power on the city?" Matheson said. "Pardon me, but I'll take my damn, sweet time before I ride in your mad trolley again."

"Don't be daft, Dan. The point of the velocity regulator is to *regulate* the velocity. One doesn't need to run at full speed to benefit." Garvey worked the board and primed the engine to build up fresh steam. "And you won't have to worry about another ride. The three of you are getting off here."

"Not you?" Anna pushed her hood back, revealing wind-burned cheeks.

"I'm going to deal with Chenét and Zonbi while you open our door home. Have it ready by the time I get back here, will you?"

Garvey sounded the trolley's whistle, a dying soprano's last breath, and then rang its bell. He commenced back the way they had come. A glance revealed LeFarge and Matheson dragging Anna up the street, urging her to let him go and get about opening the door to the living world.

The trolley rounded a corner, and Garvey spied the horses.

Blowing fog from their nostrils, they stopped when the trolley rolled into view. On the sidewalk, Baron Kriminel stood, laughing, spectator to the brewing contest between underworld beasts and hard steel and brass. Garvey built the steam to maximum pressure and ratcheted open the regulator all the way. The dark city became a blur. Wind sliced by so fast it achieved silence.

The horses stamped and then charged.

Baron Kriminel's amused uproar cut through the air.

In a cloud of steam and fog, the trolley and the horses collided.

Garvey leapt free in the moment before impact, rolling on the cobblestone, pain shooting up his left arm as it cracked against the curb. The Baron's laughter sounded like hail. His horses screamed. Iron squealed and snapped as the trolley car demolished itself against the animals, who attacked it with hoof and tooth, attempting to devour whatever part of it they could grasp with their bite.

Garvey coddled his broken arm against his abdomen and raced to the brownstone.

Matheson held the front door, waving him in, his expression telegraphing that Chenét and Zonbi followed not far behind him.

They slammed the door shut and bolted to the cellar.

Anna chanted a spell inside the ring of corpses.

Upstairs, hooves beat against the door, which crashed and splintered, and the Baron laughed.

LeFarge handed the fetish doll to Garvey.

"Take dis. I have blessed it and begged Papa Ghede's intervention. When you reach de living world, cut de hairs. De door will close if it is Papa's will."

"If not?" said Garvey.

"Den death comes to New Alexandria, and dat be his will."

Footsteps sounded overhead like canonfire. The cellar door shattered and showered down the stairs. Within the circle of the dead, light bathed Anna. The living world existed in its brightness, contained by corpses and the underworld gloom. "Into the circle with me!" Anna cried.

Chenét and Zonbi jostled down the stairs, tripping over each other, snapping off bits of bannister with their teeth. Garvey and Matheson leapt over the corpses into the circle, the sudden light stinging their eyes.

"Come, LeFarge!" Garvey yelled.

Instead, the houngan stepped into the horses' path. Chenét clamped down on his arm, and Zonbi seized one of his legs. They chewed, tore, and pulled, until LeFarge's body ripped apart in gory, uneven halves. Baron Kriminel's laughter reached a horrifying volume that resounded even after Anna ended her spell and closed the way between the living and the dead. His voice and the stamping of his horses hounded them across the Veil.

"My sweet god! I still hear that murdering bastard laughing," said Matheson.

"Not for long, Papa Ghede willing."

Garvey opened a pen knife and sliced the ring of hair.

It dropped from the fetish doll.

The laughter ceased. The doll split at its seams. Clumps of rotted stuffing spilled out, among them thirteen stones that dropped to the floor. Garvey kicked them, scattering them apart, revealing them as thirteen shriveled, hardened hearts. He ground each one to dust beneath his heels.

Cigar smoke and apples. Papa Ghede's scents filled the room.

A handful of shocked police officers trampled down the steps.

"Papa answered LeFarge's plea," Garvey said.

"And Anna's curse was fulfilled," said Matheson. "A good man died."

"Simply because one does good, does not make one a good man, Detective," said Anna.

"I have my doubts about your curse working," Garvey said.

"You doubt *my* powers?" said Anna.

A porter escorted them to a cabin onboard the *Port-Au-Prince* still docked at the pier.

Anna and Matheson quit trying to persuade Garvey to explain himself, resigned to following him to the answers they desired. He knocked on the cabin door. A hearty voice from within bid them enter. They did and found Ricard LeFarge, alive and well, awaiting them inside.

He sat in a high-backed wicker chair, a thin, frail vision of the man they had all seen devoured by Baron Kriminel's horses. A young, black girl in a yellow dress stood to his right, and to his left a stocky, bald man with one leg and an eye-patch leaned on a fat crutch.

Anna approached and poked him, one eyebrow raised, dubious.

"Yes, Madame Queen, it's me, alive and in de flesh," LeFarge said.

"Explain," said Anna.

The two attendants busied themselves with a table set with a bountiful lunch and bottles of wine.

"I knew your curse would strike me dead de moment I set foot in New Alexandria. But I had to come because Papa Ghede willed it. I arranged another way to enter de city. Baron and Papa are not de only Loa wid power over life and death. A few of de others owe me favors. All de time I was wid you, my body lay on dis ship, dead to de world, while my spirit joined you, and I never really touched ground inside your city. You saw only my ghost devoured by Chenét and Zonbi. When de door closed, Papa left a crack for me to escape and return to my body. Never underestimate de power of de very Minister of Hoodoo himself. Now let's eat! All dat running around, I'm so hungry, I could eat a—."

"I swear, Mr. LeFarge, if you say 'horse,' I'll carry you ashore myself so Anna's curse can work its business," Matheson said.

"What do you say, Anna? Temporary truce?" Garvey said.

Anna's eyes darkened, and she frowned. "Well," she said, "I find myself with quite an uncharacteristic appetite so for this one time I'll restrain my natural inclinations."

Beyond the Familiar

JEFF YOUNG

"The departed have better things to do than talk to you."

Kassandra met that statement from Madam Foss with a canted eyebrow.

"Look at me like that all you want, girl, but it's still the truth." The old medium tipped her teacup back and drank down the last dregs as Kassandra waited for her to continue. "It may sound absurd, but the dead don't always have an interest in the price of butter. They've moved on. They've joined the grand choir. They've earned their reward. They've other concerns."

Kassandra couldn't help but notice that as Madam Foss delivered her last comment her eyes drifted off to the right and she lifted the cup for another sip only to find she'd already emptied it. Kassandra enjoyed her time with her new mentor, surrounded by the scents of old book leather and candle wax, which made her feel at home. However, she often found that what Madam Foss avoided was as important as that which she relayed. Kassandra's father was the one who'd set up this apprenticeship, rather to her amazement. He'd told her that

despite whatever he felt, it appeared she was taking after her mother's spiritual prowess, and the least he could do was introduce her to someone who could keep her safe.

Because it was expected of her, she asked, "Well, Madam Foss, how does one engage with the departed? My former teacher had the poor taste to rob graves, then force the spirits to speak."

Madam Foss's dark, wrinkled visage puckered up even farther, as if she'd been offered something scraped off of the road outside. "You and I will be avoiding any such wrongdoing. What we do is like a tool. You can build a house with it or lash about doing all sorts of damage. Such behavior has the potential of not only hurting others, but also yourself." With that, one of her brown fingers shot out and dug into Kassandra's chest. "You will be better than that wretch."

Leaning away, seemingly so she could reach for her tea while conveniently putting herself out of range of that finger, Kassandra considered her mentor. Madam Foss kept her hand outstretched for a moment longer and then settled back into her own chair. "We speak to the dead through intermediaries. There are those that are just as restless in death as they were in life. They can find the spirits we need to speak to and if those are unwilling to speak, the intermediaries can carry messages."

"They are familiars," Kassandra said suddenly, pleased with herself at the realization.

The chair creaked as Madam Foss lunged toward her once again, finger pointed, and then thought better of the action. She clutched her hands together, staring at Kassandra. "I keep forgetting that you are so much older than most who are brought to me." She shook her head, the gray curls swaying under her bonnet. "You like to think for yourself instead of listening like a younger apprentice would. Girl, if you say 'familiar' to anyone else, they'll be crying witchcraft in no time at all. What we do has nothing to do with the darkness we were discussing before. Perhaps spirits do become familiar and perhaps that's why they take such a name, but the common man knows that term only as evil. We speak to *intermediaries*, and to intermediaries only. We are mediums. The dead speak to us and we speak for them. That's all that matters. When someone decides they know better than we do, that's when words like 'evil' and 'witch' get tossed about. That's when they start gathering tinder."

She considered Kassandra for a moment longer, her dark eyes squinting as if she could see inside her charge. Then the passage of a dirigible droning by overhead broke her focus. She stood up suddenly and gestured for Kassandra to follow her. Setting aside her teacup, Kassandra brushed the front of her brown dress down and then stepped after her mentor as she crossed the sitting room and walked through the foyer.

A large staircase rose into the dimness of the upper level, dividing the house. Past it were a pair of large wooden doors. Kassandra had spent most of her time in the sitting room and the kitchen during her visits. They hadn't ventured beyond that until now. Madam Foss pulled out a large brass key, unlocked the doors, and then threw them wide. Dark curtains covered the windows in what appeared to be a converted dining room. Wooden chairs with caned bottoms had been spread around the perimeter, and a rich rug covered the floor. But what drew Kassandra's attention was the table at the center.

It was circular and draped in deep red velvet. A wooden disk lay on top only slightly smaller in diameter. At its center was a hole through which braided copper wires rose from inside the table to latch on to the Jacob's Ladder that climbed halfway to the ceiling. Copper threads chased across the wooden circle in strange patterns and two brass handgrips were mounted close enough for easy use. A leather-backed chair was pushed up to the table in front of the grips.

Madam Foss pulled back the chair and said to Kassandra, "Sit."

Before they'd merely been conversing. The tone that the medium took with her now was one that dropped Kassandra into the chair before she even considered rebelling. Instinctively, she reached out for the grips. They were so cold to her touch that she almost pulled away, but a sharp glance from Madam Foss made her keep her hands in place. The older woman reached down and turned a large crank that was just visible under the edge of the tablecloth. As she did so, a crackle snapped through the air and a flicker of static flew up the Jacob's Ladder, then another and another until visible arcs ascended toward the top and dissipated into the surrounding air. The copper wiring on the tabletop danced with fat blue sparks until the current hit Kassandra, shooting her hair out in all directions. Her red curls unfurled like a corona about her.

"Now you know why I wear a bonnet," came Madam Foss's dry comment.

But Kassandra scarcely paid attention. Her skin, her pores, her mouth, her eyes, her ears—every exit from her wept thin, translucent streams. Not water. Ectoplasm. Madam Foss had called it the insulation between worlds at one point. There it was, real as real could be, right before Kassandra. Gradually, the silver substance collected in a sphere over the table. When Kassandra looked down at the design in copper with its circles about the handgrips, she realized that it was designed to help keep the ectoplasm contained. The Jacob's Ladder overhead bled off just the right amount of static to keep the circuit she completed safe. More and more ectoplasm poured from her until the sphere swelled to twice the size of her head. She looked at it closely and discovered that it was spinning ever so slightly. Instinctively, she lunged forward out of the chair, and without a thought to Madam Foss's concerns plunged her head into the silver mass.

At first she didn't notice anything. It was almost as if her eyes were adjusting to a dark room. She definitely wasn't sitting at the table any longer. There came a faint sound that might be footsteps and a light breeze blew across her face. Gradually, she realized that she was looking down what she could only describe as a path. It was so straight and long that perspective vanished into the distance. She could see a little of what looked like woods to either side but couldn't actually move her point of view. It was as if her head weren't with her any longer, only her eyes. There were shapes and shadows ahead of her, however they were so far down the path they were more like suggestions or imperfections in the overall pattern. Then one of the shadows off to the side grew darker and became more defined. It stepped onto the path and crossed it quickly. Briefly, it hesitated. For the tiniest part of an instant, Kassandra had the impression of a dark cloaked form turning to stare at her before it faded into the other side.

The last time Kassandra had seen the shade of her mother, Anastasia, she'd worn a dark cloak. If there was any spirit she wished to speak to most it was certainly her. If Mother were to become her familiar spirit...pardon...her *intermediary*, it would be almost perfect. But the figure was gone. The path faded as Madam Foss's iron grip pulled her forcibly back into the chair and thus the mortal realm.

As Kassandra sat there gasping, her hands torn from the brass grips, Madam Foss considered her, hands akimbo. "Should've known you were going to do that. From now on, you head-strong girl, you listen to me, if you plan on staying on. The other side doesn't take kindly to intruders. There are things that keep us out. That's the important part. We *talk* to the other side. You don't get to visit unless you're planning on staying. Now you just sit back and I'll get you another cup of tea. Your heart's gonna race and be out of rhythm for a little and it's likely you'll have trouble catching your breath. You're young, so you'll do fine, but it'll hurt."

With that she reached underneath, pulled the handle she'd cranked into place against the underside of the table. As the apparatus threw out a few stray sparks, she patted Kassandra on the shoulder and wandered off after the tea.

While Kassandra sat there blinking, black spots chased across her vision as her heart thumped away like a swallow trapped in a chimney. She knew she would have a few moments to herself while Madam Foss fiddled away with the new autobrewer that she'd bought to make her tea. Her mind was racing. Kassandra had seen what she would dare say was heaven. Well, she'd seen the other side, anyway.

It wasn't anything like she'd expected.

In the weeks that followed, Kassandra continued to take a carriage across town from her father's home to call upon Madam Foss. Their relationship, however, had definitely changed. In short, Kassandra's task was to observe everything. While she hadn't been invited to sit at the table again, she found herself instead introduced as Madam Foss's assistant and was called upon to help the medium with her clientele. She took coats, made tea, and seated herself demurely behind Madam Foss while the woman asked questions of the departed. She noted, that while Madam Foss did the talking, the strange apparitions, which appeared over the table, had no voices. It didn't take her long to realize that Madam Foss was in fact reading the lips of her spirit guests. Kassandra soon began to learn the art herself.

One morning, she'd stolen into the sitting room to discover what her mentor had been looking at during their initial meeting. The bookshelf across from where she'd sat had a conspicuously empty spot. Reaching into the void, she'd found a small daguerreotype image. In the scratchy image a small ebony-faced child with heavy brows and a long nose held a cicada in their hands. The likeness reminded her of Madam Foss and the black curly hair could easily have turned gray.

Kassandra carefully replaced the picture, brushing the dust back into place.

Two days later, while Madam Foss was cursing at her automated tea brewer, Kassandra slipped into the table room. She noticed that all of the chairs in the "working room," as Madam Foss called it, were attached to the floor and the various knickknacks were affixed to the surfaces they rested upon. She'd felt the odd lightness produced by opening the way with ectoplasm and imagined things might become chaotic if not controlled. She'd taken an unsupervised moment to examine the table further and found the name Emond Ressex engraved on the wooden panel where the crank fitted in. Kassandra had heard of his reputation as a spiritualist and artificer.

After watching several sessions, it was obvious to Kassandra that when she'd sat the table that first time, she'd merely begun the process of contacting the other side. Once Madam Foss had the requisite amount of ectoplasm collected, she would call out seeking an intermediary. Someone she referred to as Jasper often answered her. A caricature of a vaguely familiar face would then form on the surface of the ectoplasmic sphere. His answers were given by the motion of his lips without the evidence of any sound.

Madam Foss's intermediary appeared well informed. After a short wait, he told an elderly man that his wife had sold off her jewels before she passed away and where she'd hid the money. Another was informed that the property line that he believed was incorrectly drawn was accurate, however there was no way to prove it. A loved one was assured that their lost child was happy. The woman in black was told that her husband was in fact not dead but had run away.

Kassandra found herself admiring Madam Foss's ability to deal with all of these pronouncements. As far as Kassandra could tell, Madam Foss hadn't lied to any of them. She hadn't made them all happy either, but in the end they'd all paid her. Kassandra watched them as they'd left and noticed something different about each one. Something was lighter in their step; there was an absence of tension in their expressions or less of a slump to their shoulders. In each case the person who'd passed beyond—or had run off—left their supplicant with a need for closure. Madam Foss had given them that. It didn't matter whether they left in their carriage, steampowered auto, or simply walked, each left as though a weight were lifted from them. It occurred to Kassandra that this ability was one she admired.

As much as she watched and learned, it wasn't enough. She desperately wanted to call for the ectoplasm once again and seek out the dark-cloaked figure she'd seen in the way between the worlds of the living and the dead. The reoccurring image in her imagination made her want to try something reckless, only Madam Foss had shown herself to be very observant and Kassandra was certain she would know if her student had used the table.

One afternoon, after a long session with an attorney seeking information about one of his less savory clients, Madam Foss sighed heavily and put a hand to her forehead. "I feel a fever coming on. Child, could you make me a cup of tea? I believe perhaps I should rest for the remainder of the day."

Kassandra did as her mentor asked, choosing the chamomile in the hope that it might make Madam Foss feel better. After a few sips, the old woman leaned back in her chair with a sigh. "I don't think I am up to dealing with the remaining appointment I have today. Can you be a dear and stay on to let them know that I won't be available? If you can, please reschedule them." She gestured offhandedly at the ledger clipped to the table behind her. "It won't be but an hour. Then you can go home." Then she pulled herself up to her feet unsteadily. Kassandra came to her side and helped her to the foot of the stairs. As she turned to ascend them, the old woman's hand clamped onto Kassandra's wrist. "I can trust you to take care of this, can't I?"

"Of course," Kassandra said, "It's no trouble at all." She watched the old woman make her way up the stairs and then went to recover the cup with its remaining tea.

Once she was in the working room again, Kassandra turned and faced the table. It would be so easy to sit down, but to do so would violate Madam Foss's trust. She tamped down the temptation and turned for the tea. It wasn't where she expected it. Instead the cup sat on the same table as the ledger. Shaking her head, she grasped the cup and found it oddly cold. Something moved on the edge of her vision and she turned quickly to find herself staring at her own image in the large mirror on the wall there. She was definitely nervous being left alone in the working room and it was starting to play on her nerves. Kassandra shook her head to clear her thoughts and started back to the kitchen. Tired herself, her feet shuffled across the carpet. She stared down at the teacup trying to martial her thoughts. Once again she felt that strange sense of being observed. But this time when she looked back to the mirror, her image had changed. Silver covered her lips and spun in wisps down her chin. Ectoplasm.

She rushed over to the mirror in fascination. As she did so more ectoplasm flowed from her. Only then did she look down at her feet and realize why. Static. She'd been rushing across the carpet and building up a static charge. Somehow this, like the charge of the table, brought on an ectoplasmic discharge. The tea cup in her hand forgotten, she leaned closer. The ectoplasm didn't flow like water. It was oddly wispy, almost like spider silk. A trickle came from her ears and nose as well as from her eyes. When she ran a hand over her face it clung unevenly to her fingers. That was when she noticed the first strands flowing from her to the mirror.

As she opened her mouth, a gush of silvery filaments splashed onto the glass in front of her. Gradually, the ectoplasm spread over the entirety of the surface. Webbings of light and shadow laced the distorted reflection. A frisson of panic ran through her. What had she done? And how could she undo it? A finger drawn across her lips assured her that no more ectoplasm gathered there. Perhaps it was time to confess to Madam Foss. As much as she was loath to admit it, Kassandra was definitely out of her depth.

She strode across the carpet, careful to lift her feet. At the doorway, she hesitated. When she turned back to look at the mirror, she watched in amazement as a black-clad figure swept through the opening as though it were a window. Her fingers spasmed and the teacup fell to shatter across the floor. In that second, the specter dissolved into a mass of black mist that flew up to the ceiling. It clung there roiling like a black thundercloud and then shot out of the room. Kassandra followed it through the doorway.

Sliding across the tiled floor, she scrambled for the staircase seeking Madam Foss. As her foot struck the first riser, something crunched beneath her shoe. She grasped the banister to steady herself and felt things crackling and falling to pieces under her hand. A light brown object swung in front of her view. It caught in her hair as it fell over her face. She pulled it out and came to a halt staring at the cicada skin with a strand of her red hair still caught in its claws. When she turned around, she brushed aside more and more of the casings. They covered the stairway underfoot and clung to the threads of her brown tweed dress. As her head turned she felt more of them caught in her hair, spilling down her back and her blouse. The experience was so unexpected, she briefly forgot about the apparition she ran from. That was when she heard the humming above her, echoing in the stairwell.

It was a rustling sound, like leaves, but it also had a strange note to it reminiscent of a dynamo as it swelled and ebbed. When they began to sing, Kassandra knew what she was facing. The reason she could not see the lights in the upper hall was because it was filled with an enormous mass of cicadas. A sheer wall of glistening black carapaces, flickering veined wings, and tiny red eyes. It rippled as the insects clambered over one another in a constant twitching dance. Then the center of the mass pushed outward toward her. Starting at the top of the stairs, a shape began to emerge, coalescing from the horde of cicadas. Clutching at the banister, she saw the cloaked figure from the mirror emerge from the wall of insects, its form made up of the same clicking accumulation. She was gasping now, heart racing. As she retreated, it stepped forward, the rest of the cicadas dropping from its shoulders like an obscene cape.

Kassandra felt her foot strike the tiled floor of the foyer. Was this the same spirit she had seen during her trip under the ectoplasm? The one she'd thought was her mother? She reached down and pulled off her mother's gold ring on her right hand, holding it before her. The whirring mass of cicadas continued to block her path. It had not reacted to the ring. Did that perhaps mean this wasn't her mother's shade, but rather something that had mimicked her to gain Kassandra's trust? Sucking in a breath, she stepped forward and in sync with her, the cicada shade stepped down the staircase. The shroud of insects parted to reveal its face, a mask of silver. The ectoplasm limned it in fine relief bringing out the long nose and heavy brows of a young man.

She understood now, this was a test. She might have convinced Madam Foss that she was worthy of her apprenticeship, but had she convinced the spirits? The features she'd seen covered in ectoplasm snapped into place in her memory. The picture. What if it was a relative... a brother...a nephew...a *son...*? One who had died. A spirit that would be eager to come when she called. Add fifteen years and the child in the picture could well have grown into the form before her.

"Jasper," Kassandra said on a taut breath.

The cicadas shifted uneasily.

Placing her empty hands out in front of her, palms up, Kassandra said, "Jasper, your mother believes that I have potential. I hope that you do as well."

The mass of insects continued down the stairs step by step until it stood before her. Gradually, the cicadas parted until the rest of the silvery form came to light underneath their bodies. Its hand reached out and a sharp finger poked her once above her heart in a very familiar gesture. Then it walked past her, turning toward the working room. The long cape of cicadas swept the floor as it passed through the doorway. Everywhere the insects touched, the shells that littered the ground vanished in silvery bubbles.

When she was finally able to breathe, she saw the cloud of cicadas stripped away from Jasper's ethereal form launch itself through the ectoplasm-hazed surface of the mirror. Jasper turned toward her and beckoned. Steeling her courage, she approached the spirit. When she stood before him, Jasper reached for her. Kassandra did her best not to flinch away. The silvery hands covered her face like a mask blocking out all light and Kassandra felt a water-like chill coat her skin. When at last something impinged on her senses, she once again found herself looking at the same strange path as when she'd thrust her head into the ectoplasm sphere.

She could feel Jasper beside her. His hands touched her face again, turning her. Now she could see that beyond the path and the stands of white-barked birch trees, rose towers and walls of alabaster. Open doorways, porticos, and gates led into the buildings. From everywhere came the ringing sounds of hammers and a white dust hung in the air. She wanted to speak, but found that here she had no voice. In a reversal of fortune it was Jasper who read her lips to answer her questions.

"No, you can't hear the choir. It is not for mortal ears. But what you can hear is the work."

His fingers lingered on her lips, drawing forth more questions. "What do we do? Why, we expand the mansion within the pearly gates. There are always more dead. Some imagine that the afterlife is nothing but the absolute in pleasure. How long at any given time have you truly been completely happy? And how long have you stayed that way? We're human. We don't know how to do that. Instead some of us find that the truest reward is to have a purpose. A purpose even like mine, protecting my mother and aiding her. There are as many purposes as there are the living and the passed on. It could be that even *you*, Kassandra, have a purpose."

That was when she felt them. The others lurking among the doorways, just out of sight. Waiting, waiting for her. The voices who would gladly answer when she called. She bowed her head. Then Jasper turned her once more. Pointing her back toward the light of the familiar. Nudging her toward life. But before she returned, Jasper had one last comment, "Your mother has a purpose as well. She has, however, realized that being close to you could draw dangerous attention. So she will be there for you, Kassandra, but it will be from a distance." With that, Jasper pushed her back through the portal to the mortal realm. When she opened her eyes, Madam Foss stood framed in the doorway of the working room.

She nodded approvingly at Kassandra. "You have a lot of work ahead of you, girl, but my son is a good judge of character. You will do just fine." As she turned away, she threw over her shoulder, "If you listen to me that is."

Glass Shades

David Sherman

"Mr. Walker, sir?"

The man in the well-brushed frock coat looked up from his luncheon in the Placer's Poke restaurant to see a young man in an Eton jacket and brimless square cap.

"Yes, Jack," gambling man Cheyenne Walker said with a nod.

"A Babbage clack for you, sir." The bellhop extended a silver tray with an envelope on it.

"Thank you." Walker took the envelope and dropped a silver dollar in its place. He waited for the bellhop to back away before using a small folding knife to slit the envelope open. It contained a single sheet of paper with a message delivered via the Glittering Nugget's Babbage Analytical Engine. It read:

Mr. Cheyenne Walker
c/o the Glittering Nugget Hotel
Colorado Territory

My Dear Mr. Walker,

Mr. Pinkerton has given me an assignment on which I would most assuredly appreciate your assistance. It is of a nature similar to the several assignments on which we have co-operated in the past, and I cannot imagine acquiring such aid from another soul. Kindly respond to me as to whether or not you can join with me in this en-deavor at the Dragon Bones Hotel, Zapotec, New Mexico Territory where I will sojourn in a week's time.

[signed,] Miss Kitty Belle
The Pinkerton Agency

Walker folded the message and inserted it into an inner pocket of his coat before hastily finishing his meal. Sated, he made his way to the check in desk.

"Ah, Mr. Walker," the officious Mr. Reghaster greeted him. How might I be of assistance?

"You can first tell me when the next stagecoach to Denver will be here."

Reghaster looked startled. "The stagecoach to Denver? Are you considering leaving us, Mr. Walker?"

"I am that."

"A coach comes from Denver daily, and makes the return in the afternoon."

"I will be on it. If you will kindly give me a sheet of paper, I need to send a clack. While you are doing that, I will retire to my room to get my luggage, then return here to settle my accounts."

"The hotel will surely miss you," Reghaster said as he pushed a sheet of paper across the counter. "It's so seldom we see a gambler with your skill and ability tithe the hotel so richly from his win-nings."

Walker ignored the clerk while he scribbled out a message to Kitty Belle assuring her that he would endeavor to meet her in a week's time.

"Oh, that *woman* Pinkerton," Reghaster said with a disapproving headshake when he saw to whom the message was addressed. "A woman Pinkerton agent indeed!" He headed for the steam-operated Babbage Analytical Engine that would send a message to the Dragon Bones Hotel in Zapotec, New Mexico.

But Walker didn't hear him; he was already striding toward the Otis lifting machine that would spirit him to his room on the hotel's tenth floor.

Cheyenne Walker's room was waiting for him when he arrived at the Dragon Bones Hotel on the morning of the sixth day after leaving the Glittering Nugget. Miss Kitty Belle hadn't yet arrived, but, "We expect her daily," the hotel's proprietor assured him. Walker wasn't put off by the vagueness of her arrival time; travel across the plains and into the desert Southwest didn't lend itself to railroad timetable efficiency, not even with landships.

With hours or perhaps days to wait, he took advantage of the time to avail himself of the hotel's bath and barber. Freshly cleaned and coiffed, he dressed, with his Buntline Special discretely hidden away under his frock coat, then headed for the bar, where he was able to order a sausage and bread plate—the Dragon Bones not having a restaurant. After eating, he went in search of a card game. Not that he had to look far—the hotel's lobby also served as its gaming room. And that's where Miss Kitty Belle found him when she arrived on the next day's coach.

Walker was sitting where he could see the front door, and immediately rose to his feet on her entrance.

"Miss Kitty Belle!" he announced to the world.

"Mr. Cheyenne Walker," she replied with a dip of her head. "I'm surprised you can make me out under all this travel dust." Indeed, her long coat, bonnet, and muffler were covered with the dust of the trail.

Walker shook his head. "Your beauty of character shines through. I doubt that any thickness of dust, dirt, or even mud could disguise you from my sight."

A slight smile quirked her lips. "You speak too grandly, sir. Now I must see to my room and make myself presentable so I can join you for dinner."

Zapotec at the time was not a destination for holidaymakers, mostly a way-station for travelers passing on their way to southern Arizona or parts of Sonora, Mexico. Most of the people who stopped for longer than a meal and a night's sleep were geologists searching for the stones that some believed were the bones of giant animals that had failed to make it onto Noah's Ark.

Zapotec did, however, boast a cantina, a fact Walker ascertained while waiting for Miss Kitty Belle to refresh herself. He entered and while he had a small beer—it was obviously a local brew—he examined the interior. Manny's cantina boasted six smallish tables, each with four chairs. The room was moderately clean—no rodents scampered about the floor—and the scents wafting from the kitchen suggested the food was on the good side of palatable. The only language he heard spoken by the few customers present was a doggerel mix of border-Spanish and one or more local Indian languages.

Satisfied, he returned to the Dragon Bones to await the Pinkerton agent. He didn't expect to have to wait long, as he knew that Kitty Belle was of a practical bent. He was right. In hardly more time than he would have expected to wait for a man to bathe and dress, she descended the stairs from the hotel's upper level.

"Miss Belle," he said as he stood from an otherwise unoccupied table. He looked with approval at her garb; a simple gingham dress, just short of ankle length, with sleeves that reached mid-forearm. A bonnet of the same material perched on her head

"Mr. Walker," she said brusquely. "You were right about the bath-water. Now, I am famished. Have you torn yourself away from the gaming tables long enough to find a place to eat away from prying ears?"

"I have," he assured her." He offered his arm and led her to the exit.

They took a table next to an open window where they would garner the benefit of whatever refreshing breeze might pass their way. The young senorita who took their food and drink order tittered at Walker's hesitant Spanish, even though it was better than her broken English.

Cheyenne Walker positively beamed at Miss Kitty Belle while they waited for their dinner to be served. "It is such a delight to see you again, Miss Belle. The three times in the past when I have joined with you on your detectiving were marvelous exercises. I look forward to this one, even though I have no idea what your mission is."

They paused when their food and drink were delivered, and then Kitty Belle broached the reason she wanted Walker with her on this assignment.

"Local lawmen, both town marshals and county sheriffs," she began after tasting the stew and nodding approval of the dish, "have of late been assiduous about bringing law-breakers to justice. Three are serving lengthy prison terms for bank robbery, one is waiting the gallows for the murder of a coachman in commission of a robbery, and several others are either in jail for short sentences or have fled to distant parts.

"But," she said, waving her spoon about like a conductor's baton, "then there is the matter of the Hannity gang. Four of the five members of the gang were killed when they chose to fight a posse rather than surrender when they were caught. They are the gang leader Bloodstained Ralph Hannity, Lonesome Georgie Throckton, Hammerhands Sue Blackson, and a Zinni Indian only known as Scalptaker."

"So what is it about the matter of the Hannity gang that has aroused the interest of Mr. Pinkerton?" Walker asked when Miss Kitty paused to spoon more stew.

"As I said," she resumed, "four of the five members of the Hannity gang were killed fighting the posse. The fifth is incarcerated in the territorial penitentiary in Santa Fe."

Walker put his spoon down and spread his hands questioningly.

Miss Kitty Belle bestowed a small smile on Cheyenne Walker. "Mr. Pinkerton's attention has been aroused because it appears that the gang is still active."

Walker leaned back from the table. "An Indian is a member of the gang? Is Hammerhands Sue then a woman, like Calamity Jane perchance?"

She shook her head, causing her locks to bob about. "He uses his hammer-like hands to bring low anyone who laughs at his name."

Walker nodded, accepting her explanation, then mused, "Four are dead and the fifth is imprisoned. It's not possible for them to still be engaged in banditry."

"Now do you understand how this attracted Mr. Pinkerton's attention?"

"I do indeed."

"Now that we have eaten," she said, "we must hie to the town marshal and learn what we can about these supernatural banditries from him. Then to the newspaper office." She looked about for the young senorita and signaled her to join them. Miss Kitty Belle then surprised Cheyenne Walker by speaking in rapid-fire Spanish. The girl giggled as she scampered to the kitchen.

"I told her how delicious the stew was," she explained, acting on the assumption that Walker hadn't been able to follow her Spanish.

"So I gathered," he said dourly. "To the town marshal then." He stood and pulled her chair out for her.

Had either of them bothered to look out of the window and down at the ground below it, they would have seen sitting against the wall a wizened old man wearing leggings, a breechcloth, a baggy shirt, and a reservation hat. A pristine golden eagle's feather stood up from the hat's brim. The old man eased himself from below the window before rising to his feet and ambling off.

Zapotec's town marshal had a tiny office in the municipal building. A slightly larger space was allotted to the town administrator and council. The largest of the building's three spaces had a wall of bars—the jail. Marshal Tom Peron was the town's only full time employee.

After briefly identifying herself and Cheyenne Walker and their mission, Miss Kitty Belle said, "I'd like to question everybody who was on that stagecoach. Where can I find them?"

Marshal Peron scratched his chin in a thoughtful manner before saying, "You'll have t' talk ta One-Hand Krysler t' find out where they's gone. Ya know, they all lit out on the next stage after the robbery. 'Cept fer Mr. Jim D. Andy, who got kilt by the bandits and is now residing in our own Boot Hill. Doubt he'd be able to tell you much, though."

"And where might One-Hand Krysler be?" Kitty Belle said, dismissing Mr. Andy as a possible source of information.

"Par'bly somewheres 'tween here and Aztec City. Don't rightly know when he might be back in these parts again', on account'a because he was talkin' 'bout quittin' the stage drivin' business after getting' robbed by mechanicals what shot and kilt one a his payin' passengers." The marshal stopped talking for a moment while he pensively scratched at the stubble on his chin. "That might have had sumpin to do with him quittin' stage drivin'."

"Mechanical men?" Cheyenne Walker and Kitty Belle exclaimed simultaneously.

"Thas what One-Eye said."

"What did the passengers say?" Miss Kitty asked.

Peron shook his head. "They was all in too fired a hurry to git outta town to say anything. 'Cept, o' course, fer that Mr. Andy, what weren't in no hurry to go nowheres nohow. 'Course others as witnessed the robbery still claims it'twere the Hannity Gang, though they's mostly dead."

Miss Kitty made a moue at the unhelpful news. "All right, do you at least have pictures of the supposed highwaymen?"

"That I do!"

Marshal Peron's pay was little enough that he found it necessary to supplement it in various ways. One of which was to charge admission to the jail for the curious to see captured miscreants. Another was...

"Yep, Ah has pitchers of the Hannity Gang when their bodies was brung in," he said. "We stood 'em up right nice again' the wall of the 'nicipal building." He pointed to the right of the entrance. "We took pitchers of each of 'em and a pitcher of all of 'em."

"Wonderful. I'd like copies of each of the pictures."

"Thas right kindly of you, Missy. Since youse buyin' all of 'em, I'll give you a cut price; all of the singles fer thirty cents 'stead of ten cents each, and thirty cents fer the four of 'em together. Why I'll even throw in a pitcher of Lefty Lazlow what's in prison fer free, seein' how youse a lawman, ah, I means a law *lady* yersef."

"Marshal Peron," she gasped. "Why that's robbery."

He shook his head. "I know Mr. Pinkerton sent you here to investigate, but Mr. Pinkerton don't pay me to take them pitchers. You want 'em, you gotta pay fer 'em."

"You want sixty cents for five photographs, and another one for free. Is that right?"

"Yes'm. That'll 'bout do it."

"Do you take the pictures yourself, Marshal?" Walker asked.

"Nossuh. The photography man is Wendell Kleghorn."

"And where might Mr. Kleghorn be?"

Peron waved a hand, indicating nowhere in particular. "Out there somewheres. Par'bly sellin' pitchers his ownself." He screwed up an eye to peer sharply at Walker. "Don' think you can get 'em fer nothing from him. He'd charge full price fer alla them, and wouldn't give you the Lefty Lazlow fer free, neither. He'd make you pay ten cents fer it."

"I'd expect nothing less. Photographing is a hard way to make a living. How do you come by your copies?"

"Ever time Wendell come through here, he prints out new 'uns fer me. I gives him half the money I got from sellin' the las' bunch."

"Does Mr. Kleghorn carry the glass plates with him?"

"Nossuh!" They's too val'able fer that. They's locked up in the bank vault."

"Mr. Kleghorn seems to be a very wise businessman."

Peron started to reply, but Miss Kitty cut him off. "Marshal, I would very much like to see a place where people reported the Hannity Gang committing banditry after they were killed or incarcerated."

Peron harrumphed at the interruption and muttered something about Kleghorn being very wise, then talked.

"Don't know what you think you kin find. Las' week they robbed a stage a few miles from here. If'n it were the ghosts of the Hannitys, there ain't nothing to find no how. Not even if they's mechanical men, like One-Eye Krysler said. If'n it were other highwaymen, they's likely long gone from these parts. Either way, you're wasting your time."

"What do you mean, by mechanical men?" Kitty Belle asked.

Peron shrugged. "Thas what ole One-Eye said. 'Course he stunk of whiskey when he said it, so who knows."

"And those passengers?" Walker asked. "What did they say?"

Peron shook his head. "They was too scart to say nothing. They jis wanted t' move on as fast as they could." He shook his head again. "Don't think you'll find nothin'"

"When Mr. Pinkerton tells me to investigate something, I do it no matter how unlikely it is I will find anything. So where do we go?"

Peron shrugged. "Take the south road till it turns east, then go...."

"Now the newspaper office?" Walker suggested when they left the municipal office.

"Indeed. The newspaperman might know something more."

But the office of the *Zapotec Herald* was closed.

Two hours later and five miles southeast of Zapotec, Walker pulled back on the reins to stop the horse drawing their hansom carriage.

"That doesn't look much like the tree Marshal Peron described," Kitty Belle said of the tree next to which they'd stopped.

"But it is the only tree within two miles in either direction," Walker observed.

"And there does seem to be trace of a wagon stopping and something happening to the side of the road," Kitty Belle added. "Let us look more closely."

Before leaving Zapotec they had changed their garb. Walker doffed his frock coat and ruffled shirt in favor of a denim shirt. Kitty Belle had changed from her gingham dress to denim culottes and waistshirt.

Before stepping down from the hansom, Walker took his Buntline Special in its belted holster from the satchel he'd carried them in. He donned the belt as soon as his feet were on the ground, and immediately reached up to help Miss Kitty dismount. She didn't need the assistance. Her Colt Peacemaker remained in its satchel, but the carrier was unlatched and in her hand.

This was a landscape of Fairy Dusters and Jacob's staff, dry awaiting the next rainfall. There were two sets of wheels. One was obviously from the stagecoach. The other showed that a wagon had angled across the road to block the passage of the stage. An area of some square yards on the north side of the road had been smashed flat.

They stepped carefully through the Fairy Dusters around the smashed down area and looked carefully into it and at the ground between the plants. When their circumnavigation led them back to the road they spent a moment in thought before discussing what they'd just seen.

"The horses were cut loose and sent on their way, then the coach was toppled onto its side," Kitty Belle said.

Walker nodded agreement. "The hoof prints around the fallen coach are far too small to be the prints of dray horses."

"The footprints in the trampled area are obviously those of the men who righted the coach. There," she pointed at well-defined set of hoof prints on the road, "is where the new team was attached to draw the coach away."

Another set of footprints showed where the driver, his shotgun guard, and the surviving passengers had begun their trek to Zapotec.

Walker squatted in the road to examine other footprints that led from where the blocking wagon had stood to the coach. What he saw made him grimace. "These are far deeper than the other prints. Could it be that One-Eye Krysler was right about mechanical men?"

Kitty Belle didn't answer, instead looking east, away from Zapotec, toward some low mountains in the middle distance. After a moment, she said, "According to Marshal Peron, the only thing missing from the coach's cargo was the Wells Fargo strongbox. It's odd that the robbers didn't take the passengers' valuables from their persons."

"Odd and unusual," Walker said. "I've never before heard of highwaymen leaving passengers with their valuables untouched." He looked back in the direction of town, and saw, faint with distance, the figure of a standing man, with what might be a feather sticking up from his hat.

With nothing more to be found at the site of the robbery, they got back into the carriage to drive back to Zapotec. When Walker got the rig turned about, the faintly seen man was nowhere in sight.

"Maybe the newspaper office will be open this time," Belle said.

Cheyenne Walker and Miss Kitty Belle heard the *klickety-klatter* of the newspaper's hand-cranked printing press before they reached the office of the *Zapotec Herald*. The noise, they discovered on entering through the unlocked door, was far greater inside than out. A man, closer in age to sunset than sunrise, stood at a printing press furiously cranking its handle as it spat out broadsheet after broadsheet. Between the noise of the press and the mufflers he wore over his ears, the man didn't hear them enter. It wasn't until Walker stepped to the printer and lifted a just-printed page that the man noticed his visitors. He pulled back the sheet feeder and continued cranking until the paper currently going through the machine cleared the mechanism.

He took off his ear-mufflers and wiped his hands on an ink-stained cloth.

"Maxwell Kirkpatrick, at your service," he said in too loud a voice. "Publisher, editor, reporter, and," with a wave at the press, "chief mechanic of the premier newspaper of Zapotec and surrounding territory. And you," his gaze swept up and down his visitors, "must be Miss Kitty Belle of the Pinkerton Agency, and her sometime companion-in-arms Mr. Cheyenne Walker!"

"We are," Kitty Belle said. "How did you guess?"

Kirkpatrick shook his head. "Guessing's got nothing to do with it. Among other things, I'm the top investigating reporter in this part of New Mexico Territory. Between that and being the publisher of the paper, it's my business to know who's stopping by. And," he raised a quizzical eyebrow at Walker, "might you be carrying your Buntline Special?"

Walker raised an equally quizzical eyebrow at the question. "It's in my room at the hotel."

"Dime-novelist Ned Buntline had only commissioned half a dozen of the Colt Army revolvers with 12 inch barrels, which he gave to top lawmen. I don't expect you'll tell me how you came by yours." He turned to Kitty Belle and asked, "And you have your Colt Peacemaker?" That .45 caliber pistol was often preferred by lawmen.

"I do," she replied. Then, "We came to see you this morning, but the office was closed."

"Of course it was. I was up in the hills interviewing some of the geologists who are digging up the dragon bones buried there." He continued talking more loudly than necessary.

"Dragon bones," Walker said. "Surely you don't believe they are finding the bones of real dragons that didn't make it onto Noah's Ark."

"Course not. That might be what the unlettered denizens of this region might think, but not everybody does. The name caught on, though. Anyway, it's easier to call them that than to use that made up name, *dino-saurers*."

"But you aren't here to find out about the dragon bones, you're investigating the reports that the deceased members of the Hannity gang are still committing robbery."

"Yes we are," Kitty Belle said. "All of the witnesses are long gone. We hope you might have interviewed them before they left town, and can give us information."

"I did, and I wrote it up in the paper each time the mysterious robbers—be they mechanical or spectral—victimized folks. I don't imagine you've had opportunity to read my stories. Most people hereabouts use the paper in the outhouse, even if they don't read it first." He shook his head sadly. "But! I have archive copies, and you're more than welcome to sit yourselves down and read them while I continue printing out the new edition."

"Do you mind if we take them somewhere else to read?" Kitty Belle gestured at the printing press.

"What? Oh, yes. Of course. I'm so used to the noise of the press I hardly notice it anymore." He went to a cabinet and shuffled through stacks of broadsides, occasionally pulling one out. When he'd assembled half a dozen, he handed them to Walker.

"Kindly remember to return them after reading," Kirkpatrick said to Kitty Belle, still at high volume.

"We surely will," she said with a smile. She gave him half a bob as she turned to leave the newspaper office.

"One more thing," Walker said before following her. "What can you tell us about Mr. Kleghorn's background, has he always been an itinerant photography man?"

Kirkpatrick paused as in thought, then said, "Don't know if it's true, but there's a story that Wells Fargo foreclosed on his family farm back in Iowa. Could be true. Could be not." He shrugged.

"Thank you, Mr. Kirkpatrick." Walker exited and joined Miss Kitty on the boardwalk. They'd hardly gone a few yards before the *klickety-klatter* of the hand-cranked press took up again.

At Manny's Cantina, it being late in the afternoon, they sat at the same window-table as the day before, and ordered the beef stew over rice and a small beer before looking at the broadsheets. It was a simple paper, just one sheet printed on both sides.

"Priced at one penny," Walker noted.

Their reading disclosed that there had been six instances since the Hannity Gang's demise. Four were stagecoach holdups out on the road, two were in Zapotec when the coach was stopped to let off geologists. In each case, the only thing taken was the Wells Fargo strongbox. The box was always found along the road at a later time, broken open, its lock shattered, and contents missing. During the two robberies in town, the bandits had fired enough bullets to keep everybody ducking for cover and not shooting back.

Walker and Belle stopped reading when their stew arrived. After, when the bowls had been taken away and their small beers replenished, they resumed reading and discussing what they read.

"There doesn't seem to be a pattern to when or where they rob the stagecoaches," Miss Kitty said when she finished reading the last of the stories.

"None that I could discern either," Walker said. "Random times and intervals."

"Random places as well."

"But it's most interesting that rumor says Kleghorn's family farm was foreclosed by Wells Fargo, and the only thing stolen from the stagecoaches was the Wells Fargo strongbox," Walker said. "And I do note one other little piece of coincidence."

Kitty Belle shot him a look. "And what might that be?"

"The two times the Hannity Gang robbed in Zapotec, Mr. Kleghorn was here in town."

"I, too, saw that coincidence."

They sat in silent contemplation for a few minutes when something indistinct caught Walker's attention. He stood and stuck his head out of the window. Looking down he saw crouching a wizened old man in leggings, breechcloth, and baggy shirt. A golden eagle's feather stuck up out of the hatband of his reservation hat. The man grinned at him before scuttling away.

"What has your attention?" Miss Kitty asked.

"An old Indian. He brings to mind a figure I faintly saw after we examined the site of the latest robbery.

It being past dusk now, they returned to the Dragon Bones Hotel. Miss Kitty Belle retired to her room to await sleep and dawn, when they might head into the badlands in search of any geologists who might shed light on the robberies.

For his part, Walker went to the lobby-gaming room, where he was careful to not win too much from any one person.

The next morning, after a hearty breakfast of eggs, shredded pork, and potatoes with several cups of coffee, Cheyenne Walker was in the livery stable seeing to the lease of two horses for the day, when a clatter of hooves and excited shouting from the street drew his attention. He stepped to the stable doors to see what the noise was about—a stagecoach was pulling up and raising a cloud of dust.

"It's the Hannitys!" the driver shouted, jumping down from his driving bench. "Everbody out!" he screamed as he sped from the coach.

The shotgun guard had dropped down from his place and yanked the cab door open to let the passengers out; a man and two women stumbled onto the street and followed the guard as he headed for the nearest doorway.

Just then four fiercely bellowing horsemen, pistols drawn and firing into the air, surrounded the abandoned coach, sending the lathered horses bucking and screaming, in a panic to break free from their traces and flee from the bandits.

Walker spun about and in three rapid strides was at his valise, opening it and yanking out his Buntline Special. Before he got back to the door, he heard the powerful blast of a Colt Peacemaker from the direction of the hotel. Sure enough, when he looked he saw Kitty Belle in the window of her room, raining bullets down on the bandits. Walker wasted no time adding his .45 caliber bullets to those fired by the Pinkerton agent.

To no evident avail. None of the quartet seemed in the least discommoded by being so shot at!

"It's the Hannitys," someone shouted, and was echoed by other voices.

Shouting and laughing, one leaped onto the coach and pulled the Wells Fargo strongbox from its place under the driver's bench and held it over his head like a trophy. He leaped directly into the saddle of his mount, and the four lit out so fast Walker could hardly tell into which direction they disappeared.

Marshal Peron appeared from the doorway of the municipal building with a shotgun, its double-barrels still smoking in his hands.

"Marshal!" Walker shouted, reloading. "I will join your posse to go after them."

"As will I," Miss Kitty cried as she spun about to leave her room.

Peron sadly shook his head. "Ah cain't raise a posse. Ma jurs'diction ends at the town line."

But neither Walker nor Kitty Belle heard him; Walker had run back into the stable to saddle the two horses he'd been preparing to lease, and the Pinkerton agent was pounding down the stairs to the ground floor while the Marshal said he couldn't raise a posse.

Walker led the two saddled horses out and was mounting up when Miss Kitty joined him and leapt on the other horse. Only then did they notice the town marshal standing in the doorway of the municipal building and that the other armed men who had also shot at the gang were just standing about.

"Well, Marshal," Walker shouted, "get the posse together and let's go after them."

Peron shook his head again. "Like Ah said, Ah cain't. Ma jurs'diction ends at the town line."

Miss Kitty Belle glowered at him, then stood in her stirrups and shouted out, "I am an agent of the Pinkerton Detective Agency, *my* jurisdiction goes beyond the town line. Who amongst you will join my posse?"

There was some hemming and hawing among the armed men, then half a dozen of them grudgingly agreed to join up.

While Walker and Belle waited for them to get their horses, they examined the ground around the stagecoach.

"I know I hit at least two of them," Kitty Belle muttered.

"As did I," Walker murmured. "Then why isn't there any blood in the street?"

"And why did I hear what sounded like bullets striking iron?"

The old Indian Walker had seem scuttling away from Manny's Cantina suddenly appeared between them.

"They be spirits *inside* metal men," he intoned. "Mortal bullets cannot harm them. The picture man has stolen their souls. You will not find them. Only ancient magic can put an end to this."

"We have to try," Kitty Belle answered him. Then to Walker, "Which way did they go?"

"I think west."

She looked at him. "You *think*?"

He shrugged. "They moved so fast I couldn't tell for sure."

Then the six men who volunteered for the posse arrived, joined by Marshal Peron.

"Ah cain't raise a posse. Don't mean Ah cain't *join* one."

Kitty Belle stood in her stirrups again and shouted, "Let's go!' she dropped into her saddle and led the way west. The Indian had disappeared. On the way out of town the posse passed a wagon with fancy lettering on its side, proclaiming it to be the Photo-Graphy studio of Wendell Kleghorn. A twenty-foot pole holding an array of parabolic mirrors jutted from its roof, and its street-side panel was dropped down, to display a collection of photographs for sale.

It was going on sundown when the posse returned to Zapotec. They were all dirty and sweaty and tired. All day long they'd searched without success to find any sign of the stagecoach robbers.

The hotel's bath had fresh water. Miss Kitty Belle bathed first, and the water wasn't too muddy when Cheyenne Walker took his turn.

When they were both bathed and dressed in clean clothes, they met in the lobby and decided to return to Manny's Cantina for dinner.

The young senorita still giggled at Miss Kitty's rapid Spanish, but politely curtsied and promptly brought them roast chicken with black beans and rice, and a small beer, along with a large cup of freshly boiled water that had been off the fire long enough to cool down.

They were too tired and hungry to talk immediately, but drank the boiled water and asked for more before touching the beer, which they drank while eating.

"So, Mr. Kleghorn was back in town at the same time as bandits appeared to purloin the Wells Fargo strongbox," Walker said halfway through eating his portion of chicken.

Kitty Belle nodded. "I do believe it is incumbent on us to talk to the photography man."

Walker nodded agreement, but was too tired to talk.

After eating they had another small beer

Kitty Belle casually swept her gaze around the other tables, three of which were occupied by locals digging into their food with gusto and giving no indication that they were aware of the presence of the two gringos. Assured that no one was listening to them, she said in a low voice, "I am brought to mind of that old Indian who spoke to us whilst the posse was assembling." When she saw that Walker was absorbing her words she continued, "You are aware of the belief held by some Original Peoples of the American West that photographs steal souls, as he said?"

"Indeed. I have even read that Doctor Livingstone has reported such beliefs from darkest Africa."

"If such beliefs can be thought true, then it is possible that someone has stolen the souls of a notorious gang of miscreants and has them posthumously continuing their lives of crime."

Walker blinked at that, and looked into a space only he could see. After a moment he began to pensively murmur. "We have dealt with gremlins, Coyote and Raven, Rock Trolls and Dwarves." He shook his head sharply. "That given, I do not find stolen souls to be totally preposterous."

She gave him a small smile. "My thoughts precisely."

"So we must find whoever is stealing the souls..."

"And discover how he is using them to enrich himself."

"And finally put those souls to rest..."

"...In whatever Hades they are properly consigned to."

"And the person to start with is Mr. Kleghorn."

It was just as well that they were too tired to confront the photographer that evening, as he was ensconced in his room at the Dragon Bones Hotel, and had given the desk clerk strict orders that he was to be undisturbed before the next morn's breakfast.

In the morning, Miss Kitty responded immediately to Walker's knocking on her door.

"Kleghorn hasn't risen yet. So we have time to break our fasts before talking to him," he said.

"Good. I'd rather speak to him on a full stomach than an empty one."

They again went to Manny's, where Manny's wife served them *huevos con carne*.

Back at the hotel they discovered that Winston Kleghorn had already departed.

"Heading west and then north into the badlands, I suspect," the desk clerk informed them.

At the livery stable they were able to lease the same horses they'd ridden the day before; riders and mounts were thus familiar with each other. In soon after discovering that they'd missed their quarry, they were mounted and headed west out of Zapotec. Two miles on, they saw the wagon tracks they'd been following turn north onto an ill-used trail. They followed them.

The land they traversed gradually changed from flat to gently rolling to more like a heaving sea. Arroyos began to appear between the heights. More than an hour after turning north, they saw a flashing in the near distance.

"I suspect that's sunlight sparking off the mirrors on the wagon's spire," Miss Kitty Belle said.

"I do believe you're right," Cheyenne Walker agreed. He stood in his stirrups to look ahead. When he sat again he said, "Mr. Kleghorn has stopped his wagon. Unless he starts again, we should reach him in less than half an hour."

Walker was right in his estimation of when they caught up with the photography man's wagon. Four crudely-formed iron statues of men with glass plates in place of their heads stood alongside the wagon. A beam of light from the bottom mirrors of the spire was aimed at the back of each of the four statues, and a faint hiss of steam seemed to emit from them.

"If you are here to rob me," Kleghorn said when Walker hailed him from the wagon's left, "I put all of my money in the bank yesterday. I have nothing for you to take."

"No, Mr. Kleghorn," Kitty Belle said from the wagon's right, "we have no intention of robbing you."

The photographer jerked when he heard her and twisted. He peered sharply at her then said, "Ah ha! You're that Pinkerton who's come to investigate the robberies that some folks attribute to the Hannitys."

"You surmise correctly, Mr. Kleghorn. I am indeed that very Pinkerton agent. And I would have you answer some questions."

"Oh, you would, would you?" Kleghorn said, twisting about on the bench in attempt to keep both of his interlocutors in sight. "And what might be these questions you'd like answered?" He scrambled to the top of his wagon where, even though Walker was still on one side and Kitty Belle on the other, he felt less surrounded.

"Mr. Kleghorn," Kitty Belle said, "I could not help but make note of the fact that each of the times that the Hannitys committed a robbery in Zapotec, you were there as well."

"And we'd like to know where you were on the occasions when the gang struck elsewhere," Walker added.

"Maybe I will not tell you." As he said that, Kleghorn turned a crank on the spire, realigning the mirrors to focus their beams on the glass plates atop each of the metal men. Abruptly, the metal of the four flowed into the shapes of well-formed, fully clothed men bearing the familiar, if ghostly, features of the Hannity gang.

Kleghorn laughed wickedly and cackled at the quartet. "Kill them!" he shrieked, pointing at his antagonists.

Two of the Hannitys turned to Kitty Belle and moved in her direction. The other two did the same toward Walker.

Kitty Belle turned her horse about and galloped the short distance to Walker's side before spinning about to face the spectral bandits.

Walker drew his Buntline Special.

"Your bullets can't hurt them!" Kleghorn crowed.

Suddenly they heard the *DUM-da-da-dum-dum* of an approaching drum, and a keening singsong below the drumming.

Kleghorn looked in the direction of the drumming and singing, as did the resurrected Hannitys.

"What's that?" the photography man demanded of the air.

Walker and Miss Kitty glanced quickly at each other, both mouthed, "The old Indian?" They turned to look toward the approaching sound.

The drumming and keening grew louder. The old Indian appeared, walking up the side of the arroyo in which he'd been hidden until now. He stopped drumming when he reached the flat, and pointed his drumstick first at Scalptaker, then at the others one at a time. His keening turned into a different song.

"Kill that redskin!" Kleghorn shrilled at the bandits.

They ignored him, instead after a long moment of listening, the four bandits reached up to their heads and pulled out the glass plates that jutted from beneath their shoulders. Abruptly, the four figures melted into naked, crudely formed mannequins, and a ghostly image arose from each of them to waft into the sky. The glass plates shattered into fragments glittering in the sun the apparitions rose out of them, and shortly vanished.

"You can't do that!" Kleghorn shrieked. "You are my creations!" He collapsed onto his hands and knees and wailed with his head hanging down. "All I wanted was to make Wells Fargo pay for stealing my family's farm." He raised his face to the sky. "Is that such a bad thing?"

Kitty Belle urged her horse to the side of the wagon, and she clambered to its roof.

"Mr. Winston Kleghorn, you are under arrest for robbery, and possibly for murder as well."

Walker joined her. He knelt next to the photography man and quickly frisked him, checking for weapons. Kleghorn had a small pistol and a knife hidden in his coat, which Walker relieved him of. He used the knife to cut a strip from the photography man's shirt to bind his hands behind his back, then lifted the man and dropped him onto the bench of his wagon.

"Sir, I believe you have rid this territory of a menace," Walker said to the old Indian.

"They are now with the Great Spirit," the old man said. "What was done here was a great evil. Now those souls can rest." He turned to the arroyo from whence he'd come.

"Do you want to drive, or shall I?" Walker asked Miss Kitty when the Indian was gone from sight.

"I will drive," she said. Walker tied her horse's reins to the back of the wagon.

Back in Zapotec, they handed Kleghorn over to Marshal Peron, who dispatched a rider to the county seat in Aztec to inform him of the arrest and the remarkable events surrounding it.

The town council met briefly and decided to relieve the Marshal of his duties until they could determine whether he knew about the magical glass plates. They then called a town meeting in the street in front of the municipal building to tell everybody what had happened.

They concluded with, "Somewhere out there are several Wells Fargo strongboxes. We are sure the bank will richly reward anybody who finds them."

"My job here is now done," Miss Kitty Belle said to Cheyenne Walker over a dinner of pulled pork with black beans at Manny's Cantina. "So I will be on the next stagecoach east tomorrow. Are you going to stay and join the search for the strongboxes?"

"No. I don't hunt treasure. I make my way with cards. Maybe I'll try my luck in Aztec."

"Luck?" she asked with a twinkle in her eyes.

"...Is a lady," he said, smiling.

Spirits Calling

Jody Lynn Nye

STEPHEN MORRELL DID NOT RAISE HIS EYES, EVEN AS THE fellow mourners patted him on the arm or the back as they left the graveside. A few steps behind him, hovering an inch or two over the near-frozen ground, Arabella Morrell watched him with anxious eyes. How would he manage to cope without her?

"They were like two halves of an apple," Miss Nickson, her former next-door neighbor, said in an undertone to Mrs. Baskell. The surgeon's wife's black coat and hat virtually dripped with jet beads—but then, she had cause to attend many funerals. This time, the death was not her husband's fault. No, the consumption had taken Arabella's last breath. But, perhaps, not her last word. He had vowed to invent a device to communicate with her. But could he?

"Come along, dear one," the angel said, putting an arm around Arabella's back. She—he?—had a clear, sweet voice like one that might have issued from the long golden trumpet in her—or his—other hand. The angel's long, flowing red hair spread out over the shoulders of a robe like those worn in a church choir, only the pure white fibers emitted rainbows as

the fabric shifted. Behind, huge golden wings spread, blocking Arabella's last view of her husband. "The Most High awaits you."

Arabella tried to peek between the glorious feathers. "I hate to see him with all the joy sucked out of him," she said. "I hope he can keep his promise."

"We shall see," the angel said. "Come." He—she?—beckoned to another figure, this one short and plump, clad in a most unsuitable jacket and skirt of oxblood red. "Your reward awaits you, my child."

Arabella almost gawked.

"Harmony Fuller? I didn't know you were ill, as well."

The irascible young woman leveled a gimlet eye at her from a round, florid face.

"No, I was not *ill*. How dare you suggest it? I never ailed a day in my life! But that delivery driver from Morison's—he should never have been on the street with a hand cart, let alone a heavy-goods dray with four out-of-control horses!"

"I am so sorry," Arabella said. "I hadn't heard...."

"Of course not!" Harmony snapped. Her unfortunate parents had utterly misjudged the personality of their second daughter when they had bestowed such an unsuitable name upon her. "Your fool of a husband seldom lifted his eyes from his ridiculous inventions to see what was happening around him!"

"That's not true!" Arabella protested. She stopped the next words that would have tumbled off her tongue. Of course it was true. Stephen did get wrapped up in his wonderful ideas, so much so that he had once walked slap through a wedding party coming out of St. Francis's and never even noticed that his own cousin was the groom. However, Stephen never neglected her. Even when a commissioned invention threatened to be late, he was at her bedside a dozen or twenty times a day, asking if he could do anything for her, rotating her pillows, even inventing a steampowered instant-freezer in a handsome wooden chest so she could have ice in her drinks and iced-cream to tempt her ever more capricious appetite. Still, as brilliant as he was, he could not forestall the progress of her disease.

She remembered the wail he raised when she breathed her last, like one of their babies, now long grown to adulthood, crying for comfort. It only just occurred to her how strange it was she had been able to hear him after she had died.

"...And *my* fool of a husband—*he* thought that I had stepped out into the street against the light, as though you couldn't hear the clanking of the signal-automaton a mile away. That driver should be fined! Imprisoned! If I could only tell Wilfrid the truth! But, no, I had to stand there while he berated my broken body on the ground for being *careless*! I'll give him *careless*!"

Arabella wondered, not for the first time, how long good manners dictated that she listen to an endless screed of woe. The woman was a born faultfinder. Bless him, Stephen commented on it only once, that if he could harness Harmony's talent, she would be the finest quality-control manager industry would ever see.

She sighed. How she would miss Stephen! She pined for the little details that she loved about him, like the lock of brown hair that fell into his eyes whenever he bent over his drafting board or his work table; the quirky, shy smile he had when showing her his latest invention; but most of all, she would miss hearing his voice. He had sworn she would hear it again, but how? He must not follow her too soon into the afterlife. True, their children were grown and scattered as far across the Earth as any train, ship, or dirigible could take them. They didn't need him, but the future did. His wonderful inventions would make life easier for all humankind.

"Take my hands, dear ones," the angel said. She—or was it he? — enclosed her cold fingers in a warm, smooth grasp. Harmony gripped the angel's other hand with both of hers.

A moment later, the temperature of the air changed, as did the light. Arabella gasped. The bleak winter weather and the monochrome graveyard had vanished. She stood upon grass again, but of the brilliant yellow-green of spring's new growth. Burgeoning banks of flowers of colors so intense that they were almost rude bloomed high around her, but not so high she couldn't see the extent of the garden. It rolled away from her in all directions. The flowerbeds and bright green hedges delineated a maze of little bowers and wide, smooth fields. People of every shape of body and every hue of skin strolled or sat, alone or in groups. They looked happy and healthy, unlike her, of course.

She heard a sharp intake of breath to her left.

"I declare that I have not seen you with color in your cheeks for six months!" Harmony said, openly staring at her.

Arabella touched her own cheeks with wondering fingers. The skin felt soft and moist.

"A trick of the sun, perhaps?" she speculated.

The angel laughed, shaking those magnificent red locks so they danced upon its shoulders.

"The only sun and center here is the Most High. You are cured of all your mortal woes, my children. Be at peace. You are safe now. There are many waiting to greet you." A slim hand, so perfectly shaped it must have inspired those long-dead Greek sculptors, gestured at a lush glade filled with people.

Could that... no! ... Could that tall man with the sweeping mustache and the thick, shining black hair really be Grandfather Robert Phillipson, the great explorer? He had left Philadelphia the day after her fifth birthday on an expedition to the South Pole with a team of clockwork dogs, but never returned. He had on a jacket and knickerbocker trousers, gaitered boots, and a shirt with a bow tie under his chin, all colored the same rainbow-shedding white that the angel wore.

"Bella!" the man shouted, beaming. One bound and he stood beside her. "Child, you've grown up! But I could never mistake those bluebell eyes."

"Harmony, my dearest," a slender woman whose delicate face was surrounded by tresses of wheat-gold hair held out her hands to Arabella's companion. "How good to see you."

"Mother-in-law," Harmony said, tersely. She put her hands into the late Vanessa Fuller's for the shortest possible length of time, then withdrew them, moving out of range before the senior Mrs. Fuller could kiss her on the cheek. Arabella kept herself from frowning in disapproval. By her own observation, Vanessa didn't judge or disapprove of her daughter-in-law. Rather, the discomfort came from the other side.

"Come with me!" Grandfather Robert said, hooking his arm into Arabella's and drawing her along. To her delight, the sorrowful deep gray grave clothes in which the undertaker had dressed her had changed into her favorite walking dress, now changed from cornflower blue to white. She worried for a moment about soiling the hems, then laughed. If Grandfather Robert could keep his exploration clothes pristine after thirty-five years in Heaven, laundry was no longer going to be an issue for her ever again.

With Grandfather Robert's sure hand guiding her, they flew like swifts, sailing over five hedges into a grove of pink roses the size of her fist. Eager arms reached up to help her out of the air. Arabella's eyes filled with tears as she embraced favorite cousins, beloved friends, long-missed great-aunts and grandparents and, finally, her father. He looked thirty-five again, instead of the frail, bent seventy-two he had been at his death. His hair bloomed brown once more, and his cheeks were filled out and rosy.

"Mature enough for youngsters to ask my advice, not old enough to be ignored," he said, with a twist of his lips that had always served him for a smile. Arabella rested her head upon his chest, feeling like a little girl again. He stroked her hair. "You'll choose the form that suits you, my dear. You don't have to keep it forever. One day, you'll go into the light of the Most High." He tilted his head toward the heart of the garden, where a brilliant whiteness bigger than a cathedral pulsed like a living being. She ought to fear it, but felt an outpouring of the most all-encompassing love coming from it. It drew her, not with a mindless, irresistible compulsion, but with overwhelming joy.

"We don't stay in heaven forever?" she asked. "Are we… destroyed? Does going to God mean we cease to exist here as well as on Earth?"

Father let out a bark of laughter.

"Not at all. We will join in the most intense togetherness, all of existence in one place. The Most High gathers us like eggs under a setting hen and nurtures us forever. But I'm not going without your mother."

"Then, I'm not going without Stephen," Arabella said, sitting down with a decisive thump on a settee. It had looked like white marble, but when her bottom touched, it proved to be yielding and very comfortable. Father beamed.

"That's the spirit! I knew you were a Phillipson to the heart!"

"But, what does one do, now that one is here?" Arabella asked, looking around at the endless expanse of green and white. More people entered the garden as she watched: a dazed couple with brown skin and long black hair patiently guided by a golden-haired angel, an entire troop of men in green and brown mottled uniforms all but staggered in formation behind an incredibly handsome armored angel with flowing black hair and a silver-bladed sword raised high, and a very young woman whose tiny baby was in the arms of an angel with marvelous, curling white hair and the most tender expression she had ever seen.

"Greet your loved ones again," Father said, with a smile. He squeezed Arabella's hand. "Make peace with your soul. Absorb the joy that's all around you. Meet figures from history. Some of them are too interested in the new arrivals to go to their own rewards. Heal from your labors. Have no regrets. Mourn the life that was and rejoice in the one that is to come."

"Be bored out of my mind! If I had known what Heaven was like I would never have come," Harmony said, with a derisive snort. The small woman crossed her arms over the whitened jacket. It looked no more fashionable than it had in red.

Arabella couldn't reckon days or nights as she had known them in life, but surely no more than a week had passed since she had died—she still found it difficult to think of that event in the past tense, yet either she was still alive and hallucinating, or in Heaven on the threshold of eternal peace—and she couldn't imagine ever being bored there, despite hoping desperately for word from Stephen

"Haven't you sought out any of the marvelous people who are here?" Arabella asked, swinging her skirts to and fro. "Just a while ago, I listened to a choir of black people from the South. They sing so beautifully I thought they were already angels. I have a lot to learn from them, and they are kindly willing to teach me. *They* want to know how I do the French embroidery on my shirtwaist. I wish that I could say I did it by hand, but I used one of Stephen's twelve-needle mechanical marvels."

"Hmmph!" Harmony twisted her neck to avoid looking at Arabella. To her surprise, she saw tears in the smaller woman's eyes.

"You miss Wilfrid," Arabella said, with sudden enlightenment.

"Who says I do?" Harmony glared defiance at her.

"Well, I miss Stephen," Arabella replied, keeping her voice level. She was surprised how sorry she felt for the other woman. They had never much seen eye to eye in life, but Harmony kept seeking her out here.

"He loved you," Harmony said. The tears overspilled and poured down her cheeks. "Wilfrid never really cared. If he did he never told me so. He was always berating me for one error or another."

Arabella couldn't hide her surprise. She had always thought that the criticism in the Fuller marriage came from Harmony. She put her arm around the smaller woman and pulled her close on the bench, crooning as one would to a small child.

The moment lasted only a brief time, then Harmony pulled away and fled the rose garden, skimming over the hedges and ducking between groups of surprised souls until she was out of sight. Arabella sighed after her. If one could not find peace here, then where?

Unlike Harmony, she did indeed enjoy Heaven. She had missed visiting with others because of her illness. The few who had come to see her never stayed long, fearing that their presence made her weaker. She did her best to make up for lost time, meeting new people, listening to concerts and lectures, seeing dramatics performed from every era. Shakespeare had moved on to his eternal bliss, but his work lived on in Heaven as well as on Earth. The only thing lacking in her happiness was Stephen.

"Dearest Arabella!" The red-haired angel appeared suddenly at her shoulder.

"Gabriel!" Arabella took the outstretched hands with a genuine smile. She had become fond of her escort from Earth. She—or was it he? Its sex was never clear, not that bodily things mattered here—shared her passion for music of all kinds. "What have you come to tell me? Is the Commedia del'Arte going to perform today?"

"No! A *gift* has arrived for you," Gabriel said, its beautiful face lighting with the novelty. "The Most High has permitted its ascension, but I believe its substance has stretched as far as it can into the ether. Come with me to the underclouds." The wide wings beat mightily, and Arabella was lifted in the shelter of the angel's arm, thrilling to the sensation of flight.

Stephen's device! It had to be!

"Hello? Hello? Are you there, my love? I am seeking the spirit who was known as Arabella Morrell. Can anyone hear me?"

The tinny sound filled Arabella's heart with joy as she and Gabriel sailed underneath the mass of puffy whiteness. Though her vision of Heaven existed as a philosophical construct, or so Mr. Locke had said in his latest lecture, enough of the souls believed in it to give it a coherent and consistent structure. Few ever cared to venture beneath the beautiful gardens, or sought their limits, above or below. Odd little creatures, like the multi-winged seraphim; sable-hued, blue-eyed lwa; and childlike putti, seemed to use this as their nesting place, undisturbed by most of those waiting for their moment to pass into eternal bliss.

For the first time since her ascension, Arabella could see Earth below. It looked dark, worn and dingy, almost shop-soiled. Scudding clouds the color of lead cloaked most of the land masses. Yet, passing upward through them was a wisp of bright golden thread. At its apex, a small, translucent object hovered, held aloft by whirring rotors. The voice issued from a conical black horn on the upper surface. Arabella all but threw herself from Gabriel's arms to fly to it.

"Stephen!" she cried.

"Arabella, my darling!" The voice rose to a crescendo, then dropped into what Arabella always thought of as his professorial mode. "Thirty-seventh device, ninth attempt, contact has been successful — at least I hope so. Is that truly you, my love?"

Arabella fluttered around the floating device. It looked much like any of the machines that he had constructed in his workshop, except that it very nearly didn't exist. The sides of the device were of the same bronze hue that he favored for casings, but these were transparent, with the sheen of celluloid. The translucent gears she could see turning inside were cut into the finest and smallest cogs of any she had seen outside of a pocket watch and nearly as small. The whole object could not have weighed more than an ounce, if that.

"You will see that my voice comes up through the wire," Stephen continued. "It is amplified by the use of successive tympanums of rice paper, controlled by clockwork of the lightest and most refined of purified vegetable fiber. The power source is here in the mortal world with me. My gauges indicate that the output to run the mechanism is less than one thousandth of an ampere, so I've had to step down the generator to almost nothing. Speak to me, my darling, so I can assure myself that that is enough."

"I can hear you!" Arabella said. Her heart no longer pounded in her chest, but the upwelling of love she felt there fulfilled the same purpose.

"What is it like where you are, my love? It's raining in Philadelphia — of course, it always does."

She laughed.

"It is always light here, though you can see the constellations as bright as M. Claude's neon lamps. Everyone is happy. My father is here! We spend part of each day together. My grandfather, Robert Phillipson, greeted me when I came."

"Phillipson! What happened to him and his expedition?"

"A horrible ice storm engulfed him," Arabella said. "The tale is really thrilling. I will tell you all about it some time. And, oh, the most beautiful of angels escorted me here! Gabriel, speak to my husband, please." She beckoned the angel toward the small cone.

Gabriel lifted an admonitory finger.

"He would not hear my voice, my dearest Arabella. It is not his time."

"It's your words I must hear, my love," Stephen said. She stared at the cone as if seeing his face in it. "...I hate to ask such a mundane question, but where is our bankbook? I wanted to transfer some funds to pay the man who supplies my vacuum tubes, but I simply could not find it."

Arabella smiled indulgently. Wasn't that just like Stephen?

"It's in the bottom of my jewelry box, under the blue velvet flap. I'm sure Elizabeth and our daughters-in-law emptied the box once I'd gone, but they wouldn't want the box itself, it's so dowdy."

Stephen's voice was bright.

"You're right, my love! It's been in the middle of your dressing table all this time. Hold the line a moment."

All this time. How long had it been? It was on the tip of Arabella's tongue to ask when Stephen came back on the line.

"I found it! What a neat hand you have — had. My own scrawl is chicken scratchings in comparison."

"Stephen, how long...?" Arabella began.

"Wait a moment, my dear! The device is overheating. Back away! Don't let it harm...!"

Like lightning, a red flash crawled up the golden wire. Before Arabella could do anything, the cellulose device burst into flames. Fire licked out along the four small rotors. They burned in an instant to black flakes that broke up on the wind. Without their support, the device plummeted downward. Arabella dove after it, but Gabriel pulled her back. Crying out, she stretched out a helpless hand.

"It's gone, my dearest. Come back with me."

"He'll try again!" Arabella said, her voice thickening with sorrow. She cuddled into Gabriel's chest, her tears wetting the white samite of the angel's gown. "I know he will!"

And he did try. Four more devices ascended through the skies. Four times, the angel brought Arabella down to them, but each time, something went wrong, and they fell. Arabella's heart fell with them, but she did her best to keep hope alive.

The fifth time, a new object floated in their place. Instead of a speaker, a featherweight stylus quivered nervously over a translucent slate, supported by four transparent pairs of wings no bigger than those of a wren.

Arabella glanced at Gabriel for guidance.

"It's novel," the angel said, with a smile. "The Most High is pleased by his intelligence and drive. Take up the pen. Let Stephen know he has succeeded."

She floated close. Would her spirit fingers be able to touch an earthly object? Well, why not? She had heard stories from some of her fellow souls that they had attended séances both before and after their deaths. It had indeed been fashionable in her circle, though she had never been to one herself. Slates sealed front-to-front by elastic bands were sometimes inscribed with mystical words, or so Mrs. Baskell had told her.

If they could do it, so could she! She grasped the pen gently. It weighed almost nothing, but she felt resistance when she moved it. Applying the point to the slate, she wrote, *I am here.*

The pen quivered again, trying to leap from her hand. She let it go. Below her words, it inscribed a word in Stephen's terrible, idiosyncratic handwriting,

Success!

Gabriel raised the long trumpet and blew a lyrical fanfare.

"What a piece of work is man!" the angel said, beaming in triumph. "I will leave you here, my dear. You will be safe. Enjoy your communication."

She scarcely heard him as she kept her eyes on the remote-writer.

This version seems more stable than the others, Stephen wrote. *It was a mistake trying to add sound transmission to such a fragile device. I hope you will not miss my voice.*

Oh, I do, Arabella wrote back, *but your handwriting is almost as good. It's so very you.*

I love you, my darling. I will never stop loving you. How much do we pay the coal-gas merchant?

Arabella laughed.

Back and forth went messages both loving and mundane. The words stayed for a moment on the slate, then faded as soon as they were read, leaving room for the other to write. Arabella had to explain to him all the elements of householding that she had performed, even while on her sickbed. She included the small tweaks that a straightforward mind like Stephen's would not have anticipated.

Be certain that you check the housekeeper's accounts weekly, she wrote. *She has a tendency to add her own groceries to our bill. A leg of lamb and new peas that never appeared on our table last Easter. If she's straight for a month at a time, give her a small bonus.*

She would have continued forever, but suddenly Stephen paused.

It is nearly two in the morning, my love. I must sleep. I will write you again in the morning. Early. I can get up at dawn.

Arabella chided herself for her thoughtlessness. She never tired any longer. How funny that she was now stronger than he.

Don't, my love. If you will set aside a short time each day to write to me, that will be enough. I feel so blessed that you are such a genius! Not even death can sunder us.

Don't make me blush, Stephen scrawled, his writing even more atrocious than usual in his embarrassment. *Save me the best tales of your life there, and I will give you news. Tomorrow. Teatime. Is that all right?*

Arabella wondered how she would distinguish teatime from any other time, but she would find a way.

Yes, that will be wonderful. I love you, my darling.

I love you. Good night. Almost good morning!

The stars had spun a few degrees overhead by the time Arabella returned to the overside. Her family sat chatting in their favorite bower, the roses now interspersed with white jasmine. She felt lightheaded with joy as she settled onto the soft bench.

"You've been gone a long while," Great-Aunt Enid said, clasping her hand with both of her heavily veined ones. The old woman had not troubled to take on a younger image. "You're the ones who have to look at me," she had always said. "You missed a spectacularly talented team of acrobats. They were reunited at last with the ascension of their last member, and off they went to the light. I don't know why anyone would be in such a hurry."

"Once they were together, why wait?" Father said. "I looked for you, too, my dear. You must have been having a private conversation with someone."

Arabella couldn't wait to reveal her secret.

"I was! I was talking—well, writing—with Stephen!"

"That's impossible," Grandfather Robert said, his big brows drawing down over his strong nose. "Except for the odd medium, and I doubt their sanity, the living can't speak to the dead."

"Not this fellow, Dad," Father said, cocking his head. "He's got a brain on him. How did you talk, or write, Bella?"

Arabella explained Stephen's many attempts to contact her before lighting on the remote-writer. Aunt Enid snorted.

"Can't be bothered," she said. "My children didn't listen to me in life. Why would they want to hear from me now?"

Father looked thoughtful.

"I wouldn't mind exchanging a few words with your mother," he said, attempting to sound diffident, but Arabella knew him too well. He was dying to try it. "Assure her I'm fine, you know."

"I'm sure Stephen would bring her to the remote-writer," Arabella assured him. "But will Mother believe it's real?"

He cocked his head. "Well, you know, she did like to go to séances and consult seers. Not that I ever went with her. I think she'd be open to it. I sure hope so."

"Come down with me tomorrow," Arabella said, bouncing with eagerness. "We will ask him."

"I'm sure you're too busy to keep escorting me," Arabella told Gabriel when the angel appeared some time later and took both of them by the hand.

The angel smiled, lifting them off their feet and drawing them along the garden to the edge of the cloud mass.

"Time does not pass for me as it does for humans on Earth. I can be in many places at the same moment. Your husband's experiments interest me, as do all forms of communication. What he has set in motion the Most High has proclaimed a good idea, and I am to support it."

Arabella was overawed, as usual. "We will not waste the privilege."

Gabriel smiled that overwhelmingly beautiful smile, pure white teeth gleaming behind shapely red lips. "The Most High knows you won't."

Stephen agreed at once to bring Mother to the remote-writer. Instead of a long passage of time, it felt like mere moments before another style of handwriting appeared on the slate. Bella felt the warmth in her chest swell at the familiar shaping. Mother!

Benjamin, are you there? This is Nelly, your wife.

"Thank God!" Father reached for the pen. A beatific expression crossed his face as his hand closed around it. "Bella, just for a moment, I felt like I was holding her hand."

I'm here. Bella is with me. Are you well?

Father released the pen. It trembled for some long moments. Bella knew Mother must be overcome with emotion.

I have missed you so. Why did you leave me?

It was the disease, my dove. Nothing else could have torn me from your side.

Except the prize fights, Mother wrote, in crisp letters. Father snorted with laughter.

Guilty! Nothing but that and the cancer.

Arabella floated some distance from him and turned her back, to let him have privacy. Gabriel stayed close to her shoulder. She stared down at the broad face of the Earth, trying to follow the tiny thread of gold down to the middle of Philadelphia, where Stephen sat. It was too far away, but she felt close to him, thanks to this wonder of the machine age. At last, she heard a single sob followed by a deep intake of breath, as Father pulled himself together.

"Say goodbye to your man," he said. His eyes were red and puffy. "I need to go back up. Now."

"I will take you," Gabriel said, putting a tender arm around his shoulders. He smiled at Arabella, who returned to the slate.

Is Mother all right? she asked, nervously.

Happy, Stephen wrote. *Well, sad, of course, but comforted to know Heaven is real. It's late, my love. Good night.*

Good night, my darling. Be well.

Be… I know you are.

Arabella took her time floating upward. The stars were so lovely that she stopped to admire the constellations. Capricorn pranced with hooves of fire overhead, making way for the Water-Bearer with his overspilling burden. It would be Christmastime below. It was uncharitable, she knew, but she was grateful not to have to undertake all the tasks of the holiday, preparing feasts and writing endless cards to relatives, waiting frantically for delivery of presents from the shops. Would they or wouldn't they come in time? How nice not to have or need possessions, except for the remote-writer. It was a lifeline, quite literally, a line to those still living.

When she neared the garden, Harmony Fuller catapulted toward her, nearly bowling her over. Her hair flew everywhere and her eyes were wild.

"You have a means of communicating with home? Show me! How could you keep that a secret from me when you know how desperately lonely I have been?"

Arabella's eyes flew to her father. He shook his head. Arabella sighed. She knew what had happened. The young woman had been lurking near the Phillipsons, waiting for her to return, so she could pour out her misery into Arabella's sympathetic ear. *If only Wilfrid this! If only Wilfrid that!* She had overheard Arabella's secret.

"I'm afraid that wouldn't be possible right now," Arabella said, summoning all her patience. "It is night at home now. Stephen has gone to bed. Perhaps tomorrow...."

"No! Now! I must speak to him! To Wilfrid! He must get him!"

"Tomorrow," Arabella said, firming up her voice. She sat down on the bench beside Great-Aunt Enid, and crossed her arms. Harmony's imperious attitude was one reason they had not been friends on Earth. If she became unduly importunate, Arabella could plead weakness and flee to the privacy of her home. Here, she had no escape. Still, she sympathized. Her longing for communication with Stephen had almost dimmed the joy of Heaven itself. Let Harmony deliver herself of her gripes to poor old Wilfrid, and maybe they could all have some peace.

With no meals to get or errands to run, or even sleep to take, Arabella was all too aware of the plump young woman bouncing up and down in impatience just beyond the near hedge. When at last Gabriel appeared, Harmony threw herself in front of Arabella, insinuating her hand into the angel's fingers before Arabella could.

Arabella wished for some of the angel's eternal kindness and patience as they flew underneath the cloud bank. Harmony filled both their ears, all but rehearsing what she was going to say.

"And I will demand to know what he did with my jewelry! I am sure he doled it out to his foolish young nieces, instead of giving it all to my bosom friend, Penelope, as I would have wanted."

"Did you put that provision in your will?" Arabella asked.

"No! Did I know I was going to die in a stupid accident? I wouldn't need a will until I was old, or dying like you!"

Arabella pressed her lips closed to keep from saying something uncharitable. Harmony kept up her complaints all the way to the device, where Gabriel released her to float in the air. Harmony stared in dismay at the slate and pen.

"What is this? How can I talk into this?"

"You can't," Arabella said. "You write on it. Very gently!" she cried, as the young woman seized the pen.

She was familiar with Harmony's bold, swooping hand from the few missives she had received from her by mail. Harmony only managed to put a few words on the slate at a time.

"It vanishes! Where does it go?" she cried.

"To the receiving slate, down below," Arabella said, patiently. "Let go of the pen so Stephen can reply."

I will fetch him. Please wait, Mrs. Fuller.

They all stared at the slate, Harmony twitching furiously. What seemed like an eternity passed until the pen moved again. A masculine hand, much neater than Stephen's, filled the blankness.

My dearest! I cannot believe that you have been able to contact me from your eternal rest!

To continue to haunt you when you *thought you had achieved eternal rest*, Arabella thought, with deep sympathy for Wilfrid.

Wilfrid, you fool, I did not step out in front of that goods wagon! Harmony scrawled. *It climbed the kerb. I was an innocent victim. Stop telling people that I was careless! I heard you, you know!*

I am sorry, my love. I apologize, Wilfrid wrote, when his wife paused and shook tension out of her hand from gripping the little stylus so hard. *I miss you, my love. Life*, there was a long pause after the word before he continued, *has not been the same since I lost you.*

No, how could it? Now, pay attention, because all this vanishes when I fill the page. Give my best dress and all of my jewelry to Penelope. Not your nieces!

I left two lending-library books in the bureau.... She wrote and wrote, leaving little time for Wilfrid to reply in between scolds and instructions. After yet another eternity, she let go of the pen and floated back.

"That's all I have to say to him right now," she said. Her eyes lifted. To Arabella's surprise, they were full of tears. "Thank you."

"You're welcome," Arabella said. Gabriel enveloped the smaller woman in his arm and soared away.

Is she gone? Wilfrid asked, in tentative letters.

Yes, Arabella wrote back. *She can talk of nothing but how much she misses you.*

I'd never have known that in life. Thank you.

Arabella was thoughtful on her way back to the upperside. Perhaps now that Harmony had gotten that bile out of her system, all of them could have some peace.

She could not have been more wrong. In the garden, a huge crowd of souls had gathered around the rose bower. When Arabella appeared, they surrounded her, all shouting for her attention.

"I want to talk to my son! I'm sure he's lost without me."

"The police need to know who shot me! They think it's my beau, but it wasn't!"

"My granddaughter tore up my will! She and my solicitor are conspiring to defraud the rest of the family. I must warn my wife."

"Your husband must send a telegram to Nairobi for me!"

"Arabella will be happy to help you!" Harmony Fuller said, standing on a bench with her arms outstretched. She beamed at Arabella. "Stephen will put you in touch with your loved ones, like he did mine!"

Before she could do anything, the crowd swept Arabella up in their arms. Led by Harmony, they swooped over the garden and over the edge of the cloud bank. Arabella fought to get free, but the gigantic man holding onto her waist would not let go. She pounded her fists helplessly against the bright white tweed of his jacket.

"Sir, don't! Please. My husband must get his sleep. He has tasks to do. I only write to him once a day."

"I have to hear from my daughter," he said, his fleshy face set. "She is supposed to graduate from university, the first in our family to get a real education. I want to know she did it."

"But that's trivial!" Arabella said. "It's not life and death."

"Not to you, Mrs. Educated Woman. It means everything to me."

"But…" Arabella's protests were overwhelmed by the cacophony of the massed souls, all clamoring about whom they would contact. Ahead of her, Harmony had reached the remote-writer. She seized the pen and scrawled upon the slate.

"Stephen, wake up! You're needed."

Arabella squirmed free of the man carrying her and flew to protect her husband's invention and her husband from being disturbed.

It was too late. The device at the other end must have had a clockwork alarm of some kind, because the pen began to move under its own power. Harmony had awakened him!

What's wrong? Has something happened to Arabella?

The big man came up underneath and knocked them both away from the writer. He took the pen in his massive fist. His face screwed up in concentration as he printed laboriously on the sheet. The device bounced with every stroke, the tiny wings at the corners flapping desperately to keep it in the air.

Get in touch with Miss Melissa Noks, 14 Green Xing, N Yrk. Did she grajuayte or not?

Who is this? Stephen had just enough time to write before more people pressed in between the man and the remote-writer. Arabella was pushed farther and farther away from it. Souls fought to get in and scribble their own demands.

"Please! Poor Stephen! All he wanted to do was stay in touch with me! Don't!" she pleaded, as a tall man reached down and grabbed the device out of the hands of a fat woman with dark hair piled high on her head. "You'll break it!"

"Cease!"

Thunder crashed suddenly, and bolts of lightning shot all around them. The souls sprang away, trying to find a place to shelter from the signs of divine wrath. The putti delved deep into their undercloud nests. Harmony Fuller tried to hang onto the remote-writer, but a blue-white fork of lightning cracked directly above her. She sprang back, her mouth open.

The armored angel with long, flowing blue-black hair hung there beside the device. The sword which normally hung sheathed beside his—her?—side was raised high.

"How dare you disturb the peace of the Most High?" Michael demanded, fearsome in furious beauty.

Arabella trembled, but Harmony was never one to be deterred by authority. She fluttered close by, trying to reach around the angel for the remote-writer.

"Her husband invented this device so she could speak to him on Earth, and I see no reason why the rest of us shouldn't be able to use it, too."

"Cease!" Michael repeated. The voice's very force threw Harmony hurtling into the distance. "You are in Heaven now! You must not let such matters deter you from seeking your final reward!"

"But my daughter!" the big man protested.

"My stockbroker!"

"My grandson!"

Michael's eyes narrowed.

"The Most High has decided that this device is a distraction," the angel declared in a tone that even Harmony didn't challenge. "It must not prevent you from your contemplation of eternal bliss. I am sorry, my daughter. You had a small miracle, but it is ended." With one sweep, the massive silver sword severed the golden thread tethering it to the world below. Instantly, the wire dropped out of sight.

Without the power feeding it from the steam dynamo in Philadelphia, the tiny wings began to falter. They fluttered weakly, then stopped.

"No!" Arabella cried. She dove for the falling box, and caught it to her chest. "Oh, Michael, can't I even have it as a keepsake?"

The angel smiled.

"Of course, my daughter. The Most High would never deprive you of a reminder of your love. Now, all of you, come with me! No more arguments! You will see your loved ones again when they ascend here to join you! Come!"

Reluctantly, the souls gathered behind the brilliant golden wings and made their grumbling way to the garden. Harmony Fuller pushed out in front of the group, her chin held high. Arabella couldn't help but be cross with the little woman. Harmony had ruined everything!

Father laid a sympathetic hand on her shoulder when she returned to the garden.

"At least you still have the box," he said, though both of them knew what little comfort that was. "Stephen's a clever man. I'm proud to have had him as a son-in-law, and one day I'll tell him so. There's a concert starting across the way. Why not go and listen to it?"

"Another time, I think," Arabella said, playing with the tiny wings. "Let me sit and contemplate eternity. By myself."

"As you wish, Bella." Father smiled and flitted away, escorting Great-Aunt Enid and Grandfather Robert toward the sounds of heavenly music. Arabella felt coldness in her chest, and tried to drive back the tears starting in her eyes. *If Harmony Fuller ever showed her face again, she would get an earful! Oh, Stephen!*

The pen on the remote-writer stirred and dipped toward the slate.

My love, are you there?

Hildy and the Steampowered Hounds of Hella

L. Jagi Lamplighter

When Aunt Grimgerda claimed that a hound had stolen the shade Odin had sent her to collect, we Valkyries had a jolly good laugh. I mean, really! If you were to invent a story to cover for your failure to carry out your appointed task, surely you could come up with something a bit more credible.

So when I arrived on the battlefield one bright morning to collect the hero I had been assigned to bring to Valhalla, and a hound — made of gleaming bronze and venting steam from its pointed metal ears — rushed in and snatched the fallen warrior's spirit before my very eyes, I sure as Hella wasn't going to return my sisters and aunts to face their mockery.

I'm Brunhilda, by the way, named after my aunt, but have two Brunhildas among a couple dozen women can get tedious. So they call me Hildy.

Hello. I am Hildy, Valkyrie-in-training. Pleasure to meet you.

Curtsies.

Where was I? Oh, right.

I had a split-second to make a decision. Face mockery, or pursue the miscreant, clear my name, and Aunt Grimgerda's,

too. Aunt Gerda's been a Valkyrie since before rocks began putting on moss, but I am quite new, still earning my horse's wings, so to speak. It might not go so well for me if I came home telling strange tales about why I had failed to carry out my charge. So, I chose…

Cry havoc and pursue the dogs of steam!

The hound loped at truly amazing speeds, crossing fields, bogs, and fen, but I had an advantage, as well. I was mounted on a winged horse. My fine steed, Svartfaxi, and I rocketed across the landscape, wind whipping our hair—well, mane in Svartfaxi's case—about our heads. We kept pace with the rude hound until, with a prodigious leap, the metallic canine plunged into a dark hole in the ground, vanishing from sight.

I may have said a few words I would not have voiced if Mother were present to hear.

I landed Svartfaxi. Sliding to the ground, I slipped forward, spear in hand, to peer into the hole. It was dark as the night after Managarm finishes his feast in the sky.

Straightening up, I rested my spear butt-first on the ground.

"Ghosts," I called sternly. "Attend me!"

There is always a ghost somewhere nearby.

"Yes, Chooser," came an eerie, hair-raising voice. "How can I serve?"

"Really," I sighed, "is all that drama *truly* necessary?"

"I suppose not," muttered the ghost.

A shimmering, misty figure slouched forward. It looked like a middle-aged man, partially balding, most likely died of indigestion.

"Shade," I commanded coolly, "tell me of this hound who stole my prey."

"What's in it for the likes of me?" muttered the shade.

"I won't catch you up by your heel and throw you into the Halls of Hella, where you may meet any number of unpleasant fates, straw-death-dier!"

"You don't have to be rude," muttered the ghost, adding grumpily, "Those are Hella's new hounds."

"Hella? The Lady of Hell?" I cried in surprise. "She has steam-powered hounds now? What happened to Garm?"

"If I knew the secrets of Hella's Kingdom, would I be out here to be ordered about by the likes of you?" bemoaned the ghost.

I shrugged. "Be gone, before I change my mind."
The ghost fled.

In the past, the cave entrance to Hella's Kingdom had been guarded by a great brute of a beast named Garm. Garm was not a bad sort, once you grew to know him — not like Fenrir or Hati. Garm had a spot on his stomach where, if you rubbed him there, he would go all puppyish and wag his tail and howl happily.

But, I must admit, he was imposing.

Only this time, when Svartfaxi and I arrived at the cave mouth, Garm was not there. Or rather, he was not standing guard like a proud sentinel. Instead, he sat off to one side, head down, tail between his legs.

It took me a moment to realize that the great hound was sulking.

"Hello there, Garm-Old-Boy." I tossed him a honey cake and a haunch of venison. Usually, he lapped this stuff up. Today, he hardly noticed.

I walked over to inspect him. The great hound whined softly and rubbed his head against me, nearly knocking me over. Now, I do not believe I am bragging when I tell you I am a strong young woman. We Valkyries can lift stones that no ten men alive today could lift, but Garm nearly sent me sprawling.

He is a very large dog.

Garm whimpered and looked sad, with huge puppy eyes, at the cave entrance. A gleam of bronze caught my eye. I peered closer. Deep in the mouth of the cave stood a brass and bronze hound the size of a house. Steam came from its nostrils and ears. Its mechanical tail swung back and forth, like a pendulum.

"Replaced were you, old boy?" I scratched him behind the ears.
He merely moaned softly.
I scrunched him behind the ear. "I shall see what can be done."

I have visited Hella's residence before. I came once with my mother when I was a wee lass, something about a mix-up of shades that needed straightening out. I recalled the place as the epitome of dull — quite, dismal, and, if I may be frank, boring. My best friend Rowan the Sea Witch had listed it as Number Two on her list of places in the universe most in need of remodeling.

But maybe Hella had overheard her, because I hardly recognized the place. Gleaming bright tubes of brass and copper extended from floor to…whatever one might call the blackness overhead. Gigantic gears and pistons, rising hundreds of feet into the air, whirled and clacked. The dead, who once drifted about listlessly, had all been put to work and now moved busily amidst the machines throwing switches and shoveling coal.

The Kingdom of Hella had become as busy as a factory town!

"Ah, Valkyrie, I have been expecting one of your ilk," purred a female voice.

I spun around.

Hella rode toward me in a chariot pulled by rather handsome clockwork goats. She was dressed smartly in a black and white tea gown with a white and black corset. One side of her face was fair and beautiful. The other was hidden behind a copper mask that had a complicated monocle over the eye. She carried a black and white parasol, which she snapped open and shut as she rode.

"Hi, Aunt Hella," I couldn't recall a connection by which she was truly my aunt, but I felt it showed respect. "I must say you are looking quite handsome. Might I have the name of your seamstress?" I gestured upward. "And I must say, compliments on what you've done with the place."

"You like it, do you?" Hella pulled to a stop beside me and looked up at the pipes and gears, smiling fondly. "My new suiter felt I should…lighten the place up a bit."

"Lighten?" I nodded slowly. "That's one word for it."

Suiter?

"Come," she purred. "I will introduce you."

Hella's new suiter was a large fellow with truly enormous biceps and a big bushy black beard he'd made an attempt to tame with pomade. He sat in a contraption that was like a cross between a chair and a cart. It moved him along without even the pretense of mechanical goats.

"Helli, who's this intruder?" rumbled Bushy Face.

"This is my niece Brunhilda…or maybe it's Rossweisse. I do get them confused," Hella purred in her throaty voice.

"Hildy," I extended my hand.

He grasped it and shook.

Good grip!

"Hephaestus's the name," said Bushy Face. "Heph for short."

"Ooooh!" I murmured.

"And that means…what?" his equally bushy eyebrows drew together suspiciously.

I gestured at the new décor. "This is…"

"My idea? Sure! Helli has a huge work force down here. Why should they be flitting about, purposelessly, when they could be acting and achieving!"

"Isn't it magnificent?" purred Hella. "I feel as if I have a new lease on life. Should have done this centuries ago."

"But how?" I asked. "Aren't they, well, dead?"

"Psychotropic metals," explained Heph, banging on the brassy surface of his motorized cart. "Spirits can touch it."

I blinked. "That's quite…clever."

It was clever, though I could not help feeling pity for the poor spirits, condemned to work again, after their hard lives.

Though, truth be told, they looked happier than they had last time I was here. On the other hand, most likely anything would be better than to have no purpose and nothing to which they could look forward for all eternity. Still, there was the matter of why I had come.

"Um, Auntie, there seems to be a bit of a mix up. I believe your new hounds are…somewhat confused as to which spirits they are supposed to be fetching. They've made a few mistakes."

"Ah yes," Hella made a languid gesture. "I thought you might get around to that."

After some haggling, it was decided that a contest would be held — myself against the shades and their new contraptions — best three out of five. If I won, the shades that the Norns had destined to become Einherjar would be returned to Valhalla. If I lost — which was not in the cards, I do say! — I would stay in Hella's realm as her personal guard, training her new elite force of hero shades.

The challenges were to be discus, wrestling, footrace, high jump, and swimming. I would lose the swimming contest, of course. No fleshly form could swim faster than a shade in the water, but I was pretty sure I could win the other four.

I had full confidence in my triumph.

The first contest was the discus put. The slain heroes that Hella had captured went first. Each clanked out wearing a different steam-powered contraption. One had pistons that moved the arms. Another looked like a walking catapult. A third carried a discus made of this psychotropic metal, and so on.

They all threw tolerably well. The unaugmented fellow tossed the discus three times farther than any normal man could. I applauded him. He had done well. Truly.

Then came my turn.

I threw the discus so far it could not be found.

Next came wrestling. Their steampowered outfits were gaudy and, if I do say so, quite amusing. It took quite a bit of effort not to laugh. I might have accidentally let a bit of a chuckle slip out when the fellow with the lobster claws clanked forward. But I did try to be kind.

I hope they appreciated that.

Against a full-fledged Einherjar in Valhalla, I admit I might have found myself in a bit of trouble. But these poor blokes were newly dead. They had not even had a single sip of Odin's spirit-strengthening mead. Even with the extra copper and steam they were hardly a challenge.

Didn't even break a sweat.

Next up, a distance race. I grinned. *This* was my specialty. Even among the Valkyrie, I was considered fleet of foot. True, Hephastus had designed a number of ingenious contraptions for the shades. One had treads. Another had gigantic wheels. A third included a hot air balloon and a propeller. But I had seen them practicing, and none of them were quite fast enough to offer serious competition.

I grinned and performed a few stretches, ready to race.

As I headed for the chosen track, a cloaked figure bumped into me heading the other way. Before I could murmur 'I beg your pardon', a very familiar voice — deep and subtle — spoke in my ear.

"Let them win."

I truly did my best not to whimper. I had been really looking forward to the foot race. I may even have made the error of vaunting in a distinctly unlady-like fashion before hand.

"But…?" I gaped. "Grandfather? A-are you certain? Foot races are my forte."

"Let her win this one," repeated Odin, "And the next one."
And then he was gone. The sly dastard.

So, I let her men win. The whole thing was ridiculous. I practically had to run in place. True, the treaded vehicle made surprisingly good time, and I am quite convinced that the mini-airship would give even a fast mortal a difficult time of it. But it was the vehicle with wheels — which won in the end — that gave me an opportunity to stretch my legs a bit. But really!

There I was, running beside the slain heroes in their coppery contraptions, pumping my arms and picking up my legs so high — in an effort to look as if I made an effort without covering territory — that I nearly kneed myself in the jaw.

It would be a downright miracle if anyone was fooled.

The high jump was easier to lose. The slain, unencumbered by bodies, could leap quite high, especially the one wearing Hephaestus's custom-made, piston-powered jumpers. Frankly, I am not certain I would have won that one, even if had I tried.

But if I had won the foot race, it would not have mattered.

What was Grandfather up to?

But, of course, people have been wondering about *that* since before the dawn of time. If I wanted to know the answer to "What is Odin up to?" I was going to have to stand in a very long and illustrious line.

As I rested after the exertions of the high jump — leaning over and doing a spot of stretching — the mysterious cloaked figure with my grandfather's voice returned.

"You'll need to win this last one," he murmured. "Only be sure to renegotiate first: loser must give the winner a boon. She'll go for it, because she believes her chances are good."

I raised my head and stared into his single eye, what I could see of it under the hood.

"Are you mad?" I replied. I am embarrassed to say I may have sounded rather tart. "What if she asks for my life? Or for me to stay down here forever? I may like what they've done with the place, but…"

"Win," his voice was deep, "and there will be no problem."

"Against swimming shades?" I waved my hands like frightened birds. "Grandfather, it really would have been more expedient had you mentioned that you wanted me to win the last contest *the first time* you spoke to me! Back then, there was still time to rearrange the events!"

He shook his head. "If this last one were not swimming, she would not have enough expectation of winning to tempt her to try for a boon."

"But she will win!" I cried. "And I will be forced to spend the rest of my life drilling ex-heroes in invigorating calisthenics!"

The hooded head shook. "Be assured, *you* can find a way to win."

And he was gone again, leaving me standing there with my mouth agog. I was fortunate that there were no flies in the land of the dead, or I surely would have caught a mouthful.

Hella went for the boon. Who wouldn't?

I managed to talk her into holding the last contest in three days time. This gave me a bit of a breather—a short stretch of time to practice and think. And mayhaps to have my last meal as a free woman.

The first thing I did was a few practice runs, but even ordinary, run-of-the-mill, straw-deathers could beat me in the water—much less heroic shades with Hephaestus's steampowered inventions.

I swam pretty fast, if I might say so myself.

They zoomed by me so quickly that I could hardly make them out.

By day two, I sat slumped against a huge copper pipe, warm from the heated water and steam that coursed through it. I must tell you truly I was rather melancholy. I had come here with such confidence, convinced that I could solve this problem all on my lonesome. Now I faced the very real danger of spending the rest of eternity inside what amounted, when all was said and done, to an oversized grandfather clock.

What in Bestla's name was I to do?

I was still ruminating when a shade came to let me know that Hephaestus required me presence for a *private* chat.

I had a fair idea of what he wanted to… *discuss*. Men. So predictable.

Rising, I followed the messenger. As an airship floated by overhead, I glanced at the shade that had been sent to fetch me, a young woman. I did not recall ever having seen her before, but there was something of the familiar about her.

"Do I know you?" I asked.

The young woman beamed. "You do, Brunny! I thought perhaps you had forgotten your old nurse."

"*Nanny Shara*? But you're not…"

"Old?" She smiled with kind amusement. "I was back then. But I've been here a while now. We shades tend to revert back to the time we remember most clearly."

"What is this like?" I asked, gesturing at the pistons and gears, the towers and airships. "A steampowered nightmare?"

"Oh, 'tis not so bad," Her sweet smile was quite reminiscent of my old nurse. "At least it gives us something to do."

"You'd rather slave away than rest?"

"One can only rest so long before all the pleasure goes out of it," sighed Once-Nanny Shara. "Besides, no one slaves. We only work if we wish."

"Why would you wish to?"

"To have something to do. And we can earn things."

"What could the dead earn?"

"Manna. Ambrosia. Nectar. Trips to Elysia," said Nanny Shara, "and — my personal favorite — chances to look in the reflecting pools and watch our loved ones back in the daylit realms."

"Oh." I considered. "Doesn't sound so bad."

"No," Shana agreed. "Not for the dead. 'twould be terrible for a live one, like yourself."

Somehow, that did not make me fell any better. "Seems I'm going to be joining you — if I can't figure out how to win the swimming contest."

"How to win?"

"Grandfather seems to think I can. But I seem to be lacking the correct physique — or lack thereof."

"Then, maybe your grandfather does not mean for you win by physical prowess," said Nanny Shara. "He is a tricky one, is Odin."

"But what else do I have?" I must admit that I may have sounded a bit on the querulous side. "I am a Valkyrie. Strength and brawn are our gifts."

"What do you normally do when you have a problem that cannot be solved by force of arms?" asked Shara. She suddenly looked very much like my old nanny. I could see it in the concerned crinkle of her eyes and the kindness of her smile.

"I ask my friend Rowan, the sea witch."

My old nurse's eyebrows shot upward. "Are you the only Valkyrie who is friends with a sea witch?"

Just then, we reached the place where Hephaestus waited. I had thought I knew what he was about, that one. I had encountered my share of cads. Only, when he came around the corner in his steam-powered cart—gears *whirling* and *clacking*—he did not look the least bit like a lothario.

He looked…

Angry.

Hephaestus's cart stopped beside me. He glared down. Shara curtsied and hurried away. I'm not often intimidated. I am fleet of foot and blessed with inhuman strength, able to hold my own against anything smaller than a blue whale.

But he was a *god.*

And not a puny one, either. The man had biceps larger than some bulls.

"Listen, Valkyrie," he growled, glaring down at me. "I don't know what you are about, but a blind goat could tell that you threw those last two contests. Hella doesn't believe me, but," He pointed at his face, "these eyes don't lie." He pointed his finger at me. "You do anything to hurt her, and it will be the last thing you do. Clockwork hounds and hawks will follow you to the ends of the earth and tear you limb from limb."

"Right!" I croaked, recalling the speed of the hound I had followed from the battlefield. "Don't hurt Hella!"

Only…*was I going to hurt her?*

I hadn't a single clue what Grandfather had planned in that mysterious head of his. If I was going to hurt her, I hoped Odin had a plan to keep those steamy hawks and hounds from making mincemeat of me.

"It's the real thing, then?" I asked Heph. "Between the two of you, I mean?"

Hephaestus leaned back, scratched his beard, and grinned. "Sure is. Man like me. Been unappreciated all my life. I know a good thing when I find it."

"That's…very nice?"

"We're two of a kind, her and I. Half crippled, half whole. I'm cripple on the bottom half." He flipped up the leather cover over his lap. His legs were on the thin side, puny even. "And her on the left half.

But together." He spread his hands indicating the clockwork towers and gigantic pistons, the spinning gears the size of hills and the airships with their oversized propellers. "We make beautiful music."

"Great," I squeaked, trying my best to look cheerful. "Glad to hear it."

His eyes narrowed. "You just remember what I told you."

At the place where the World Tree touched the Ocean of Dream, a young woman in a simple blue gown stood on the beach, singing. Her long, glorious, red locks streamed out from her head in all directions. She held a distaff in her hands, with which she spun seafoam into thread.

She looked so lovely. I wondered if I could carry off that over-a-yard-of-hair look. *Probably not.* It would be problematic during battle.

I landed Svartfaxi on the pale sands of the beach. My flying steed snorted sparks and tossed its black mane and tail. I gave him a pat and an apple and slipped to the ground.

"Greetings, Rowan."

"Hello, Hildy," The young sea witch waved, a sweet little smile on her lips.

The moment she stopped singing, her hair floated slowly down, until it hung normally, brushing her ankles. The sea foam that had not already been spun into thread dropped back into the salty waves.

"Oops," Rowan Vanderdecken pressed her hand against her mouth in mirthful chagrin. "Ah, well." She held up the distaff, peering at the fluffy white yarn already wound around it. "I guess that's enough for now. Here, be a dear and hold this, will you?"

Handing me the distaff, she pulled from a little cloth pouch a device made of gold that looked like a cross between a hair comb and a spider. She placed it on top of her head. The little golden contraption unfolded six spidery legs and rapidly moved down her long hair, using its legs to braid the thick, luxurious locks. By the time it reached the bottom, it had formed a handsome braid. The spiderish-device then folded into a pretty golden hair clasp.

"Isn't that amazing?" My friend beamed.

"If I might hazard a guess," I drawled. "Captain Remington made that for you?"

"Yes, he did! He's so much fun."

"Remmy's is such a character." I laughed, adding teasingly, "He must like you to visit so often and make you such clever gifts."

Rowan made a face. "Not really. He was a man of many talents — not just military ones — before he died his hero's death. Now all he does is lead a band of Einherjar. I think he's bored. Besides," she looked at me sideways, a sad little smile haunting her lips. "I'm not the one he holds a tender for."

I had not the slightest idea what she was implying.

"I have a problem," I said, and explained, ending with, "Can you help me?"

"Most certainly!" declared my friend. "Easy-peasy!"

"Really?" I perked up. "What did you have in mind?"

"Well," she tapped her chin as she thought. "How about getting a bunch of shades to push you? Shades like Valkyries. They listen to you."

I tried to picture that. "Not fast enough, since they'd have to lug my fleshly body, and they would be slower than the hero shades to begin with."

"Oh. Good point. Scratch that," said Rowan, as energetic as ever. "How about I give you some warding powder. You throw it in the water, and the shades can't swim there." She held out another pouch, a leather one this time. Sea witches carry many of pouches.

I shook my head. "No good. Then they couldn't swim through the water at all. That strikes me as unfair. I have a feeling Hella would agree. She might disqualify me and I would lose by default."

"Hmm." She rolled her eyes upward, thinking. "Oh, I know! Lightning grease!"

"Lightning…I beg your pardon?"

"Lightning grease. You cover your body with it and…*ffu-umme!*…you shoot through the water with the speed of a shooting star."

I grinned. "That sounds like exactly what I am looking for."

"Great! I'll mix you up a batch. But I may need a few ingredients. Any chance you could fly over to Olympus and catch me a few lightning bolts?"

Something in my expression must have conveyed my answer.

"No worries. Lightning grass or even an electric eel will serve instead!"

"I really hope this works," I muttered. "Otherwise, this will be the last time I see you…or the ocean…or the sky."

"It'll work." She waved comforting a hand at me. "Have I ever let you down?"

Glumly, I mumbled, "There could always be a first time."

As it turned out, I need not have worried.

The lightning grease worked splendidly. I moved through the water as if it were made of dream stuff. I left the hero shades in my wake.

Hella looked pale as I climbed dripping from the Cocytus, paler, I mean. She held her beau's arm as if I was going to demand that she end things with him.

I hoped to Valhalla that I was not.

When I reached my towel and armor, a familiar cloaked figure stood beside it.

"Well done," he nodded.

"Um…thank you?" I murmured, toweling my hair. "Glad you are pleased that I demeaned myself and lost a footrace of all things. Even Hephaestus didn't fall for it, you know."

He chuckled.

"I do hope you are going to explain," I sighed. "For what am I to ask her?"

He leaned over and whispered in my ear. My eyebrows leapt so high, they may well have been attempting to abandon my face.

"Just…that?"

I could not help feeling relieved. At least, Heph would not feel the need to hound me to the ends of the earth with his steampowered hunting giraffe or whatever his latest contraption might be.

Hephaestus was holding Aunt Hella's hand tightly when I came striding back.

"I am ready to request my boon!" I announced.

Their faces went even paler.

"Yes?" Hella gripped her beau more tightly.

I crossed my arms. I am sorry to say I might have enjoyed that moment. "As the winner of the Valkyrie/Shades of the Dead challenge, I request for my boon that the goddess Hella limits herself to stealing only one hero's shade every seven years."

"Just…" Hella moistened her half-black, half-white lips. "Just that?"

"Quite right."

Very slowly, the right side of her mouth curved upward, forming a smile.

Recalling their desire to have me stay and train their troops, I added, on my own initiative, "Oh, and you should request an Einherjar to come train your men. We would not want them to grow rusty. Ask for Captain Remington. He will love this punky steam stuff."

There. That should help Remmy fend off the horrors of boredom. Only, as I turned to go, I suddenly grasped what that little sad smile of Rowan's had been intended to communicate.

Did she believe that Remmy liked *me*?

Oh, no! That would never do.

Definitely not my type!

I turned back to Hella and Hephaestus. "Perhaps you two lovebirds would do another couple a favor? When Captain Remington comes, do tell him that he was recommended by Rowan Vanderdecken."

As I left the cave mouth, Svartfaxi trotted forward and nuzzled me. My flying steed seemed no worse for the time without me, but I was very glad to see him.

"Well done, Granddaughter."

I jumped. Odin stood beside me. He was dressed in his ordinary garb now, a huge gray cloak and wide-brimmed hat. His one eye gleamed from beneath its brim.

"Grandfather, whatever was that all about?" I asked, one hand still grasping the dark mane of my steed protectively. "My whole point in coming here had been to bring those shades back to Valhalla. And, yet, you want us to leave them here?"

"My child, it is never a good idea to keep all your eggs in one basket," Odin replied, a gleam in his one eye. "Should something ever happen to Valhalla, we now have a backup plan—and one of which few will know. A small force, true, but an elite one. Nice touch, recommending Captain Remington. It's wise to busy clever minds with useful projects."

I nodded, relieved and yet still, if I might speak frankly, a bit shaken. I glanced around. The enormous brass hound still gleamed in the cave mouth. To the far right, the real thing lay dejected, ignoring his food.

"Oh no!" I sighed. "I forgot Garm! I was going to make her do something for him."

Odin tilted the brow of his hat up, glancing left and right. "It doesn't look as if he is needed here anymore. Why don't you take him with you?"

And that, my dear readers, is how I came to own a hound.

Windows to the Soul

Danielle Ackley-McPhail

30, October, 1870

The crows are what I remember most clearly of the day they say my father died. They wheeled in the sky, a black whirlwind of feathers, beaks, and talons, dipping and diving over the remains of Papa's cherished courtyard. They screamed their outrage. My heart cried with them, though my voice remained mute, shocked at the destruction that surrounded me. I had turned a slow circle before dropping to my knees at the center of what had recently been a garden oasis once tended by my mother's gentle hand. It laid in ruins around me, rose bushes torn from the ground, their petals bruised and stained, other flowers, for which I did not even have names, had been crushed into the dirt. The fountain at the heart of the garden lay toppled and shattered, while blood marred the white marble cobblestones beneath me. But of my beloved Papa… there was no sign.

A.A.F

Aleta Angelina Fabricio set down her quill, her hand only slightly trembling. It had been many months, but not until now had she found the strength to document what she had

discovered that day. It hardly seemed necessary, the memories were so crisp, but she could not risk overlooking anything. All Saints' Day drew near, and with it *Día de Muertos* — the Day of the Dead. If there was any time to prove what she suspected it was now.

No matter what she had been told, she would not believe that her father was dead when she had cause to doubt. No body had ever been found. And a month ago, on a rare trip into nearby Oaxaca, Lina was certain she had seen him in the distance, though he had gone before she reached where she thought he had been. There were other times she would swear she had seen him, but none as certain as that day. She could not say what kept him away from his family, but she would use a device of his own creation to prove it was not death.

Before his…*disappearance*…Papa had been working on his grand invention, one Lina hoped to employ. The device was intended to grant the wearer the ability to part the Veil between life and death, to see beyond the physical world into that of the afterlife. In his journal, Papa had claimed to have finally achieved success. If he had, Lina could not say. Above his worktable there were two boxes, one empty, the other containing only a partially constructed device. Her father, however, was always meticulous in documenting his process. Using his journal, it should be a small matter to complete his work. Lina prayed that was so, and that she knew enough to put practice to his theory.

Setting aside her journal, she drew her father's to her. The pages were filled with diagrams drawn in a fine hand in clear and precise detail. Surrounding the images were intricate notations, but also amongst them tender passages giving insight to what drove him. The pain. The longing. The love. She read of aether and lenses and windows to the soul…that was how he put it. So poetic. His grand plan. Her mother had been the other half of his heart. His soul. And he had been determined to look upon her once more, and the son lost with her. To know that even death did not part them. Lina frowned. He had been so focused on that goal that Lina herself may as well have been a ghost, for all he saw her, always there, always tending to his needs, never noticed.

Faint bitterness bit at the back of her throat. Early on, when she was younger, it would have festered, but as an adult she forced it away. Even had she not read his journal she would have known the love her father had for his family, including her. If Mother had not died so suddenly, without warning… The loss had been terrible, leaving

Father half a man and that half driven to be whole again. Love for him kept Lina rereading long into the night. Checking and rechecking the science of his work, making sure she fully understood before she took his watchmaker's tools to the delicate machinery half-finished in its box above his worktable. Her eyes burned from reading and she had already filled the lantern twice over.

Closing her eyes, she massaged her scalp where she had pinned back her dark locks to keep them out of her way. Behind her Papa's pet crow, Beltran, gave a broken croak. She rose and went to him, careful to make a *shh*ing sound to announce her presence lest the bird startle and bring his beak against her. Slowly, gently she ruffled his crest, as Father used to do. She marveled at how the feathers felt both soft and slick to her touch. The crow made low moan-like sounds and leaned into her fingers.

Faithful Beltran. She had found him beneath the remains of her mother's favorite rose bush, battered and near to death, his eyes gouged from his head. Lina marveled that he still lived, regardless of her efforts. Her heart broke to see the still-angry red lines of scars layering his face, bald of feathers around the sockets where his eyes had been. Somehow she had restored his health. Now to restore his vision. Beltran was the key, if her father's notations were correct, for many believed that crows possessed the gift of seeing into both worlds, that of the living and the dead. This was the crux of her father's premise.

In a box beside the crow's perch lay a brass cowl the size of a child's bracelet or a large man's ring but bent slightly outward, thin, with wires and ocular lenses suspended in the center. Next to that was a small bottle of laudanum. The traveling doctor had given it to Lina weeks after that day in the garden to aid her rest. The nightmares had been relentless. They still were for she would not drug herself, not at the risk of dimming her thoughts and disassociating herself from the world when she depended on the sharpness of her mind more now than ever. She suffered the pain of those dreams for they drove her to success here in her father's workroom.

"Are you ready, *pequeño?*" *Little one.*

On his perch, Beltran bobbed up and down and ruffled his feathers before settling once more. Lina stroked down his back, not certain if she was soothing herself or the bird. The premise of what she was about to attempt had been outlined in her father's journal in precise detail. She had grown up at his side, observing, if not helping, in this very room on one invention or another. Nothing of what he wrote was beyond her. Drawing a deep breath and releasing it slowly, she first moved to the washbasin and cleaned her hands. Then she dusted the work area carefully, capturing any dirt on a cloth before taking out the folding pouch containing Papa's prized tools. Unrolling the worn leather, she set the implements to the side within easy reach then took down from the shelf above her head a wooden box edged in brass plates studded with rivets. As she opened it her breath caught in her chest. She smelled the faint musk of oiled leather as the lantern light glimmered off a set of intricate goggles. The lenses shimmered silver with faintly rainbow-hued swirls. In truth, they were dual lenses of clear polished glass. The tint came from the gas trapped between them. Her father called it aether and claimed it the substance of the beyond. How he had captured a sampling was and always would be a mystery to her. Attached to one of those lenses inside the leather frame of the goggles was a fine filament of copper wire that ended in webbing adhered to the thinnest of curved glass plates Lina had ever seen. Here she shuddered faintly before steeling herself. Per her father's notations, that minute disc must be applied direct onto her eye, but only one of them, else her vision would be completely filled with the afterlife, blinding her to the mortal realm around her.

Beltan's cowl was of the same design, now minus their even smaller curved discs. Lina had removed them, given his lack of eyes. She only hoped that the wires themselves set into the sockets where the crow's eyes had been would function the same. If any remnant of the nerves remained, there was hope.

"Aleta Angelina Fabricio!"

Lina jerked around, catching the edge of her lip between her teeth as she met her grandmother's eye. She forced her head to remain level, rather than dipping in instinctive guilt at the use of her full name.

"Yes, Abuela?"

"You promised me you would sleep, and yet here I find you in this infernal workroom," Grandmother said, with a disapproving *hmph* at the end, as she drew her shawl tighter about her shoulders. Lina frowned as she noticed how threadbare the nightgown beneath it was. "It is nearly dawn, child. If you have no care for yourself, do you not at least remember you are to help me with the ofrenda in the morning?"

"Yes, Abuela," Lina answered respectfully, but with no intention of going to her rest. There was no time, which her grandmother had just served to remind her. Besides, she exaggerated. The clock on the shelf above the worktable read barely one.

"*Ay Dios mio*! You are as bad as your father. I know you will do as you please. Just like Vasco. And you see where that got him…"

Lina's jaw clenched at that, for even were she to believe her father dead, she would *not* believe it any fault of his own. And for her grandmother to say so… Forcing her expression to relax she walked to her mother's mother and placed a kiss on her weathered cheek, while smoothing a hand over her silver-shot braid as she had Beltran's feathers.

"I am sorry, Abuela. I am almost done. I will go to bed shortly."

31, October, 1870

I do not know why Abuela pushes me to sleep. It never ends well. I am better rested by closing my eyes throughout the day, as I am wont to do, than to subject myself to the nightmares. This night it was the vision of a skeletal dog. No. More wolf or coyote than dog. Fur hung from its bones and the eyes burned like coals in a brazier. All of it was weathered and aged but for the teeth, which gleamed sharp and bright to my sleeping eye. Rising from it was the musty scent of the grave and the metallic tang of spilt blood. Beyond the beast stood a shadow without the form of a man, but with the feel of one. It watched intently as the canid hounded me, chasing me through a graveyard full of souls, past families feasting at altars with their deceased loved ones. I woke just as they tried to force me below to the realm of Mictlan, of which my Abuela often tells tales, the underworld of her Aztec ancestors. Tales where the spirits of the dead journey the underworld with dog-companions. I woke choking on screams this morning feeling the phantom slice of wind-blown knives shredding my flesh while at my back a jaguar snarled, about to devour my unworthy soul. Before they could consume me the very image of Santa Muerte rose up to usher me home, her robes fine and the delicate lines of her exposed bones beautiful as she menaced the cats with her scythe. Even so, I may never sleep again.

A.A.F.

By the time Lina left her room in the morning, her grandmother had already pulled the bare *ofrenda* into its place in the central room of their *hacienda*, not above using what was convenient even while she derided the memory of the one responsible for its making. Lina's Papa built the altar, simple, but ingenious, made to be sturdy. Made to be as easily raised up as folded down and stored for the next year. They had been using it a long time. This year Lina would watch to see if Papa came to feast from his own table. Her heart could not believe he would.

Her grandmother's disapproving look followed Lina as she shuffled from her room and into the kitchen. On the back of the cast-iron stove a pot of *frijoles* simmered. The rich scent of garlic and onion and chili caused her gorge to rise. Breathing shallow and swallowing hard, Lina quickly prepared herself a cup of willow bark tea heavily laced with honey. Grit burned in her eyes and her head ached, feeling tight, as if the demons of her nightmare hung from her hair. She said nothing of this. To what end? Abuela would never give credence or sympathy when she was fully confident she already knew the cause of Lina's discomfort.

"Good morning, Abuela," she said as she hugged her grandmother. "*Hmph*. Nearly noon."

By the sun coming through the window it could be no later than nine o'clock. Lina again said nothing, merely moving past her to the leather-banded chest against the wall, lid open and waiting. "The *papel picado* are looking a little faded. Shall we make new or use these another year?" she asked her grandmother as she shifted the paper banners to the side to lift the snowy-white altar cloth from the chest.

Grandmother sniffed. "No time. We've the *calavera de azucar* to finish."

Lina had always loved decorating the little sugar skulls, so bright and festive and full of love. This year she had no heart for it, though she knew she must. As they sat at the table in the kitchen she dutifully drew flowers and swirls and crosses in colorful icing on the glittery skulls her grandmother had molded. Upon each one she wrote the names of those loved ones passed: Angelina for her mother, after whom she was named; Maximo for her baby brother, who never had drawn breath; Tio Luis and Tia Lucia, her mother's siblings, who died as children.

On one, Grandmother wrote in her shaky hand "Papi Orlando" for Lina's grandfather.

Finally, one skull remained. Lina drew it to her, staring overlong into those empty eye sockets and the cheerful toothy grin. This one was meant for her father. Carefully, in golden hue, she iced the skull using the approximation of gears in place of flowers and spanners in place of a cross, because it would have made him smile. That was as far as she could bring herself, though Grandmother waited expectantly, her brow drawing down the longer Lina hesitated.

"Well? There is work to be done beyond this."

"I am sorry, Abuela," Lina answered with the quickness of habit. As she stared at the almost-finished skull she reminded herself that the names written upon them were not always those of the dead. With that she was able to scribe her father's name, Vasco, in good faith. She set the skull aside and finished helping her grandmother decorate the altar.

From the other room, Beltran cawed stridently.

1, November, 1870

The nightmares grow worse, until I am better rested from a siesta spent only in part napping on the cot in Papa's workroom, than I was after most of a night in my own bed. Though I must confess, I spent more time making adjustments to Beltran's cowl and the newly finished goggles, than I did in slumber. I do believe I am more intimately familiar with Papa's device than even he is. After, I joined Abuela in the courtyard, where she gathered the flor de muerto. *The marigolds have grown large and well, despite the near destruction of the garden mere months ago, bright and golden and pungent in their scent, surely fragrant enough to guide our beloved spirits home. They are the final decoration we need for the* ofrenda, *already heavy with sweets,* pan de muerto, *and, of course, the* calaveras. *My mouth waters even now at the thought of the sweet bread dipped in a cup of Abuela's rich and spicy chocolate, a special and costly treat only to be had this night. Abuela claims it is her only chance to spoil her grandson, who she never held, but she always looks at me with particular fondness when she says so. While Grandmother was at her work, I examined the fountain, the sole aspect of the courtyard so far beyond my means to fix. I was startled to find among the rubble a torn piece of leather strap, brass-riveted and distinctly familiar. This very day I attached its cousin to the goggles stored on my father's shelf.*

As I turned the puzzling strap over in my hand, I would have hardly noticed the cries of the wild crows, if not for Abuela's grumbling and Beltran's answering croak. I looked up to spy them perched almost like sentries on the courtyard wall. Though their presence was somehow comforting, I shivered despite the warmth of the sun.

A.A.F.

The scent of crushed herbs, spices, and roasting meat filled the *hacienda*, enticing Lina's appetite as Abuela cooked her younger children's favorite meal. The aroma mingled with the rich heavy perfume of burning copal resin tempered by the sweetness of the beeswax altar candles. Their family, in the old tradition, observed *Dia de los Inocentes* in the privacy of their own home, out of respect for those little ones lost too young to know any but their family or, like Maximo, did not get to dance with life at all. Tomorrow night, *Día de Muertos,* she and Abuela would trek to the nearby graveyard to celebrate the adults at the family plot, as most did.

Lina's thoughts lingered on Maximo. She had only ever known the thought of him, but she held a deep love for her brother in her heart and had often as a girl made up tales to tell her father, stories of her adventures with Maximo. What he looked like and things they had done. Though Papa had laughed or showed proper awe, as was fitting to the tale, all the while the hint of tears glimmered in his eyes. For *Dia de los Inocentes,* they had always built something special as a gift for him. In the workroom an entire shelf held the tinkered offerings from past years, kept carefully dusted.

Earlier that night Lina had placed on the altar a tiny steampowered wagon. The first gift she'd built alone.

Tears glimmered in her own eyes when she imagined she heard Maximo's laughter as he played.

The echo of that sound tempted her to fetch Beltran and the goggles from the workroom, only to do so — on this holy day in particular — would bring down Abuela's wrath. She loathed the bird and would not countenance him in her home, anywhere beyond the workroom. (At times when her patience was worn thin, Lina had to restrain herself from pointing out this home belonged to Vasco Fabricio, *not* Aleta Cuacuas.) Just as well; part of her feared to test Papa's invention too soon, as if to do so would rob her of the chance for which she so desperately held out hope. Tomorrow she would don the goggles, during the trek to the graveyard where the spirits mingled with the living at public altars, and none would notice a crow in the dark, no matter how unusual.

To distract herself, Lina murmured stories of their father to Maximo.

That night Lina paced her room as a coyote's howl mocked her from the darkness beyond the courtyard wall. Though she knew it was impossible so late at night, she would almost swear she heard the wild crows cawing back in challenge. Even without those mournful sounds, she felt anxious…by some means watched, the shadows on her wall looming in menace. With the howls reminding her of her nightmares there was no hope of sleep. She sighed and crept from her bedchamber to her father's workroom as quiet as she could. Once there she draped a thick canvas—sporting burns and nicks and other testaments to its service—over the doorframe to block any sign of the lantern light that might betray her. She then crossed to the perch where Beltran rested, his cowl still in place. She would have thought it uncomfortable, but earlier when she had attempted to remove the mechanism the crow had resisted. She ran a light finger over the glossy feathers along his neck before pouring some seeds and nuts into the bowl beside his perch. He stirred and looked up at her through faintly red-tinged lenses before ruffling his feathers and settling to rest once more.

Smiling, she took a carved wood mask from the cabinet below him. It was smooth and contoured beneath her touch, shaped as a sugar skull, but lacking any color. Though such masks were traditional, a means of mocking death and robbing that specter of any power to be gained through fear, this was the first year Lina had thought to wear one. She wasn't sure why. Maybe it was the nightmares, or maybe she felt the need for courage as she tested her belief… In either case, until now she had been undecided, though earlier she had made a makeshift scythe from a shoulder-high walking stick and a blade of tin from among Papa's scrap pile, in honor of Santa Muerte…Saint Death, who showed her favor to rescue her in her dreams.

Taking out the paints she and her father had used for Maximo's various gifts, she began to decorate the mask. While the symbols of the *calaveras* took shape, flowers and filigree, intermixed with the gears and tools of her inventor's trade, in her thoughts she sent a prayer to the Saint of Death, also called the Lady of Shadows, petitioning for her protection.

Whether for herself or for her father, Lina could not say.

2, November, 1870

I do not know which fills me with the most dread. The thought that I will see my father tonight, or the thought that I will not.
A.A.F

From a distance, the light of a thousand of flames glowed in the twilight. As Lina approached the wall surrounding the graveyard she saw the candles perched upon gravestones, nestled among flowers, held in the hands of those walking among the plots. Illuminating *calaveras*, portraits of lost loved ones, the joyous faces of the living, families celebrating everywhere, disturbingly like the memory of her nightmares. Lina shivered and continued on. Even before she reached the graveyard proper, bright marigold petals sprinkled the flagstone path she followed. The dizzying scents of rich food and incense filled the air as quiet laughter and conversation came to Lina's ear. It was late and she walked alone, her right hand holding her scythe while a basket of *pan de muertos,* roasted goat, and *huevos con nopales* hung over her other arm. When it had been time to leave she and her grandmother had fought over Lina's manner of dress — *calaveras* mask, a faded blue cotton robe, goggles perched atop her head like a diadem — and Beltran on her right shoulder with his metal cowl. Though it upset her grandmother, Lina had remained steadfast, earning Abuela's ire. She could not say why, but Lina felt called to honor Santa Muerte in this, no matter the strife caused.

In the end, her mother's mother refused to come.

Lina frowned and rubbed at the ache in her chest as guilt weighed on her heart. She was torn between the need to find her father and showing respect to her grandmother. Though Lina was not without regret, Papa won.

Stopping beside the entrance to the graveyard, she leaned her scythe against the stone and setting her basket on the ground to slide the goggles down into place over the mask, fumbling a moment as she placed the thin glass disc on the surface of her right eye. The cold, hard sensation caused her to flinch. It was an effort not to blink furiously, sending the disc fluttering aside, but she managed.

As she looked through the aether lenses Aleta Angelina Fabricio gasped. Slowly she turned a full circle, letting her gaze trail over the family gatherings.

It worked.

Papa's invention worked!

Through her left eye, with her mortal vision, Lina saw the family groupings as they were, but through her right eye she saw the guests of honor seated at those feasts. Flickering and translucent, the spirits silently laughed or smiled or occasionally looked on in faint disappointment as they breathed deep, drawing their sustenance from the heady steam wafting from the warm meals prepared for their enjoyment, as if perhaps the dish made had not in truth been their favorite.

She laughed with their success — hers and her father's — though the split vision made her sway and almost stumble as she gathered her things and continued on. Occasionally, she had to stop as Beltran looked elsewhere and half her vision diverged from what was before her. She was glad of her walking-stick scythe as she traveled through the graveyard. Still, her hope blossomed a bit more with each step.

Nowhere she looked did she see her father. Surely she would have, were he dead.

She did notice, from a distance, that Abuela must have come down to the gravesite earlier to set up an altar, beautifully arranged, with a silver-backed mirror propped against the headstone to reflect the candlelight. Lina's heart ached at the sight of the unlit candles and remorse soured her belly. She had not realized she'd learned more than inventing at her father's side. Her grandmother should be here, and it was to Lina's shame that she was not.

Silently, she prayed to the Virgin Mother for forgiveness as she turned back to fetch her grandmother. Lina reached up and caressed Beltran's wing as she headed back along the marigold-strewn path. At her touch he turned and groomed a bit of her hair with his beak, oddly comforting. But even as she drew her hand away, the crow tensed, then mantled, crying out the harshest caw she had ever heard him utter. Jerking, she looked up but could see no reason for his anger.

Beltran continued to scream from her shoulder, fluttering violently as someone stepped onto the path, blocking her way.

Lina peered at the shadow before her. Perhaps the goggles were to blame, but the looming presence served as another echo of her nightmares. It stood there without the form of a man, but the feel of one. Shaking her head as if to clear her vision, she swayed and blinked, first closing her right eye, then her left. With her left eye open, what stood before her was clearly a living, breathing man. But with her right eye, a gleam encased him, as if spirit and body were not one. She could not see his features or expression, but the feel of him was unnatural and his posture showed clear menace.

Slowly she backed away, toward the bright light of the festivities.

The man's hand shot out, his hard grip halting her. He drew close until candlelight revealed his face.

Lina gasped, too shocked to cry out as she looked upon her father's face only to find something else staring through his eyes. Was it a spirit? A demon? However this being stole her father's body, Lina believed it had happened that fateful day in the courtyard, but she doubted she would ever know for certain, the what, the how, or the why of it.

She tried to pull away, but the basket and scythe hindered her movement.

"Not so fast, *mija*…" His tone was cruel and mocking.

Even the voice differed from Papa's, though she scarcely understood how. Then she realized what he'd said. Lina scowled and bared her teeth behind her mask, jerking her arm from his grip. On instinct, she dropped the basket, but took a firmer grip on the scythe.

"No daughter of yours, *ladrón*." *Thief*.

The shadow man laughed, the sound harsh in contrast to the families celebrating not too far away. "Who else knows but you and I?"

Tension ran through Lina like a firebrand. He was right. None would believe her claim. Almost without thought she swung the scythe, not menacing him with the blade—which held no true edge—but with the solid wooden shaft. Even so he leaped to the side as if she would cut him, stumbling over a worn tombstone.

Lina turned and fled before he could regain his feet. She had to close her right eye to better focus on the physical world, all the while praying she did not fall herself. Behind her the villain called out, "You meddle where you shouldn't, girl. This vessel is *mine* now, and I will have that tattered crow as well." She hurried her steps as much as she dared, tripping and catching herself half a dozen times, all the while hearing him scramble after her. As she ran, Beltran dug his talons into her robe, mantling to keep his balance.

Her eyes fell on her family's gravesite. Some kind soul had lit the candles on the altar and all around other families celebrated their dead. Surely there was safety among so many.

Before she could reach the warmth of the candlelight a heavy hand came down upon her shoulder, spinning her around. Only his grip kept her from falling. With his other hand, the man that was and was not her father drew a *tecpatl* from his vest, the obsidian blade gleaming black on black in the darkness.

"When you reach the Underworld, tell Xolotl I won't be coming back. I have no wish to test my... 'worthiness' in the realm of Mictlan, when there is power yet to be had here in the Overworld. Once I've that crow, I will make this world mine to rule."

As he raised the sacrificial knife he sneered at her and brought the blade down toward her chest. Lina brought up the scythe to force him away. At the same time she twisted, renewing her effort to escape.

The breath went out of her as her gaze fell full on the mirror backing Abuela's altar.

In the glass she saw her own reflection, but at her back, seemingly against her right shoulder, where Beltran should have been, stood her father's spirit.

Of course, she had not seen him anywhere among the dead...she had been looking through his eyes!

Thin threads—like the wires attaching the lens she wore to the goggles—ran from the reflection of her father to his body. Lina moaned as she realized part of how her attacker bore Papa's face, but not his soul. And why the thief had tried to capture the crow.

Her father spoke to her, distracting her from her thoughts, the movement of his lip vehement, but his words silent. In perfect synchronization with his actions, Beltran's wings beat against Lina's head.

"Oh, Papa," she cried. She didn't need to know what he said. It was clear to her what she must do.

In the mirror she saw the demon in her father's body lurch toward her, blade raised once more. Lina gripped the scythe with both hands as she would in the fields at threshing time. She braced herself with care as her vision threatened to unbalance her.

For a moment she couldn't move. Her grip white-knuckled on the scythe as she stared with longing at her father's spirit. Then, out of nowhere — or perhaps out of the aether — a woman's voice, hollow and beautiful and unworldly all at once, spoke to her, like a gentle whisper, somehow sounding in her ear and her heart both at once.

"Let him go, my child."

Sobbing as she listened to Death, Lina's hands clenched tighter on the haft. Eyes closing against the pain, she turned back toward her attacker. She brought her scythe slicing down through the space between the crow and the demon breaking the threads still linking her father's spirit to his physical form. At the same time, she brought her right hand up to cradle Beltran's body before it could fall. Her eyes opened at the sharp sound of the obsidian blade shattering against flagstones, followed by the thud of a body falling to earth.

An angry, tortured scream echoed in her head, fading quickly to nothing.

Lina barely noticed. As the life went out of the crow she cradled, she turned back to look into the silver-backed glass. Despite the tears streaming down her face she saw clearly before her a double image, her own skull mask and coarse robe mirrored by a stately figure in need of no mask, wearing rich robes of soft blue velvet. Their scythes overlapped until Lina could not tell one from the other.

The Lady of Shadows reached out and brushed her hand across the crown of Lina's head, as if in benediction, before stepping back among the spirits behind her. To Lina, it appeared she left without her scythe. She wondered at that until she realized what the mirror now reflected.

Again, guilt tempered Lina's joy. *Oh, if only Abuela were here to see...*

Beneath Santa Muerte's draped arm stood Vasco Fabricio, faint and shimmery, but unmistakable; beside him stood Lina's mother, her expression both proud and joyous. But between them…between them stood a small boy with Papa's eyes and Mama's smile. Maximo, looking exactly as Lina had always pictured him, though he'd never had the chance to grow so big. Lina's heart swelled with the love that shone in all four gazes. A part of her wondered how she could still see them without the aid of Beltran's vision. The rest of her didn't care as it drank in the sight.

She smiled back through her tears as the spirits waved farewell.

The Sun Worshiper

David Lee Summers

Dinella Stanton had a rapport with the dead. She couldn't explain it and didn't necessarily want it, but she could feel spirits and channel their voices. When Professor Augustus Harriman invited her to a mummy unwrapping party, she couldn't resist. She'd known many wealthy people around London had acquired mummies from Egyptian expeditions and hosted unwrappings. She so wanted to go to one. Much as spirits frightened Dinella, they also fascinated her. She had never encountered a spirit as ancient as that belonging to a long dead Egyptian pharaoh. She wondered how long they lingered and what secrets they could impart.

She followed Harriman's butler, Talbot, down the hallway to the parlor. She'd never met the professor before and wondered what possessed him to invite her. Nevertheless, a thrill of excitement fluttered through her and lightened her steps.

Talbot announced her and Dinella bristled as she realized the parlor was filled with scientists, all of whom had slandered her at one time or another. Near the punchbowl stood Martin Mitchell, a chemist with slicked-back hair who once said the

spirit voices that spoke during her séances were made by an accomplice behind a curtain. At the buffet, toad-like Nigel Pogson chatted with Desmond Llewelyn, who once said she used wires to lift tables. Ornithologist Maurice Swift caught her eye, then dared snort a laugh as his eyes shot away. He once said she accomplished spirit writing with her feet.

All those statements the scientists had made about her were patent lies. Her fists clenched and unclenched. She began to suspect Harriman invited her to be mocked by these cretinous chemists, astronomers, and biologists.

She steeled her nerves and continued into the room, curiosity about the mummy driving her forward despite her irritation. Fortunately, she didn't have to wait long. Soon curtains parted and a man with a full beard and a mop of black hair rolled out a wooden gurney on squeaky wheels. A blanket covered what appeared to be a body. The scientists fell silent and all eyes turned to the gurney. The man introduced himself as Professor Harriman.

"Thank you all for attending." The professor moved behind the gurney so he could address the audience. "As many of you know, I recently acquired the mummy of one Prince Neferamun from an associate in Egypt. His name means 'the good of the sun god.' Shall we meet our sun worshiper?"

He grabbed the corner of the blanket and paused to make sure he had everyone's attention, then yanked it away, revealing the mummy underneath.

"Fake!" All eyes fell on Dinella, but she couldn't help herself. "Fraud!" she cried. She knew what mummies should look like. The bandages should be brown and ancient, nearly falling to dust. The bandages on this "mummy" were white and new as though they'd come from a modern hospital. Her worst fears now seemed justified. Professor Harriman had indeed invited her just to make a fool of her.

"I say," croaked Professor Pogson, "your mummy doesn't look very ancient at all."

Dinella appreciated that someone else in the room also seemed taken aback.

Harriman handed the sheet to his butler. "Please, please, I do not intend to deceive." He held his hands out over the mummy. "This is a real mummy. I have taken the liberty of unwrapping it in the privacy of my laboratory and conducting some studies before this public event."

"To what end?" Maurice Swift leaned forward and narrowed his skeptical gaze on his colleague.

"All shall soon be made clear." Harriman glanced down at the body before him. "I assure you, I have conscientiously rewrapped the mummy, returning the artifacts where I found them."

Without further ado, the professor began unwrapping the mummy, handling it with great care. Talbot rolled out a trolley and placed it next to the professor. Below the first layer of bandages, he revealed an elaborate collar of gold and polished coral. He placed it on the trolley.

He unwrapped another layer and came to a pair of amulets. One looked like a cross with a loop at the top. He declared it an ankh, a symbol of life. The other amulet looked like the English letter "A." Harriman explained that it was a plummet, which would bring balance to the deceased.

Dinella walked up to the trolley and examined the amulets. They looked genuine. She dared to reach out and touch them. Love and pride of artisans long dead rolled off them, setting her hand tingling. She stepped back, blinking and wondering why the professor perpetrated this elaborate hoax, wrapping real artifacts in such obviously new wrappings.

Professor Mitchell stepped up beside her and retrieved a monocular from his coat pocket. He made a show of examining the artifacts.

At last, Harriman reached the bottom layer. He revealed the mummy's face to be no fraud at all. Brown and wrinkled like parchment, it still appeared lifelike. In spite of herself, Dinella reached out to touch the skin. Realizing what she was doing, she yanked her hand back.

"No, no, it's okay," said Harriman. "Go ahead, touch him."

Dinella did so and gasped. She expected the skin to feel dry and rough. Instead, it proved soft and supple. "So lifelike," she whispered.

"That's the reason for the new bandages," explained Harriman. "The Egyptians wanted to preserve life and they sustained Prince Neferamun's form, but allowed him to dry out, removed his organs and stored them in canopic jars." He glanced around at the scientists who hung on his words. "What if we could bring the prince back to life?"

Llewellyn scoffed and Mitchell gave a derisive snort. Pogson narrowed his gaze, interested but clearly uncertain.

Harriman produced a set of shears and clipped the rest of the bandages, pushing them away from the mummified body of the prince.

Dinella's hand shot to her mouth. The action left no doubt at all about the mummy being male.

Mitchell looked down his nose and smirked at her discomfort.

Then the mummy's eyelids sprang open revealing hollow eye sockets beneath. Mitchell stumbled backward into Pogson. The two scientists nearly tumbled to the ground.

With a tick and a whir, the mummy sat up, rotating on the gurney as it turned to face the audience.

"What kind of trickery is this?" This time Professor Swift revealed his ire.

Dinella noticed an incision on the mummy's abdomen. Harriman stepped around the gurney and peeled the skin back at the incision with a wet, sucking sound. Inside, gears turned, cogs whirred, and springs throbbed like a heart beating. "I've replaced the organs with clockworks. I can give the prince the illusion of life again." He glanced over at Dinella. "This is why I had to wrap him in new bandages. I rehydrated his skin with special chemicals and ointments so he won't crumble to dust when he moves."

"But he has no spirit." Dinella shook her head. "I feel no life from this…*thing*."

Harriman nodded. "That's where you come in. Do you think you could summon Prince Neferamun's spirit? Bring him back to his body? Allow us to talk to him again?"

"This is outrageous!" Maurice Swift turned and flew from the room.

"You want me to summon his spirit, in front of the very men who have derided me and my work all these years?" Dinella put her hands on her hips, tempted to storm after Professor Swift.

Harriman shook his head. "No, Miss Stanton, I will only invite those to stay who will keep an open mind." He cast meaningful glances at Pogson, Llewellyn, and Mitchell.

Mitchell shook his head, tucked his monocular back in his jacket, and, with a derisive snort, followed Swift from the room.

Llewellyn clasped his hands together and bowed his head. "I accused you of using wires, madam, but I must confess, I had no basis for my claim. Science is the process of learning and if you're willing to let me sit in on a séance where you attempt to resurrect the good prince's spirit, I'm willing to retract my hasty words."

Dinella put her hand to her chest, surprised at the scientist's offer. She nodded. "Keep an open mind, and you will be welcome."

Harriman folded the flap of skin back over the clockworks. "What do we need for you to proceed?"

"A quiet, dark room," said Dinella. "If you have some items the prince had in life, that would also be helpful."

"Several items from the tomb were sent along with the mummy." Harriman smiled and clapped his hands. He reached out and took Prince Neferamun's hand. "Please enjoy the refreshments we have laid out. I'll prepare the room and summon you shortly."

He led the mummy, ticking and clicking, into the other room. Dinella found herself glued to the ghastly sight, not really wanting to see the hip bones protruding above the mummy's sunken buttocks, but intrigued by the view, nonetheless.

An hour later, Talbot summoned Dinella, along with Pogson and Llewellyn. They followed the butler to a small, dark dining room with green wallpaper. The mummy was now dressed in a pair of trousers and a smoking jacket. Such dress was certainly more appropriate to the somber occasion than allowing the mummy to go about in the nude. Had Harriman sutured up his belly? Dinella turned her thoughts from such improper considerations. She nodded her approval with the setting.

An array of items had been spread out on the table. Pogson picked up a strange wooden figurine. A man kneeling on the ground, holding up a U-shaped block.

"That is the god, Shu," said Harriman. "The god of air. I gather our friend here—" he inclined his head toward the mummy "—would have used that as a headrest or a pillow, if you will."

Dinella found herself attracted to the figure of a cat. She picked it up. "Such an odd carving," she remarked.

"It's actually a little sarcophagus." Harriman held out his hands. She handed him the cat. He opened it and within lay an oblong form swaddled in ancient brown bandages.

"So small and so sad." Dinella felt a lump in her throat, even as she thought this was what a proper mummy should look like.

Llewellyn sniffed as though the objects were below his notice. "How do you propose to communicate with the spirit of our dear prince?"

"I hope these personal objects, along with the prince himself, will help me build a bridge across time and space to talk to his spirit."

"And you speak Ancient Egyptian?" Llewellyn lifted an eyebrow.

Dinella frowned. "You mock me, sir!"

"Not at all." Llewellyn took a step back as though she'd struck him. Even his bristly muttonchops seemed to wilt. "I'm honestly curious how you propose to speak to a person who never learned English."

"Ah." Dinella took a deep breath to cover her discomfort. "Some time back, a Dutch woman who'd settled in Croydon hired me to channel the spirit of her husband. It's at that time I learned that spirits don't use language as such. They make their meaning clear and then speak through me."

"Perhaps they learn the language from the Medium," suggested Pogson as he reached down and moved a silver token on a board that resembled an oblong chess set.

Dinella nodded. "Perhaps. I sense the spirit as a presence that enters my mind. It is possible that it learns from me even as it speaks through me."

Harriman leaned forward and steepled his fingers. "Do you think you could encourage the spirit to occupy its former body?"

Dinella swallowed. "I've never tried, but if it's a physical presence, it seems possible…if the spirit is willing."

Harriman's smile, although satisfied, wasn't altogether pleasant. "Do you require anything more in order to proceed?"

Folding her arms, Dinella inventoried the room. "I think the room is in good order. I could use a candle. It would help me focus."

Harriman gave a curt nod to the butler at the doorway who disappeared behind the curtain. He returned a moment later with a candle, set it in the middle of the table, then struck a match and lit it. "That will be all," said Harriman. With that, Talbot retreated from the room.

"Let us all be seated," said Dinella. "Please understand, when the trance comes over me, it will be the spirit speaking, not I. I may not be able to respond to queries."

Llewellyn held a chair for Dinella and she sat. The scientists then took their places at the table.

"Now, place your hands on the table and focus on the antiquities — the mummy's possessions."

Harriman reached out and placed Neferamun's hands on the table, then placed his own on the table. The other scientists followed suit.

"Think about Neferamun. Welcome his spirit. Think about how he used these items in life." She followed her own instructions. She imagined his head cradled by the image of the god Shu. She watched him playing a game on the board. She visualized a sleek cat jumping into the prince's lap to have its ears scratched.

A presence made itself known to her. Hesitant, it kept to the corner of the room. She continued to face the candle's flame, but lifted her eyes slightly. The spirit manifested as a faint, green miasma. From previous experience, she doubted the others in the room could see it. "We seek the spirit of Neferamun. We welcome the spirit of Neferamun to join us."

The green miasma slunk around the room and disappeared from sight. She calmed her breathing, hoping she hadn't lost the spirit. Sometimes they grew skittish. Sometimes it wasn't even the spirit she sought, but a curious ghost inhabiting the house.

"Neferamun, you have traveled far from your home," intoned Dinella. "You have traveled far through time. We seek your wisdom. We seek your knowledge. We seek your experience." She had spoken those words at other séances before, but she couldn't help but feel they held special significance for the men around the table.

A presence sprang at her from behind. For a moment sharp pain, like pinpricks, needled her, but soon the spirit settled into a quiet contentment. She tried to speak, but no longer could. She assumed spirits needed time to adjust and to find words after their time in the grave, or like the Dutch spirit in Croydon, they needed to find words in a new language. How different from Ancient Egyptian must English be?

"Where am I?" Dinella felt the air pass over her own vocal chords, but she never thought the words and they emerged with an unearthly high-pitched timbre. She remained powerless to speak on her own.

The men sat in stunned silence. Dinella feared the spirit would grow bored and leave. "Is that the spirit's voice?" asked Pogson, eyes wide. She wanted to respond, but couldn't.

"I believe it may be," whispered Llewelyn. She thought the hairs of his muttonchops stood on end.

At last Harriman responded to the spirit. "You're in England, in a city called London. We've summoned you because we would like to know about your life."

"Yes," piped in Pogson, "what was life like for you?"

The spirit remained silent. Dinella thought it must be thinking how to answer. "Life was worship of Amun-Ra who shed the warmth of the sun on all righteous creatures. Life was being groomed by my followers. Yes, grooming was quite nice."

"And the hunt?" Llewellyn leaned forward. "I've seen depictions of the hunt in Egyptian art. Did you hunt?"

"Ah yes, the hunt," said the spirit in Dinella's unearthly voice. "The hunt was a great joy. I hunted nearly every day and the feasting was joyful when the hunt succeeded."

Harriman glanced over to the mummy. "We have prepared this vessel, your former body. Perhaps, if you would allow Miss Stanton to guide your spirit into this body, we could continue our conversation at leisure, without taxing her."

Dinella sensed the spirit's confusion at first. Perhaps they did have the wrong spirit. Then she sensed intrigue. At last, a warm wash of agreement came over her. She found herself pushing back from the table.

Llewellyn and Pogson rose on either side and helped her to stand. Her feet carried her toward the mummy. She put her hands on its head, felt the wispy hairs clinging to its lifeless scalp. The presence left her mind. The green miasma traveled down her arms and into her hands, before vanishing into the skull.

Once again, the mummy's empty eye sockets opened. This time, they glowed green. The mummy looked from side to side, then rolled out of the chair until it landed on all fours. Harriman pushed back from the table, then reached over as though to help the ancient prince back into the chair.

The mummy pushed itself up onto its legs and wobbled, as though unaccustomed to walking upright, then jumped through the curtain into the other room like Spring-heeled Jack. Harriman shot after him. Dinella fell into a faint, supported by Pogson and Llewellyn.

Dinella awoke with her arms folded under her head on the table. The curtain at the side of the room had been pulled aside. Through them she could see daylight. Had the séance taken the entire night? Or had she simply fallen from her faint into sleep. That had never happened before. Then again, Neferamun proved to be a strong spirit. She didn't expect that from a spirit so ancient.

Did spirits gain strength as they aged? Perhaps the strength came from royalty. She had no idea. She pushed back from the table and rose unsteadily to her feet. She found her way to the main hall where the curtains were pushed back and a rare beam of British sunlight filtered in from outside.

Lying on the floor, curled up in the sunbeam, was the mummy, its internal clockworks making a strange rasping noise. Dinella's hand rose to her chest as she steadied her breathing. A moment later, Augustus Harriman appeared and rushed to her side. He helped her to a chair, then sat down opposite her. "Professors Pogson and Llewellyn send their regrets. They had to return to their respective duties." He smiled at her. "This has been a most illuminating evening, but I must say this Egyptian prince is nothing like I expected."

"What happened when I…when I became indisposed?"

"Well, the prince found his way to the cellar. After about an hour, he captured and killed a rat. For a mummy automated by clockworks, I must say, he looked rather pleased with himself. By that time, the sun had come up. He curled up here and has been sleeping ever since. I would think someone who has been dead to the world so long would have more on their mind than sleeping and catching rats, but then again the daily lives of ancient Egyptian royalty are still a mystery to us. We will learn much by studying him."

"I'm sure you will." Dinella tried to find words, but failed.

"Last night was clearly taxing," said the professor. "I'll have my coachman take you home. We can speak more another day. I would very much like to compose a treatise on this experiment and I believe you can provide a great deal of insight."

Dinella swallowed, but simply nodded as she thought about the cat mummy on the table in the dining room. She allowed Harriman to help her to her feet and considered the mummy's rasping clockworks, so like a purr. She couldn't bear to tell him that she had not channeled the spirit of Prince Neferamun, but rather the spirit of Neferamun's cat.

Rock of Ages

Gail Z. Martin and Larry N. Martin

"Tell me again why we're babysitting an archeologist?" Agent Mitch Storm grumbled as he got on the train for Rockland Township, in the hinterland of Northwestern Pennsylvania.

"We're not 'babysitting,'" Jacob Drangosavich, his partner at the Department of Supernatural Investigation, explained patiently. He was used to Mitch's outbursts, especially when a new assignment didn't seem to add up. "Dr. Kathryn Moser is the head of the Antiquities Department at Chatham College. She's also on record for having personally shot three brigands that attempted to hijack her convoy in Egypt. I don't think she's the typical academic."

Mitch snorted, shouldering his bag and finding their seats. "What's she afraid of out in the backend of nowhere? Snakes?"

Jacob reminded himself that Mitch was a crack shot, a brilliant strategist, and a wily federal agent. All of those were good reasons for not strangling him because Mitch was also annoying, irreverent, and had no regard for his own personal safety.

"There've been reports of vengeful ghosts near the relic site," Jacob replied, recounting what he knew Mitch had already read in the file. Then again, Mitch said that he remembered better when he heard instructions more than when he read them. Jacob felt certain Mitch really just wanted to drive him mad for the sake of entertainment. "And HQ thinks that there's a lead plate somewhere on the site that might be from an unidentified airship from Beyond."

"Plate? Like a dinner plate?"

Jacob gave his partner a withering look. "No. Like a commemorative sign. Maybe six inches by eight inches, or a little bigger. Rectangular, with raised lettering."

Some people might have snickered at the idea of flying ships from other worlds, but Mitch and Jacob knew better. Their work with DSI had involved a lot of strange revelations, and their job entailed not just protecting the country from supernatural and alien threats, but also keeping the public blissfully ignorant that those dangers existed.

"Hell, the whole rock might be from Beyond," Mitch replied. "No one knows who made those inscriptions."

"Which is why Dr. Moser is investigating, for the antiquities department," Jacob prompted. "And we're going to watch her back, in case vengeful spirits or aliens show up."

The gear bags they carefully stored in the rack above their seats held a variety of weapons, both conventional firearms and more unusual, experimental ones from the secret labs at Tesla-Westinghouse. Both men carried their service pistols in holsters beneath their jackets, a requirement for agents who were never not on duty.

"You know there isn't even a town near that damn rock," Mitch grumbled. "We've got to meet up with the doc and then get there by boat, and it's still a hike. They've got snakes out there, Jacob. Ticks, snakes, and wild boars."

"Wild boars?" Jacob raised an eyebrow. "Well, at least those shouldn't be a problem for an ex-Army sharpshooter." Jacob and Mitch's friendship went way back, before DSI, to their Army days in the Johnson County Wars.

"I just figured we had moved off the bodyguard duty list," Mitch said, leaning back into his seat.

"Think of it as guarding the experimental technology Dr. Moser plans to use," Jacob cajoled. "And if that doesn't help, remember how upset Adam would be if one of his new playthings got broken."

Adam Farber, a young genius inventor and the wunderkind of Tesla-Westinghouse, created a seemingly limitless stream of prototype weapons and gadgets that Jacob found both astounding, and a little terrifying. Mostly because no one knew exactly how the gadgets would perform until they were field-tested, and Mitch was first in line for trying all the new toys.

That got a grin out of Mitch. His bag held a Maxwell Box to call and dispel ghosts, and Dr. Moser was bringing with her an Edison Cylinder, on which she hoped to record the voices of the dead and learn the truth of their story. "Yeah, you know what that cylinder means, if it works. All we need is a medium and one of those recording machines, and the ghosts can give testimony against who murdered them."

"It probably wouldn't stand up in court," Jacob replied, settling into his seat and opening the newspaper he brought with him, although on a trip with Mitch, he didn't expect to get much reading done. The two agents were a study in contrasts. Jacob was tall and lean, with blond hair and the features of his Croatian ancestry. Mitch wasn't quite as tall, but he was all muscle, with dark hair and blue eyes and a perpetual five o'clock shadow no matter how often he shaved. Mitch looked like the hero on the cover of a penny dreadful, and Jacob blended easily into the background. They made a remarkable team.

"You're probably right," Mitch admitted with a groan. "But— if the ghosts could tell us who to look for, we can run down the evidence that the courts will accept. You've got to admit, that would take care of a lot of unsolved crimes, having the ultimate witness's testimony."

"Maybe," Jacob said, holding out just for the sake of argument. "Then again, I would have thought you'd have liked this assignment. We need a break. It's been non-stop, one case after another. What can possibly happen out in the woods?"

Dr. Kathryn Moser was waiting at the docks on the Allegheny River when they arrived. Her crisp linen suit had an unusual skirt— wide pants covered with a front and back panel that permitted easy motion in rough terrain. Kathryn's hair was pinned up in a prim bun, and the large, sturdy hat box by her feet seemed more likely to hold the Edison Cylinder than a trendy chapeau. As the two agents approached, she consulted an engraved pocket watch that looped between the buttons on her vest. Her glance in their direction made it clear that they were late.

"Dr. Moser," Jacob said, closing the distance and extending his hand. Mitch followed half a stride behind. The archeologist gave them both an appraising look, then responded with a firm, businesslike handshake.

"Agents," she replied with a curt nod. "Our boat is waiting."

Mitch offered his arm to help her aboard. Kathryn merely smiled and moved around him to board without assistance. Jacob already had the box plus his own bags, and the porters had apparently loaded Kathryn's luggage before they arrived, so Mitch muttered something under his breath and grabbed his duffle.

The boat was a private charter, paid for by the university and piloted by a man in DSI's employ. The first mate showed them to the cabin, where tea and sandwiches were ready on a silver tray. They sat down at the table and helped themselves.

Kathryn smoothed the napkin over her skirt and lifted her chin, looking first at one and then the other. "I told the university your services were not necessary."

Jacob cleared his throat. "It's for your own protection, Dr. Moser."

"I'm quite capable of taking care of myself."

"We know that, Dr. Moser," Mitch replied, breaking out the charming grin that usually got him whatever he wanted. It only took a few seconds to realize his charm did not sway her in the least. "If you prefer, consider us here to guard the equipment."

Her quiet *harrumph* made her feelings clear on the matter. "Have you been part of an archeological dig before?" she asked.

Jacob cleared his throat. "No, ma'am. But we understand not to excavate or alter the area in any way to preserve the integrity of the site." Mitch turned to look at him as if he'd sprouted a second head. Jacob smothered a smile. That book on 'Beginner's Archeology' might pay off, after all.

"Very well," Dr. Moser replied, apparently resigned to their company. "But your greatest value to me will be in making sure I'm not disturbed by any of the locals."

Mitch leaned forward, and Jacob held his breath. He never knew what was going to come out of Mitch's mouth, and while his partner was a good man at heart, he wasn't always… enlightened.

"I read about your Egypt expedition in the papers," Mitch said. He'd dropped the grin and the charm. "I haven't been to the Sahara, but I spent a good bit of time in the Army out in Arizona and Nevada. Living and working in those conditions isn't for the faint of heart."

"No, indeed," Kathryn replied, eyeing Mitch.

"I found the articles as interesting for what they didn't say as what they did," Mitch went on.

"Oh?" Kathryn asked.

Jacob found himself holding his breath and crossing his fingers under the table, ready to kick Mitch in the shin if warranted.

"I figure it took you twice as much effort to get half of the funding of your male colleagues, and that the newspapers are more interested in what you're wearing and whether or not you've found a husband than about the, frankly, mind-boggling discoveries you've made," Mitch said, utterly candid. "And I'm also betting that you made those discoveries by going against the experts' conventional wisdom, which probably got a lot of mockery before you showed them all up with the discovery of the 'lost pharaoh of Egypt.'"

Kathryn was quiet for a moment. "Thank you," she said. "You would be right on all counts."

Mitch smiled, but this time, it had none of the cockiness Jacob knew he used as a shield against the world. "I know how it goes for Agent Della Kennedy, our airship pilot, and some of our other colleagues. Both of you have the advantage of being able to shoot a squirrel's nuts at a hundred paces."

Jacob groaned at the impropriety of Mitch's statement. To his surprise, Kathryn chuckled. "Then consider the squirrels to be suitably warned," she said with a conspiratorial smile.

The rest of the trip on the river passed in quiet conversation. Jacob and Mitch pressed for details about Kathryn's latest expeditions, and she returned the interest by asking about their recent cases. Before they knew it, the boat pulled up as close to the petroglyph rock as possible, on a spit of land sightseeing boats from Pittsburgh used to bring gawkers out from the city to see the huge boulder known as the 'Indian God Rock.'"

"I hate that name, by the way," Kathryn said as they unloaded their belongings and trekked in from the riverbank to where they would make their camp. "It's so...sensational. The tribes that were in these parts didn't worship rocks. And since we can't translate the markings, we have no clue what it says. It might not be about deities at all. Maybe it's a giant genealogy or a list of crops grown nearby for traders."

"The newspapers need headlines to sell copies," Jacob said with a shrug. "You should see the way they write up some of our cases."

"To be fair, there are a lot of explosions," Mitch said, hefting his bag and moving to take Kathryn's gear, only to find she had already grabbed her things and started up the path.

"The explosions are just part of your charm," Jacob sighed.

"There it is," Kathryn said, pausing as they drew closer to the large boulder that rose from a pile of smaller rocks at the water's edge. The huge rock was about the size of a train car, sloping upward from the river, a flat, wide, slanted expanse covered completely with deeply carved symbols that extended around the sides and back.

Jacob caught his breath. "That's...amazing." Even Mitch appeared to be rendered speechless.

Kathryn grinned, with a look in her eyes of someone beholding a priceless treasure. "It is, isn't it? And even more amazing that no one's carted it off to a museum or chopped it up to sell for souvenirs." She sighed. "It's been vandalized, of course—by tourists carving their names onto that ancient surface." The anger was clear in her voice.

"Have you talked to the college about protecting it somehow?" Jacob asked.

Kathryn's expression darkened, and she turned away, heading back up the trail toward the area where they would camp. "Of course. But the landowner doesn't want to drive away the tourists, because they stop downriver in town to buy food and souvenirs. The way the college secured access for me was by promising that we'll provide information so that the newspapers can run plenty of stories. I brought a camera to take pictures. They're pressuring me to make up something fantastical to sell papers."

Jacob saw the tension in her jaw and understood the struggle all too well. More than once, he and Mitch had to either cover up details of cases or say nothing to correct salacious articles that garnered attention beneficial to the Department. "So the cylinder, it would validate how important the carvings are," he said quietly. "If you could record the voices telling the truth about the stone—and the lead plate—then you could prove the others wrong."

They reached the flat land above the river where they could camp for the night. Kathryn set down her gear and paced out the space needed for her tent. "It's so hard to tell the story the way it deserves to be told," she said quietly. "The college has an agenda. The government has an agenda, or at least it does when it comes to the story it wants told about the native people. The landowner and the newspapers—they all have their own agendas. None of them want the same story—and none of them want the real story. Just me—and maybe the ghosts."

"And maybe not all of the ghosts, if the stories about the vengeful spirits are true," Mitch said, carrying the tent he and Jacob would share to the other side of the clearing. Jacob went to make a small fire pit in the middle ringed by stones as the other two started setting up the shelters.

"Would it surprise you to find out that people might not be all that different after they die than when they were alive?" Kathryn asked. "Rivalries. Old grudges. Misunderstandings. Ambition. All powerful enough to transcend even death, maybe."

"Is that a bit of metaphysics slipping in beneath the science, Doctor?" Mitch asked with a gleam in his eye.

"As the mad prince of Denmark said, 'There are more things in heaven and earth, Horacio, than are dreamt of in your philosophy,'" Kathryn replied.

They pitched the tents while Jacob rummaged in the bags for the rudimentary cooking utensils and the provisions they brought. Before long, he had a small fire going, and a pot of coffee boiling on the flames. Jacob stood up and dusted off his hands. "There. Now we can do work."

"I like you," Kathryn said, eyeing the pot. "Let me know when the coffee is ready. I'm going to go down for a look at the inscriptions."

"We'll come, too," Mitch said. He and Jacob followed Kathryn down through the brush to the waterline. Kathryn carried a camera and tripod with her, and stopped to survey the rocky shoal around the 'god rock' with a frown. "I want to get photographs while the light lasts," she said before striding over to plant the stand and set up the camera.

While she busied herself with the camera, Jacob pulled out the EMF reader and began to adjust the settings. "Let me get a baseline before you turn that thing on," he warned. He walked around the narrow shoal with the scanner, watching the needle rise and fall as the electromagnetic frequencies varied in intensity.

"I'm getting a stronger reading over here," he called to Mitch as he moved to the downriver side of the rock. The scanner whined as the needle pegged the red zone. "But it falls when I move away, until I get to this spot," he narrated, watching the readings rise again when he came to a point on the other side of the rock.

Kathryn handled the camera with professional ease, changing out the plates and waiting out the long exposures. "Can we wait to summon the ghosts until the Cylinder is set up? In case they only want to talk once?"

"We can do that," Mitch agreed. "How are your pictures coming?"

I'll develop them tonight, once it's dark," she said. "I have a portable darkroom." She sighed. "Look at the damage the vandals have done. Some of the original carvings have been obliterated. That can't be undone."

"But with your pictures, even if you can't stop the damage, you can save what's left," Jacob said.

Kathryn gave a bitter smile. "Sometimes, in my business, that's the best we can do."

"Do you know who the ghosts are?" Mitch asked.

Kathryn nodded. "Yes. Or at least, I think so. Hans Bittner and Carl Patterson. They were researchers from about twenty years ago. Very interested in native artifacts, especially the ones that couldn't be matched to any existing tribe. But they weren't friends. In fact, they were pitted against each other trying to prove conflicting theories."

She reached beneath the leather cover of the small journal with her gear and handed them two faded photographs. One of the men had close-shorn dark hair and piercing dark eyes. "That's Bittner," she said. The other man was tall and slender with light hair Jacob guessed might have been either red or dark blond. "And Patterson."

"Who were?" Jacob asked, fascinated.

"Patterson was an ethnographer, very interested in documenting the native tribes and fascinated with taking photographs to record their way of life. As you can imagine, that made him some enemies, among people whose views were more…strident…toward the first inhabitants."

Jacob and Mitch had spent plenty of time in the West, both in the Army and since then with the Department. Jacob was well aware of how many ranchers and settlers viewed the tribes, and so Kathryn's careful and respectful language stood out to him. He had heard enough stories from his Croatian grandparents about being dispossessed when one invader or another seized territory back in the Old Country that he had always harbored sympathy for the tribes many others might not understand. Mitch understood and shared his outlook, though some in DSI did not.

"I would guess so," Jacob allowed.

"Bittner was obsessed with the idea that we aren't alone in the heavens, that there is life on planets circling other stars up there," Kathryn went on, gesturing toward the sky. "His writings showed he was fixated on the 'god rock' as a way to find these star-men and communicate with them. He believed there was a hidden metal plate that held the key to decode the inscriptions." She shook her head. "Of course, that's nonsense. There was a lead plate, left by the French explorer who first found the rock back in the 1700s. It's either washed away or been stolen—no one's ever found it."

Jacob cleared his throat, and Mitch looked away. Bittner's theories weren't as crazy as Kathryn thought, and their orders from HQ were to find and secure the plate and bring it back for study. "I guess we'll know when we talk to the ghosts," he replied.

When the light faded, they retreated to the camp. Mitch walked the perimeter while Jacob warmed up their food and Kathryn readied the chemicals in her darkroom. By the time they all regrouped, Jacob offered tin plates with beans and sausages. "Dinner is served."

Fresh air and hard work could make anything taste good. When they finished eating, Mitch pulled out a deck of cards. "Do you play?" he asked Kathryn, raising an eyebrow. "Fancy a game of Whist?"

She rolled her eyes. "Poker's more my game. If you dare."

After a few rounds of poker—two of which Kathryn won handily—they retired for the night. From inside their tent, Jacob could hear Kathryn in her makeshift darkroom and found himself curious to see what the pictures might reveal come morning. The fresh air and activity helped him fall asleep quickly, as Mitch took the first watch.

The next morning, Jacob yawned and stretched as he waited for the coffee to boil. Mitch looked just as tired since they had taken shifts sleeping and on watch. So far, nothing out of the ordinary had occurred, and Jacob feared that Kathryn might have been right about not needing their help.

"Orbs," she said as she bustled from her tent, waving several glass plate photographs. She looked as prim as she had on the boat dock, linen suit barely rumpled, hair perfectly coiffed.

"What?" Mitch asked, looking up.

"Orbs. In the photographs." Kathryn handed the plates over to Mitch and then poured herself a cup of strong, black coffee.

Jacob looked over Mitch's shoulder, not difficult given the height difference between the two. The photographs showed the petroglyph rock, the surrounding river and brush, and several very clear round white orbs in mid-air.

"Could it be dust on your lens?" Jacob suggested.

"I'd cleaned my lens before I started, and between shots. And I dare say none of us saw orbs at the time I took the photographs," Kathryn retorted.

"Phenomena like this have been explained away before," Jacob said carefully. "By itself, it doesn't constitute proof."

She gave him a withering glare. "Of course not. I know that. But it does augur well for being able to contact the spirits."

Jacob and Mitch shared a look. In the course of their work, they had seen spirit orbs that did turn out to be ghosts. But on more than one occasion, those orbs had been a different kind of presence, from an extraterrestrial source.

They ate a hurried breakfast, then Kathryn grabbed the hatbox, and the three headed down to the riverside.

"We've seen Edison Cylinders before, but not quite like that," Mitch observed as she carefully began setting up the equipment.

Thomas Edison was a brilliant man and an inspired inventor. But he also had an obsession with ghosts, and with the possibility of using science to confirm or deny the existence of an afterlife. His wax cylinders combined with a machine that used a sensitive needle to inscribe impressions from speech yielded a way to record the spoken word. With a few alterations, Edison had what he hoped would be a 'spirit graph' that could communicate with ghosts in much the same way a telegraph could carry coded taps across a continent.

"It's been modified," Kathryn replied. "Your friend, Mr. Farber, was quite enthusiastic about making some alterations."

The contraption looked like a combination phonograph and telegraph, with some extra wires and gauges for good measure. Kathryn pulled a large sound trumpet from the case and affixed it, then attached the crank that would store power in the device's coils.

Mitch had the Maxwell Box, as well as a shotgun full of rock salt, in case the ghosts the box summoned were not friendly. Jacob's shotgun had iron buckshot. Mitch laid down a circle of salt around the recording device, positioning it so that the stool and bulk of the machine were inside the protected area, and only the fluted recording trumpet projected beyond.

"What are you doing?" Kathryn asked as Jacob proceeded to set down another, larger salt circle.

"Making a place for us to fall back to, in case the spirits aren't friendly," Jacob replied. "There's no telling how spirits will react to being summoned. If they're hostile, we can jump into the circle — minding not to smudge the line — and have some protection."

Kathryn's expression told him she did not like the idea of retreating, and the brace of pistols shoved through her belt confirmed that she knew how to take care of herself. But she did not try to stop Jacob from making the circle, although the way the toe of her boot tapped against the rock made it clear that she was ready to get on with the experiment.

"Why do you think Bittner and Patterson's spirits are near the rock?" Mitch asked.

"Because neither man survived their expeditions, and the last record we have of either man comes from Patterson's journal, found in his camp. His body was discovered down here, near the rock," Kathryn replied. "Bittner's body was never recovered, but he didn't return home and was never seen again."

"You think they killed each other?" Jacob asked.

Kathryn shrugged. "Theories abound. Two rivals meet up; threats are made, shots fired. One man falls into the river, never to be seen again. The other dies of his wounds before he could get help. Or shoots himself in remorse for murdering his competitor. Or is shot by an unknown third party who wants…something. Or that Bittner shot Patterson, took the lead plate, left in a boat and changed his name — or was abducted by aliens."

"Actually, none of those are crazy — by our standards," Jacob replied. "I just hope we can narrow down the possibilities."

Kathryn cranked the Edison Cylinder, and stepped back, just a pace from the protective circle, gun in hand. Mitch turned the Maxwell Box to its middle setting, sending out the frequencies that apparently were catnip to spirits. After a few seconds, the air around them grew colder, until they could see their breath.

"Look!" Kathryn whispered, pointing to the cylinder. "It's recording."

Jacob didn't hear anything, and from the look on his face, neither did Mitch. But the stylus on the cylinder jumped and wiggled, etching a conversation only it could hear into the wax surface.

"Mitch," Jacob warned, and his partner's attention turned to the spirit materializing not far from the downriver side of the rock. He recognized the figure as Bittner, and by the looks of the man, the specter did not appreciate being dragged back from the Great Beyond.

"Over there," Mitch replied in a low, dangerous tone. His gun came up by reflex. Jacob turned slowly and saw the other ghost, a tall man with light hair and a gaping hole in his chest.

"What are you doing here?" Bittner spat.

"I'd ask the same of you," Patterson retorted. Whatever grievance had been between them in life had obviously not been eased by the passage of time or transcending the Veil.

"You're both dead," Kathryn said, in case the two ghosts hadn't noticed. Sometimes, spirits didn't realize that they were no longer living. "We want to know what happened."

"I came to try to break the code of the carvings," Patterson said, still staring angrily at Bittner. "I thought I'd made some progress, linking a few of the marks to other known languages. Then he showed up," he said, contempt thick in his voice. "And all he could talk about were air-ships from beyond the sky and monsters that talked to him in his sleep."

"Not monsters," Bittner corrected sharply. "Beings. They weren't from here, from Earth. They looked different from us, beautiful and frightening. And they told me to find the lead plate and bring it back."

"There were no creatures," Patterson argued. "You're soft in the head. That plate, it's nothing but a marker from an explorer long ago. You've spun this fantastic tale out of nothing—"

"It's true!" Bittner's ghost shouted. Jacob glanced at the cylinder, which jumped and twitched with every ghostly comment. "This is so much bigger than you imagine. There you are, trying to match symbols to one tribe or another, and you can't see that this transcends worlds!"

"Who shot you?" Kathryn asked, taking a direct approach to cut off their argument.

"He did," Patterson said, staring venomously at Bittner.

"Why?" Mitch asked.

"Because he wouldn't give me the damn plate!" Bittner retorted. "The creatures told me where it was, told me to bring it to them, and he wanted it for a piddling museum—"

"It's a historical treasure," Patterson countered.

"What is a museum compared to a race from another world?"

Bittner might be crazy, Jacob thought, *but even after death, he is completely convinced of his delusions.*

"Then how did you end up dead?" Jacob asked, staring at Bittner.

Bittner started to answer, then paused, frowning. "I'm…not sure. I found the lead plate beneath the shoal. It was covered with symbols like on the rock, and what looked like several dots with connecting lines. No French explorer left that. Maybe an explorer of another kind, from somewhere else," he replied.

"And the dead part?" Mitch nudged. Jacob spared a glance for the cylinder, which still recorded.

"Patterson tried to take it from me, tried to stop me. I couldn't let him get in the way. This was too important, don't you see?" Bittner pleaded. The whine of the Maxwell Box had become a constant backdrop. "We argued, he attacked me, we struggled. I shot him. I didn't intend to kill him—"

"Like hell you didn't!" Patterson argued.

"I didn't!" Bitter protested. "I only meant to slow you down. But you moved, and I'm a lousy shot. Then I saw you fall, and I took the lead plate and ran. I had a boat downriver—I just intended to take the plate and leave, didn't expect that you'd be here trying to translate that damned rock."

"What is it? The rock." Mitch asked. Bittner looked at him, confused. "If you talk to these aliens, then what did they tell you about the rock? Why is it important?"

"It's a 'claiming stone'—a marker they leave on worlds they discover, to say they have been there."

"They didn't 'discover' Earth. It already had people living here," Kathryn corrected in a tart tone.

"It was new for them," Bittner shot back. "And the plate—it's some kind of transmitter. At least, that's what I thought. So after Patterson and I argued, I took my boat downriver and got on the *Georgia Queen,* headed south. We were past Pittsburgh, on the Ohio River, and I remember a bright light, so bright everything else faded. And then, I woke up here again. With him."

"I remember fighting and the sound of a shot, and then I was back in my camp, like this," Patterson added, gesturing to indicate the bloody wound in his chest.

Mitch looked to Kathryn and Jacob, who both gave him a somber nod. "All right. I think we've got what we came for. We'll send a priest back here to send you on. Rest in peace, gentlemen," he said, and turned the Maxwell Box off. Abruptly, both ghosts vanished.

Kathryn stared at the god rock. "Patterson still could be right," she said, eying the inscriptions. "We only have the ranting of a mad ghost to account for the other explanation."

"I knew I recognized the name of the ship when Bittner said it, but it took me a few moments to place it," Jacob replied. "The *Georgia Queen* is one of those legendary missing ships. It vanished *en route* to the Mississippi, on a clear day with no record of storms. Witnesses said they saw a lightning bolt rise up from the deck of the ship into the sky, and there was a flare of light, and then the ship was gone. None of the crew or cargo were ever found, and no wreckage has ever been spotted."

"You think Bittner was telling the truth," Mitch said.

Jacob nodded. "I remember the story about the *Georgia Queen* because I had to go through the shipwreck lists for a case a while back. The story stuck in my mind. It sounds like what could have happened if someone from somewhere else decided to take an artifact back to where it belonged."

"But at least we have it all recorded," Kathryn replied, still looking shaken from the ghostly encounter. She moved over to the cylinder and stopped the needle, then moved levers to play back the etched vibrations. They listened to the scratch of the needle on wax, and then a chatter of strange syllables and the rise and fall of voices that did not sound human in the least.

"What the hell?" Mitch asked, staring wide-eyed at the recording device.

The voices were suddenly silenced by a high-pitched whine, the sound of the Maxwell Box. All three of them stared in horror at the persistent squeal that went on and on.

"Oh, shit," Kathryn muttered.

"We lost it," Jacob said, horrified. "It overwrote—"

"All of it," Mitch growled. "All of it!" He grabbed a rock from the shoal and hurled it as hard as he could into the river. "Goddamn!"

"So we know the truth, but we can't prove it," Kathryn said in a voice just above a whisper. "We know what happened to Patterson and

Bittner, and why they died. We know what the 'god rock' is. And we know where the lead plate went. And we can't prove a thing."

"It's kinda the story of our lives," Jacob said with a sigh. "This sort of thing happens to us all the time."

"I'm a researcher. I document and I publish," Kathryn protested. "How do I deal with this?"

Mitch flashed a grin. "Alcohol helps. But there's also satisfaction in knowing the truth, even if you can't tell anyone else."

"That's all you've got to offer?" Kathryn asked, staring at the petroglyphs and then the river with an expression of loss and disbelief.

"Sometimes, knowing is enough," Jacob replied.

The Light of One Candle

Michelle D. Sonnier

Hinata turned away from the peaceful view of the sunset over her family's small pond ringed by persimmon trees and back to her parents' bedroom. She swept her eyes over the harmonious neutral tones and traditional brushwork paintings on the walls. For all the wealth her father had gathered through his business dealings, her mother shied away from ostentatious shows of wealth and preferred traditional, simple, clean lines. The only concession Mother allowed Father was the huge wooden canopy bed in the Western style facing the sliding doors with rice paper panes that slid away to reveal the serene pond view. And in the middle of that bed, on clouds of crisp white linens, lay her mother propped up on a thick mound of pillows like a empress of old on her throne. She was dying.

Hinata's mother had actually been dying for quite some time, a mysterious illness eating away at her slowly like it was savoring a rich meal at the finest restaurant. But the time had finally come. Father sent for doctor after doctor, even expensive doctors from the West, and they all agreed—Kanna Tanaka did not have long to live and there was nothing that could be done. The most they could do was make her

comfortable as she declined. Father became so desperate at that point he even called in an old herbal woman. The moment she walked into the bedroom she turned and walked out, murmuring about Shinigami standing at the head of the bed. Father raged at her retreating back, a rare display of temper Hinata had only seen twice before, but the old woman only shook her head sadly and told him to enjoy what time left he had with his wife.

Approaching the bed with her arms around her middle, Hinata examined her mother's face. Even with all the ravages of illness, she was still beautiful, or perhaps it only seemed that way to Hinata. She could not remember a day without her mother's gentle presence, her quiet love, the steadfast nurturing that seemed endless. She sighed as she took a washcloth from the bowl of water on the nightstand, giving it a gentle squeeze to make sure it wasn't too wet. Hinata tenderly wiped the damp cloth over her mother's lips, moistening them and keeping to the old Buddhist tradition of care for the dying. Kanna's lips moved and pressed into the wet cloth, as if to a lover, taking some of the wetness. Hinata felt her shoulders ease a bit as tears gathered in the corners of her eyes. It would be soon, but perhaps not dreadfully soon.

Mother sighed and turned her head to the side, settling deeper into her pillows, her eyes still closed. Hinata returned the cloth to its dish and settled herself on her knees next to the bed and folded her hands in her lap. She tried not to weep. She tried to be good, to sit still, to be the dutiful daughter Father always told her she wasn't. But she couldn't hold still for long. She fidgeted and fingered the oil stains at the frayed edges of her kimono sleeves. Perhaps Father was right and she was and always would be a disappointment.

Hinata sighed and tried to push the thoughts of her father's quiet scowl out of her mind as she pulled her latest invention from the canvas bag on the floor next to her. She'd been trying to think of something to impress her father, something to really stand out after a long string of failures while she tried to help her mother with the household duties. Mother had always been indulgent of her daughter's absentminded ways and mechanical proclivities, but as her illness grew worse she had no choice but to coax Hinata into the kitchen and the laundry and away from her inventions.

Hinata resisted as much as her filial duty would allow in the beginning, until she realized she had a new set of challenges before her, new opportunities to invent. But things had not gone so well. The steampowered wash tub quickly scrubbed Father's favorite yukata to shreds against the washboard. The twirling drying lines she'd designed to make the laundry dry faster with gentle breezes spun too fast and flung the laundry all over the yard and into the pond. Her brother's blue linen hakama were still missing. Hinata thought she almost had the automatic rice steamer perfected, but Father would not allow her to try it again. Not after the last time when it blew off the lid and put a hole in the roof. So Hinata bowed to her father and applied herself to the traditional way of doing things. While she would admit that her domestic skills had improved significantly with the practice, her rice would still not maintain the same perfect stickiness as Mother's, and her dumplings were not quite so tasty; under her hand the laundry was clean but not quite so perfect or without wrinkles as Mother could manage.

She turned her latest invention over in her hands and examined it from every angle; if she was correct, it was finally done. They appeared a simple, if overlarge pair of brass shoes anyone could strap to their feet. In truth, the thick base contained a small boiler that powered strong steel scissor lifts that folded neatly into the sole. Hinata created them to make harvest time in her father's persimmon orchards more efficient and less costly. The metal bracing encased the wearer's ankles to give them confidence and stability, with additional leather straps that criss-crossed their way up the calf. One tap of the heels made them lift upward and a second tap paused the action. Two quick taps in succession brought the lifts down. The shoes added as much as thirty-six inches to the wearer's height, and remained stable enough even at full extension that you could walk up and down the length of the orchard in confidence. No more shifting ladders from tree to tree, tiresomely going up and down. Each picker could get closer to the fruit too, making for fewer bruised persimmons that could not be sold.

"See Okaa-san?" Hinata murmured without raising her eyes from her invention. "I'm not just a silly dreamer, I can make useful things."

"I know that, my little peony," Mother's voice came in a disused croak. "I've never doubted you could master whatever you put your mind to; you are *my* daughter, after all. You'll eventually get the rice right too."

"Mama!" gasped Hinata as she juggled the shoe in her hands to keep from dropping it, lifting her wide eyes to her mother. "You're awake! How do you feel?"

Her mother's hand lifted off the snowy coverlet and brushed the question away. "I am the same. What I want to know about is that glorious contraption in your hands. Tell me about your invention, my Hinata."

Warmth blossomed in Hinata's belly as she held out the left shoe to her mother. "I call them ascension shoes. I made them so we can harvest the persimmons without the cumbersome ladders. There's a scissor lift in the sole so that you can be any height you need to be. These are for me so I made the brass pretty." The words tumbled out of her like a river undammed and she held the brass work closer for Mother to see. Even though she said the elegant touches were for herself, they were really to make Mother smile. She'd spent so many evenings getting it perfect, cutting just the right amount of scroll work at the edges, brushing the surface to a soft gleam instead of a garish shine, and etching in flowers and swirling strokes — the proper touches to demonstrate beauty and good taste, but not enough to be gaudy or ostentatious.

"Put them on, show me how they work," Mother said with a smile.

Hinata's grin nearly broke her face in half as she bent to strap the shoes on her feet, wrapping the leather straps firmly, but not too tight. "I tried to keep the design as clean as I could, less things to go wrong..." she began.

Hinata's head snapped up as a wet cough tore through Mother's chest. The shoes forgotten, she leapt up and helped her mother sit up. She grabbed a handkerchief from the bedside table and held it at her mother's chin. She winced at the fresh, bright red droplets that stained the cloth but never stopped rubbing Kanna's back or crooning comforting words. Eventually, Mother's fit subsided and Hinata eased her back onto the pillows.

Mother sighed and slipped back down into slumber. Hinata wiped the last of the blood from her mother's mouth and tossed the stained handkerchief into a small washing basket with one hand while she grabbed the wet cloth from its dish with the other. This time when she pressed the damp cloth to Kanna's lips there was no reaction.

"Please, Okaa-sama, please..." Desperation crept into Hinata's voice along with the higher honorific for her mother. She sank to her knees next to the bed. "Just a little longer, please. Father and Brother will be home soon. Please don't go without a proper good-bye." The last words choked out around a sob.

Hinata took a few breaths to steady herself, then rose from her knees. She crossed the room to the one invention her father grudgingly agreed was useful — her illumination communicator. It had a concave lens on the front of a mirror-lined compartment on top of a graceful brass pole with claw feet and wheels the size of her palm. Inside the mirrored compartment was room for a massive candle with three wicks. Hinata opened the front and lit each wick. She had to turn her face away as the mirrors amplified the light enough to hurt her eyes. As she closed the compartment she made sure the louvers on the front of the lens were completely closed so not a crack of light peeked through.

Guiding it carefully to the threshold, Hinata tried to think of what to say. What could she say that would bring Father and Brother faster? She pointed the illumination communicator in the direction of the far persimmon orchards Father and Brother had gone to inspect. She hoped they would see the light and respond with the portable illumination communicator she'd sent with them. The louvers squeaked just a little as she opened and closed the flaps to send a message in her own adaptation of the new Morse Code. Mr. Morse's code worked fine for Western letters, but Hinata had to modify it to suit the kanji she and her family used. She begged her father and brother to come quickly, to hurry as much as they could. She held her breath and scanned the horizon for a response.

When she was about to send her message again, she saw a light winking on the horizon with a terse message from her father. She could see his scowl in her mind's eye. They were coming as fast as they could. She would have to handle things for herself until they got there.

Hinata opened the lens of the illumination communicator and snuffed the candlewicks. She returned to her mother's bedside and sank to her knees, taking Mother's hand. She pressed Mother's frail hand to her wet cheek and sobbed, "Please Okaa-sama, don't go yet. I need you."

Kanna made no sign that she heard her daughter. Hinata held her breath in hopes of hearing the barest whisper, or even a change in her mother's breath, to give her hope. There was only silence. She pressed her forehead into the mattress and held her mother's hand in both of hers, trying to breathe evenly and not sob. She wasn't ready, she wasn't ready.

The slightest rustle of the tatami mats broke the silence. Hinata's head jerked up, her cheeks damp and her hair flying in all directions, eyes full of wild hope that Father and Brother had made it home in time, that Mother would not pass with only her for company. But it was not Father or Brother she saw. Two strange men stood at the head of her mother's bed, one on either side, facing each other over her mother.

They dressed like samurai at court with full formal black kimono, topped with gray hakama and kataginu with exaggerated shoulders and knife sharp pleats in the front. They had both katana and wakizashi, the big sword and the little, tucked into their belts. Their shaggy hair hanging over their brows seemed out of place, but their stiff carriage and serious eyes matched what Hinata thought a true samurai would look like.

Hinata's gaze rose up the full height of the one who stood near her shoulder. She found her breath again and gasped. He frowned and looked down at her.

"You should not be able to see us, girl." His voice sounded like soil falling into a grave, but rather than frightening Hinata the soft sliding sound brought her peace.

"Who are you?" she whispered.

"A more appropriate question would be, what are we?" said the man on the other side of the bed. "We don't have proper names of our own. We are Shinigami."

Hinata heard a low moan and it took her a moment to realize it came from her own throat. Shinigami came when it was time; Shinigami came to escort souls to their final destination.

"Please, no," she groaned. "Please, not yet. Father and Brother are on their way. They need to say a proper goodbye."

The Shinigami next to her shook his head and gazed down at her with gentle eyes. "We have no control over the time, girl. Your mother's candle has nearly burned out, and when a candle reaches its end we must come to perform our duties."

"What candle? What do you mean?" Hinata looked from one Shinigami to the other.

"Each person has a candle that burns throughout their life," the far Shinigami explained. "And when that candle is about to go out, the person's life is at an end."

Hinata remained silent for a moment, her mind racing and the tip of her tongue tracing over her lower lip. Hope suddenly flared in her eyes.

"You didn't say Mother's candle is out, so it is still burning somewhere, yes?"

The Shinigami looked at each other with furrowed brows and slowly nodded as they returned their gazes to Hinata.

"And if I can find a way to keep Mother's candle burning a little bit longer, then Mother can live long enough for Father and Brother to reach her side, yes?" Hinata's voice rose in excitement.

The Shinigami traded looks that said far more than words, born of beings who had partnered with each other for time beyond reckoning and didn't need to speak. Finally, the one next to Hinata shrugged and the Shinigami on the far side of the bed spoke.

"If your mother's candle still burns, then yes, she still lives," he said.

"Most honorable Shinigami, if it would suit you, would you take this humble girl to her Mother's candle? Please," Hinata begged and made deep obeisance with her forehead on the floor to the pair of Shinigami.

Hinata kept her forehead to the floor, fighting the urge to spring to her feet and babble and beg the Shinigami to help her. She counted her breaths, in and out, four slow times and still there was silence. Her shoulders rounded in, hunching close to her body, as she strained to hear the smallest sound. Mother's labored breathing continued, so at least the Shinigami hadn't made off with her spirit while Hinata stared at the floor. She counted her breaths again four slow times. Just when she was about to jump up and howl at the Shinigami for their heartlessness one of them finally spoke. She couldn't tell which one.

"Because you have seen us, we will take you to the candles once, and only once. This favor may not be repeated no matter how you might beg or try to bribe us. Are you sure you wish to use this favor now?"

Hinata sat up tall, her spine straight, the tracks of tears dry on her cheeks. She looked at her mother with serious eyes and made a show of thinking carefully, but her mind was already made up. There was no other person in this world or any other she cared for more than her mother.

"I understand the limits of your favor, most honorable Shinigami," Hinata said as she bowed low with her forehead to the floor once more. "I do wish to use this singular kindness for my mother so that my father and brother may have a chance to say goodbye."

"Then stand up, child," one of the Shinigami said. "We must hurry. Our favor will do you no good if her candle dies before we can get there. Even our power is not limitless."

Hinata sprang to her feet, almost pitching forward completely as the weight of the scissor-lift shoes played tricks with her balance. The Shinigami closest to her caught her by her shoulders and helped her right herself.

"There is enough time that you don't need to snuff your own candle in order to save your mother's," he said with a gentle smile.

Hinata nodded and gave him a weak smile of her own. She stepped past him to pull the cloth from the bowl once more and wet her mother's unresponsive lips one last time before she went. She leaned over and placed a tender kiss on Mother's forehead.

"Wait for me," she whispered. "I will be back as soon as I can."

Placing the cloth back in its bowl, she bent down to flip the switches on her heels to start the boilers warming, just in case. Hinata turned to the Shinigami with a resolute nod of her head. "I am ready."

Hinata could have sworn that neither Shinigami moved, or even breathed, but suddenly they stood on either side of her. As one, the Shinigami each laid a hand on her nearest shoulder. Hinata felt the world ripple as if she had dropped into a deep pool. Everything was muffled, the evening birds in the trees, her thoughts, even the beat of her own heart. The Shinigami steered her forward with gentle pressure, stopping her at the threshold between the bedroom and the central courtyard of the house. They both raised their hands, palms flat before them, and the air in the doorway turned to what looked like a vertical opaque pool of water, with concentric circles rippling out from where the Shinigami touched it without touching it.

The Shinigami guided her forward to the water gateway. Hinata screwed her eyes shut tight and held her breath, but the feeling of water against her skin never came. The guiding spirits took her three steps and stopped. Hinata waited, fear cramping her belly as she refused to let her eyes open. The familiar scents of machine oil and warm metal came to her. Somewhere near she heard the teeth of gears meshing together, the jingle of chains.

The Shinigami on her right squeezed her shoulder before he removed his hand and whispered in her ear, "You may open your eyes now."

Hinata obeyed and could not stop herself from gasping. Her mouth hanging open in wonderment, she stepped forward without a thought that there might be rules governing this astounding place she found herself in.

It looked as if it had been a natural cave at one time, all rippling stone walls and stalactites and stalagmites. Every inch of the stone was covered with gears and struts and pulley chains in all manner of gleaming metals. Extending out from the machinery that carpeted the walls were graceful arms of brass that each ended in a small cupped platform holding one burning snow-white pillar candle each. As she watched, the gears turned, some faster, some slower. As they moved they pulled the platforms up toward the ceiling on chains that seemed far too delicate and ethereal. The ceiling soared high above her head and even in the golden light of the thousands of candles the true height was hidden somewhere in the inky black shadows above.

Hinata turned slowly in a circle taking it all in. She settled her gaze back on the Shinigami, who regarded her with small smiles and twinkles in their eyes. Hinata bowed at her waist, bringing her hands together in front of her.

"Thank you, honorable Shinigami, for guiding me to the place where I may help my mother." She straightened up and couldn't keep her eyes from wandering over the walls once more. "Has it always been like this? Who built this?" Her words came out on the breath of awe.

The Shinigami exchanged glances and the one on the left spoke. "In a way, you built it. The way the candles appear is different for each mortal who sees it, and reveals something of their soul. We never know what shape it will take until a mortal opens their eyes."

Hinata's head bobbed as she paced closer to one of the elegant candle arms with her hands clasped behind her back, leaning in close to examine every aspect, careful not to breathe out too hard and disturb the flame. The platform was just large enough to hold its candle, the edges curling up slightly to hold it firmly. Her eyes traced along the graceful brass arm that connected the platform to the chains and gears that ticked along, counting minutes and breaths.

"It's beautiful," she whispered to herself, forgetting for a moment that the Shinigami were even there.

"It's you," the Shinigami on the right said. "Or at least, it's what's in your heart."

Hinata blushed and dropped her eyes to the floor as she stood up from her examination. She gathered herself and lifted her face to the Shinigami.

"Which candle is my mother's?" Hinata asked.

As one the Shinigami pointed to a candle burned down to its last inch, high up on the wall behind her, its guttering flame barely pushing back any of the darkness. It was far above Hinata's head.

She gasped. "It's nearly out."

"Indeed, girl. That is why we came for your mother. It is almost time," said one Shinigami behind Hinata. She paced forward slowly with her head tilted to the side as she considered the problem of keeping her mother's candle burning.

"But the herbalist said she saw you before." Hinata's voice was soft and distracted as she came to a stop just under her mother's candle and stared up.

"Your mother is strong-willed. She has fought her illness fiercely. We've visited several times and her will to live has always pushed us back."

Hinata's head whipped around and she narrowed her eyes. "Then how do you know she won't push you back again? How do you know that this is finally her time?"

"Your mother is tired, child," the Shinigami on the right said.

"There is only so long that Death can be resisted," said the other. "It is her time now. We are certain."

Hinata turned quickly back to her study of the candle overhead to hide her tears from the Shinigami. She crossed her arms over her chest and ran her tongue back and forth over her lower lip, deep in thought.

"Is it the platform or the candle that's important?" she asked the Shinigami without turning her head, as she listened to the soft rattle of chains. "If I switch her candle for a taller one from a different platform, will that prolong her life?"

Hinata felt a wind rush through the cave and set all the candle flames dancing, and there was a Shinigami at her shoulder his eyes alight with anger. She clutched her hands over her heart as she watched her mother's flame sputter and then grow steady again.

"To take another's candle is to steal their life," the Shinigami growled into her ear. "We cannot allow murder."

Hinata gasped. "Oh! Oh, I beg your pardon. I meant no offense. That wasn't what I meant." She turned to face the Shinigami, making multiple embarrassed bows. "I only meant that if I could exchange one long enough to ensure mother could say goodbye to Father and Brother, then I would put the borrowed candle back."

"And the person you took it from would have already taken on your mother's death," the Shinigami interrupted with an even deeper frown.

"So it is the candle that makes the difference? Not the platform?" Hinata's brow creased as her eyes wandered back to her mother's candle again. It seemed like it was a little closer to the ceiling, and the wax a little further gone in just the short time she'd been in the cavern.

The Shinigami shook his head. "They work together. The platform represents the person, and the candle represents the life. They are bound together just like the mortal soul is bound to the flesh."

"Where is my candle?" Hinata asked.

"There." The Shinigami pointed to another candle, still thick and tall and burning steadily, on the same wall as her mother's candle but much closer to the ground.

"If I take my candle from my platform, how long will it take me to die?" Hinata asked.

"You would exchange your life for your mother's?" The Shinigami asked.

"Would that work? Would my mother be able to enjoy the life I give her?" Hinata pinned the Shinigami with a ferociously curious gaze.

"Your mother would live longer, but she would remain ill for the time you gave her. The extra life essence would not cure her," the Shinigami said with a frown.

"She would not thank me for that," Hinata murmured as her eyes jumped back and forth between the candles, measuring distance. "And you haven't answered my question. How long before I die?"

The Shinigami sighed. "You would not die here. The magic in this place is too strong. But you will grow weaker the longer your candle is not on your platform, and when we returned you to the world of the living you would die upon crossing."

Hinata nodded slowly, an epiphany blossoming in her head. "Then I should have time."

"Time for what?" asked the Shinigami, his brow furrowed.

"You'll see," Hinata said as she gave him a coy smile.

She took a deep breath and leaned down to test the bindings on her shoes. She straightened and squared her shoulders, then strode forward toward her candle.

It was easy enough to lay her fingers against the warm, waxy surface of the pillar that represented her life. The scent of chrysanthemums tickled her nose through the smell of oil on the gears and chains. The candle was not above her head just yet and plucking it off the platform was as easy as taking it from an eye-level cabinet shelf.

The moment the bottom of her candle lost contact with the platform, Hinata's heart constricted and her breathing turned to harsh wheezing. She nearly dropped it in shock.

Her grip on the candle white-knuckled and her other hand clutched over her erratic heart, Hinata moaned. "You said I would not die here."

"You will not die," the Shinigami said in placid calm. "But separating your candle from your platform is not without risks. Look." He pointed to her platform, which no longer ascended the wall so slowly that it was imperceptible. The gears spun faster, the chain clacking and rattling. It had begun a stately glide up the wall. It would not take long before it lifted up into the shadows and was lost.

"What happens if I do not return the candle before the platform..." Hinata couldn't finish the thought but the Shinigami understood her well enough.

"You could never leave this cavern as a corporeal being," he said. "If we took you back to the mortal realm you would be an *ikiryo* wandering the earth until the time when your candle would have burned out." He clasped his hands behind his back and rocked from heel to toe. "And most likely you would go mad long before your release. It is rare for spirits to resist madness for more than a short period."

Hinata pressed her lips together and gripped her candle before her carefully with both hands. "Well then, I had better leap while there is yet a place to land."

She tapped the heels of her ascension shoes together and the scissor lifts engaged, raising Hinata until she quickly passed her empty candle platform. She flung her empty arm out to balance herself. Despite the ache in her chest, Hinata felt hope warm the painful muscles. And then the scissor lifts snapped to a stop at their full height. Her mother's candle was still above her head.

Hinata stretched up as far as her arms would reach, but she still could not quite grasp her mother's candle. Her eyes darted to the right to catch sight of her own ascending platform. Carefully holding her candle steady, Hinata squatted and undid the buckles that secured her feet to the brass shoes, fumbling one-handed with the leather straps to throw them off her calves. She stood slowly, one arm extended for balance and the other cradling her candle as close to her chest as she dared without getting singed. Even though her eyes told her the shoes and the lifts were rock steady, Hinata still felt like she swayed on a high wire. She swallowed hard and blew out a steadying breath.

Hinata lifted up onto her toes. The lifts did begin to tremble out of balance then. But she persisted, stretching up as high as she could with her arms, holding her breath. She could reach, but only barely. And given that her mother's platform was still in motion, however slow, she couldn't waste a second.

Tilting her own candle, Hinata dribbled wax collecting beneath her own wick to enlarge the pool that fed her mother's. She had to gauge the strength of her mother's flame by the shadow on the wall. Her thoughts raced and she hoped that she didn't slip and pour the liquid wax right on the flame and snuff it out.

The trembling and swaying from the scissor lifts grew more pronounced until Hinata's hand shuddered. She gasped as the flame's reflection on the wall started to gutter. Hinata yanked her candle away. She hissed in pain as hot wax splashed across her hand but did not take her eyes from the light and shadow on the wall. Her mother's flame steadied and began to burn brighter.

Hinata carefully relaxed from her pointed toe stance, but not carefully enough. The scissor lifts quaked and swayed wildly. She windmilled one arm and brought her candle close to her chest again. The swaying stopped. Hinata settled her heels into the shoes as well as she could, but was unable to strap them. She glanced down at the long swinging leather straps, hoping they wouldn't tangle in the scissor lifts on the way down. Casting her eyes to the side, she again searched for her platform. It was almost even with where she stood. Extending both arms out, Hinata got ready. As the platform came within reach she slid her candle into place. The tightness in her chest eased as candle and platform were reunited. But for one desperate moment it seemed like the platform wouldn't stop. It seemed it would continue its accelerated ascent into the shadows above her head.

Then it shuddered to a stop. It held still a moment, almost even with Kanna's candle, before sinking again at a glacial pace.

Hinata didn't dare bend to redo the straps on her shoes, fearing she'd bring herself crashing to the hard stone floor below her. She tapped her heels together twice in quick succession. The scissor lifts jerked into downward motion. Hinata finally did lose her balance and toppled over.

The Shinigami were there and broke her fall with their outstretched arms, but it was still enough to knock the wind out of Hinata. She winced as she heard her precious invention clatter against the stone floor.

"Oil them," she grunted as the Shinigami helped her stand. "I really must oil them."

"Your hand," murmured one of the Shinigami as he furrowed his brow with concern. Hinata looked down at the irregular red blotch of throbbing pain on her hand.

"I've spilled candle wax on myself before, it usually doesn't hurt this much," she said.

"Magical wax full of life essence holds properties that mundane candles do not," the other Shinigami said with a gentle smile. He took her hand, cradling it gently in his own. As he blew a soft breath across her burn, Hinata felt it cool as if an unseen hand had pressed ice to her skin. "Even after this heals, you will still bear the mark of the wax. The skin the wax touched will chill, like so, whenever one of us near."

Hinata sighed and looked around the room as she shook her head. "Traveling to other realms with death spirits... Keeping my mother alive with magic.... I suppose a magic wax burn allowing me to feel spirits is the most believable thing yet."

The other Shinigami grinned and waggled his eyebrows. "This is positively normal compared to other realms we could show you."

Hinata blanched. "It is a gracious offer, most honorable Shinigami, but I must return to my mother's bedside." She turned her face back up to her mother's candle. "Do you think it worked? Do you think I gave her enough time?"

"There is only one way to know," said the Shinigami. "We take you back and see if she still breathes."

Hinata nodded decisively, her mouth set in a grim line as she cradled her burned hand against herself. "Shall we go?"

The Shinigami laid their hands on her shoulders as before and once again Hinata felt muffled as if in deep water. One leaned down and murmured in her ear, "You have gifted some of your life essence to your mother. This will leave you weak on your return. Be gentle with yourself. We do not wish to come for you too soon."

Raising their palms together, the Shinigami called the quivering doorway once more. Hinata snapped her eyes shut at the last moment. As much as she longed to see the space between the worlds, she could not bear that it would only last a moment, that it would leave her hungry for the rest of her life for something she could never see again. There was not enough time to examine whatever wonders existed in that liminal space, not if she wanted to return to her mother while she still lived. Two steps later Hinata felt the tatami mats of her parent's bedroom floor through her socks rather than the rough stone of the other realm. The Shinigami's hands fell away from her shoulders. Hinata kept her eyes clenched shut on the tears gathering there. She held her breath that she might better hear her mother's.

Did Hinata dare believe that the rasping had lessened, that Mother's breathing sounded just a bit less labored? There was only one way to know.

Hinata opened her eyes. Tears spilled down her cheeks as she met her mother's gaze, as she saw her mother's long-absent smile. The Shinigami were gone, or at least Hinata could no longer see them. Mother lifted her frail arm and held out a hand to her daughter.

"What did you do, my blessing, my child?" Mother's voice slipped out in a harsh whisper.

"I did what was necessary," Hinata choked out and took a step toward her mother's bedside.

Somewhere a sliding door clacked and there were footsteps on the gravel path in the garden. Hinata's brother pushed past her, just steps ahead of their father. Hinata stumbled and weakness sent her to the floor. They had made it, Father and Brother had made it while Mother still breathed. A great, wracking sob hitched up in her chest and tears, of relief this time, flowed anew.

Hinata's father sank to his knees next to his wife, taking her fragile hand with utmost tenderness. He lifted her fingers to his trembling lips as tears traced down his cheeks.

"My moon, my stars," he whispered. "Please do not leave me."

Mother took her hand from his and caressed his cheek as she gave him a melancholy smile. "I have delayed as long as I could, my love. My time has come."

Hinata's father sobbed and leaned into her touch, nodding. His arms crept around her waist and he laid his head against her chest. As he wept she stroked his hair and sighed.

"Her lips are dry!" growled Hinata's brother and he whirled on his sister where she shivered on the floor. His eyes flashed with anger and disgust. "Where is your honor? You could not even tend our mother properly at this of all times?"

He reached down and grabbed Hinata to pull her up, making her cry out as he grabbed her burned hand.

"You neglected your responsibilities!" he cried in shock as he gripped her wrist and thrust her burned hand forward for their parents to see. "She must have been experimenting with her ridiculous inventions while she ignored her duty."

"Boy!" Mother's voice cracked through the still air of the bedroom with more strength than she'd displayed in months. All eyes locked on her, mouths hung open in shock.

"You will not disrespect your sister," Mother's voice croaked out, her eyes flashing. "Hinata made a deal with the Shinigami and gave of her own life essence to keep me alive long enough for you and Father to get here to say good-bye. You will honor your sister's sacrifice."

Her brother dropped her hand as he turned and goggled at her. Hinata barely noticed.

"You saw?" she whispered.

Mother's expression softened as she turned her gaze to her daughter. "Of course I did, my little peony. My soul was loose and about to travel. I saw everything."

"I only wished to bring you what comfort I could, Okaa-sama," Hinata said as she brought her hands together and made a deep bow.

As she straightened, her eyes met her father's. He gazed at her thoughtfully and said, "It seems I have misjudged your strength, my daughter. You have much of your mother in you, and it is my shame to have not seen it."

Hinata bowed to her father. "Honored Otou-sama, perhaps I share some of the shame for hiding my light from you."

"You are too generous, Hinata," Father said with a shake of his head. "I will make things right."

"Come," Mother stretched out her arms to all of her family. "Come say good-bye to me in peace. I want no bickering in my final moments."

Hinata crawled up on the bed and curled against her mother's side, laying a gentle arm over her middle. Her hand brushed her father's and they smiled at each other as their fingers intertwined. She felt the burn on her hand tingle with cold and knew the Shinigami were close, even if they would no longer allow her to see them. Hinata's brother came and knelt beside their father and laid his hand over both of their's. He laid his head on Father's shoulder and let out a sob.

With a thin and reedy whisper, Mother began to sing the lullaby she'd sung to both her children from the time they were infants. Her voice faltered at the end, so Hinata sang the last line and kissed her mother on the forehead.

With her family gathered around her, Kanna Tanaka passed in peace.

The Camera

Jeffrey Lyman

I GOT TO THE HANGER LATE, STILL FURIOUS I WAS EVEN HERE, lugging my box camera and a case of fresh film plates in the back seat of my cabriole, and stopped at the top of the rise overlooking the valley.

I had to stop, it was just so impressive. For a moment I put away my anger and took in the scene. The *Tiaga* was already anchored tight to the servicing tracks on the ground and was being dragged slowly into the hanger, with a gaggle of news photographers close up under it. The *Saint Lucia* tug airship was tethered to the docking mast about a hundred feet above, and looked dwarfed by the craft below.

My, my, the *Tiaga* was big. All dirigibles are, I guess, but I'd rarely cared to be this close to one before. As one of the great ships, the *Tiaga* stretched for over a thousand feet. The police crews and newsmen beneath it were smaller than ants.

I suddenly wanted a picture of it. I don't normal do outdoorsy stuff, or landscapes, or airships, but I was already late and would have preferred to be later, and it'd give the mortuary crews time to cart the bodies off. I hate bodies. Freezes me up to even think about it. And these bodies would be worse than normal. I can't even imagine.

I carefully set up my camera on its tripod and swung out the front and rear standards and bellows, careful of the

aether-lenses inside. I had to hunt for my biggest brass lens to capture the breadth of the scene before me. I hardly ever use the wide lenses in my fashion practice, so it was still wrapped in its silk bag. The *Tiaga* was so large it had hardly moved much in all this time, so I carefully adjusted the focus, locked it down, and put a glass plate in. Since the owner, Thaddeus Greatmoore, was blackmailing me into this photographic excursion, I was going to expense every plate I took, whether it applied to the investigation or not.

Maybe I could make a little side money after this. Publish a pamphlet. I mean, how many dirigibles get lost over the Harrow Fields, and then return? Poor bastards on board probably didn't count it as lucky. I shivered. Very little ever comes back from the Harrow that one would welcome with open arms. I shivered again, and tried once more to think of an excuse to get me out of this. Greatmoore had me good, and had since our atelier days.

My only leverage would be the legendary quality of my photographs. The police always took bad pictures, and they were only ever really interested in the broad scene. The bodies and blood, and the damage. My camera was exceptional, magical even, and I lived and breathed tiny details in arranging my fashion models. Tiny details would be the thing to get Greatmoore out of this pickle. The newsmen were publicly excoriating his company with turgid and melodramatic headlines, but it would be the air marshals and the insurance men who could ruin him.

He needed me. He needed me to prove this was a straightforward accident and not negligence. And he needed me to prove that flying over the Harrow was still safe. All air traffic had ground to a halt since the *Tiaga* was lost, and his company was hemorrhaging money. Communication with the west had gotten difficult. Radiomen were trying to pick up the slack since the mail ships had been grounded, but there was only so much they could do . . . at least that's what I'd heard on the radio while driving over. I don't generally listen to the news, but this story was all anyone was talking about right now.

I folded my camera carefully back into its box, packed everything up, and made myself drive down the hill. The car bucked a bit, puffing steam, and I worried about throwing another rod. I hadn't brought my driver today, or any of my nice cars, because no one could know I was here. I was dressed as a mechanic so the newsmen would pass me by, but that wouldn't hold if I showed up in a chauffeured Drapice.

Not that I was a bad driver, I just didn't do it much anymore. I'd driven a considerable amount in my early days when I first started earning big money. I even learned how to work on the boiler and gears myself.

The *Tiaga* loomed higher and higher as my cabriole chuffed along, and when I passed into its shadow I hunkered down a bit. The temperature fell. It felt like leaving daylight and entering twilight. I still had a ways to go to get to the hanger parking lot.

There was a single, low office annex up against the hanger. A few newsmen waited by the door with a bunch of non-descript people who might have been family members of the deceased, but policemen kept everyone back. They waved me through when I showed them my temporary police papers. I hurried into the dingy airmen's lounge before any of the newsmen could recognize me through my coveralls.

The lounge wasn't much more than a few tables, a bar, a small toilet room, and the burn-reek of old cigarettes. There was a terrible chugging racket coming from the hanger that made it hard to think. Everyone was clustered at the back of the room, watching the *Tiaga's* progress through a pair of large windows into the hanger proper. The insurance people were at the left window and the airship people were clustered at the right with Greatmoore, keeping a bit of distance. The police chief and two air marshals with mammoth Haze guns over their shoulders stood between them.

Through the windows, I could see a full score of air marshals walking backward beneath the slow-moving *Tiaga* gondola. They all had their Haze guns pointed up. I stared at those heavy, iron hand-cannons, my unformed fears suddenly hardening into something much more defined.

I eased into Mr. Greatmoore's group and set my camera gently on a rickety table. Greatmoore stood with his thumbs in his waistcoat pockets, great belly straining the buttons of his vest. I counted three gold watch chains. Greatmoore had always lived to excess, even before he could afford it. Now the great industrialist could have anything he wanted.

I told myself sternly that he was the one in trouble today. Trouble he couldn't buy his way out of.

"You're late, Jack," Greatmoore grunted at me, not taking his eyes from the view.

He didn't need to be quiet. The steam crawlers out in the hanger that dragged the *Tiaga* thumped hard enough that I could feel them in my breastbone, and the air marshals shouted back and forth to one another as they covered the approach. The flight deck of the gondola was just reaching us, and I could see that most of its windows gaped open. The low air pressure at high altitudes had probably burst them outward. Hopefully it was air pressure, and not 'changed' passengers.

"I was getting a wide picture from the hill," I said.

Greatmoore grimaced. "The newsboys are getting plenty of pictures up there," he groused. "You can just pick up any daily paper tomorrow for a nice wide angle view."

"The newsboys don't have cameras like this," I retorted.

He glanced at my camera and the ghost of a smile crossed his lips. "That's Edward's camera, isn't it?"

I refused to tremble before his implied threat. "Have the mortuary retrievers been on board yet?"

The police chief turned to me in annoyance. "Does it look like we've even gotten her settled yet?" he snarled. "The morticians will go on after my air marshals have cleared the ship. Not before. You'll wait with the rest."

I made myself not glare at him or retort because I was disguised as a mechanic. Stupid public servant. I could buy and sell him, if he only knew who I was. This could take hours! But then I saw the tight set of his jaw and how his eyes flicked back and forth between his air marshals out there and the broken windows and realized he was on edge. Frightened even.

I leaned back and looked over at the insurance men, and then looked around Greatmoore's crew. They all were. My throat tightened a little bit, and I vowed to never speak to Greatmoore again after this. This was the last 'job'. I should have told him no when he rang me up two days ago. I should have found the courage, except he could ruin me.

I comforted myself that he only rang me up every couple of years for some job that demanded my photographic talents.

The *Tiaga* had dominated the dailies for the past week, so that even I in my cloistered workshop was aware of it. The loss of a great ship over the Harrow Fields made headlines because dirigibles were guaranteed to be safe at higher altitudes. The prime minister always said so. The advertisements said so. Unfortunately for Greatmoore, a number of notable socialites had gone missing with his ship. The famous Harrow Hunter, Mr. Gregory Dallbot, and his Harrow-mapping team were among the missing, and the air marshal community was up in arms. Before the *Tiaga's* return, funerals had been planned without the benefit of bodies.

And then the ship suddenly reappeared over accessible land, clearly foundering. The dailies raced to one-up each other with dramatic headlines, both plausible ones like burst valves and ruptured hydrogen bags at high altitudes bringing the ship back down, or lurid ones about 'changed' people onboard flying their own way back out of the Harrow.

The tug-ship, *Saint Lucia*, on an emergency run had snagged the *Tiaga* out near Breslin before it could hit the ground or get blown into the city, and brought it here. Away from population centers. According to the *Saint Lucia* crew, nothing living, human or 'changed', had been seen through the widows. The air marshals clearly weren't taking chances.

Greatmoore pulled me aside a few minutes later. "It's going to be a long day, so pace yourself," he said, his eyes boring into me. "The mortuary crews will clear the bodies. I don't have to tell you to stay out of their way and step carefully. If you come across a body they missed or someone who hid in a closet, don't disturb them. Just call the mortuary director, Mrs. Hammels, and she'll set up a retrieval. Okay?"

I stared right back at him; my anger and fear surging. "This is the last one, Thaddeus," I said firmly. "This is the worst one."

"Which is why I need the best." He smiled a broad smile.

"I could die up there."

"Don't be so melodramatic. You're going to follow the morticians, the air marshals, even the police photographers, for God's sake."

"Last time." I poked a finger into his chest.

He smacked my hand away like I'd hoped, his smile dropping, and I knew that people rarely poked him anymore. "I told you it would be the last time, *if* this works out in my favor. Just make sure you photograph the valves and control sticks and gauges. Develop them right away. I'll get them to Mr. Creigh to analyze what the hell they were up to when they lost control of the ship. Take pictures of anything out of the ordinary. I'll have my structural men analyzing the internal struts and hydrogen bags, and my engineers review the engines." He nodded toward the gaggle of insurance men. "And they'll have their photographers and their engineers trying to prove it was our fault. The whole industry depends on it being my fault. They're desperate to make me a scapegoat so they can resume flights over the Harrow." He finished with a mutter, "Sometimes accidents just happen."

The air marshal chief grunted. "Could have been an accident, could have been crew error, could have been the Harrow itself, reaching up like the hand of the devil. Let the police determine the cause and stay out of our way."

The steam crawlers in the hanger suddenly went silent and it felt like my ears popped. Greatmoore and everyone turned. Air marshals fanned out as the *Tiaga* came to a gentle stop while the chief and his two lieutenants quickly went out through the door with a bang, letting in a cold gust of air that smelled like lubricating oil.

A police gang loudly pushed boarding stairs out to the belly dock, though the stairs were a mismatch since a ship of *Tiaga's* size would never normally have been boarded from the ground. As it was, the rolling stairs were about four feet too short and the air marshals would have to hoist themselves up. Mortuary crews in their protective suits gathered. You didn't take chances with the Harrow.

Greatmoore was frowning, staring hard through the window.

"The ship's engineers might have moved the controls in an effort to get ahold of the ship once they knew they were in trouble," I said quietly to him. "Don't get your hopes up that this'll be cut and dried. Most likely it'll come back 'undetermined cause'."

He didn't respond for a long minute, though I could see his eyes tighten. He took a deep breath at last and said without looking at me, "I'll get copies of the police photographs. We can see where the bodies ended up. That might tell a story — whether it was quick or slow."

I turned back to the window, a pit in my stomach as air marshals in gasmasks climbed the stairs to unbolt the hatch. Haze guns were out and aimed at the hatch by the air marshals on the ground. My hands were clenched and I consciously relaxed them. I really didn't want to see the bodies. I'm intensely visual, and I knew they'd be stuck in my dreams for weeks. I didn't want to know what the Harrow had done to them.

I'd flown over the Harrow Fields twice, it's the only way to get to Drannislyn and the western cities now that it's cut the country in half, but I couldn't remember it. No one can. It does things to your memory. The Harrow mappers have to draw quickly in flight and they never remember what they've drawn afterward. But what they drew, I've read, is enough to give any sane person nightmares.

The Harrow Hunters actually go into it wearing protective gear. They're famous. There are popular books written about them that I'll never read. They even managed to recapture the city of Tyffin and push the Harrow back last year, their one significant victory. No one wants to live in Tyffin now, but still . . . it's symbolic.

The hatch swung down and the assault-lead shoved his head and Haze gun up through the opening. A moment later, he waved 'all clear' and climbed aboard. His companions cautiously followed one by one. The mortuary crew, in heavy canvas suits and full-head gasmasks, waited with stretchers and body bags. The police photographers had their cameras under their arms, and I noted that they looked battered and old. Not like my mythical beauty. They boarded after the last of the air marshals. Then the morticians.

The removal of bodies proceeded fairly rapidly, I guess, but it still seemed endless at the same time. Two morticians would stand at the top of the stairs, hands raised, and a stretcher, tightly wrapped in canvas, would descend. They would hustle down and another pair would take their place. There were just so many bodies. Forty passengers and nearly thirty crew. I wondered where they were taking all the bodies, and then decided I didn't want to know. Curiosity only ever got me into trouble.

Funny thing was that though the belly hatch and stair were crawling with morticians, not a single air marshal had yet returned. I guess they had to check every nook and cranny, even up into the hull on the spiderweb of catwalks and platforms. Once I saw two men cross on an exposed walkway out to one of the mammoth engine cars on an outrigger.

I broke into a cold sweat, my heart thumping. How was I going to go out onto that? I was hyperventilating. I closed my eyes and forced my breathing to slow. It helped a bit.

I heard muttering around me and opened my eyes to see the police chief jogging down the stairs. A number of morticians followed behind him with no new bodies.

He banged through the door, pulling his heavy, rubber gasmask off with a hard yank. "You," he barked, pointing at me. "You're up. The bodies are off and I want to quarantine this thing before the end of the day." He looked at the insurance men. "You too."

Their photographer and a pair of mechanics separated from the group, looking just as frightened as I felt. As we moved forward, the chief stepped back, crossing his arms. "They all died of asphyxiation as far as we can tell, probably due to the altitude. Any blood seems incidental to them falling on edges and corners. My detectives are still on board. Don't get in their way. Don't touch anything."

Two men separated from Greatmoore's group and followed me. Probably his engineers. Greatmore nodded to me.

I made my way through the door into the cool, diesel-scented air of the hanger and grabbed a gasmask from the police bin. It said 'Air Marshal' in yellow stencil on the side, and was uncomfortably heavy. I hadn't worn one since the scare back at the atelier — what some would call an art enclave — when I was twenty-two. The insurance photographer and I shared a look, and then he hurried up the stairs after his team, his tripod balanced on his shoulder, the camera already screwed on. I followed, lugging a case of about a twenty plates. You never know how many photographs you might need to take. Morticians continued to pass us heading down, hurrying to be clear of the derelict. More than one stared at me through their distorting gasmask lenses.

I carefully placed my camera and cases in the hold and wriggled myself up like a floundering guppy, fully aware of all the eyes watching me through the windows below. The mechanics and insurance photographer were already past the stacks of equipment and packaged food and were hurrying up an iron staircase to the main deck. I forced myself to go slow and document everything. I'd get Greatmoore out of this fix, but I had to do it properly.

It felt deathly quiet beyond my breathing through the gasmask as I set up my tripod and took my first photograph of the neatly stacked supplies and a mortician walking up the narrow path through them toward me. The flash was bright and left both of us shaking our heads and him cursing at me. The mortician shoved past me and dropped through the hatch, and I was alone. Why couldn't I hear any air marshals talking or moving above?

I felt like someone was watching, standing right beside me, following behind. My nerves, tense after the last two hours of waiting, were getting the best of me, right? Maybe I should move a little faster, even as I took careful pictures.

I hurried forward to the stairs, lingering for a moment to photograph the grand, carpeted entrance behind the stairs where guests would normally have boarded in comfort. The filigree along the molding was gilded and lovely; but the oppressive feeling of someone standing beside me was too much to linger there for long.

I hauled the equipment up to the main deck where air marshals in groups were finishing their sweep or were talking intently to each other. Thick carpeting ate all sounds of footsteps, so that explained the sepulchral silence. Behind me stretched a narrow hall to the sleeping cabins, and forward was the wide lounge/dining room. An air marshal stopped me, as he was about to start up the stairs to the crew level above. His great, bristly moustache brushed the glass of his gasmask.

"When you get to the Control Room," he called, "don't mind the blood. Looks like they toppled over at their posts."

"They warned me," I called back. "So it was a quick death?" Maybe Greatmoore would be lucky and the levers and valves would all be in their original positions.

"I doubt it," the man said. "Most of the passengers were at the front observation lounge, so there was time to gather. There are still a bunch of detectives up there, so you might check engineering first." He pointed down the corridor between the sleeping cabins.

I nodded and gathered my nerve. There was nothing here, really. The air marshals had been all through it. The Morticians had been here by the dozen. Except there *was* something here and it had me jumping at every noise. Being unable to see out of my peripheral vision with the gasmask on made it worse.

I walked down the plush, maroon carpet, moving as quickly as possible while remaining calm and in control because I didn't want to bang my camera on anything. The doors of the sleeping cabins all hung eerily open, revealing bits of abandoned personal lives, but I saw no other living person. The air marshals had finished their sweep down at this end.

I was also alone in the engineering car, which sat at the far back of the ship and below the stern cabins. It was claustrophobically tight, with windows on either side that looked out on the ship's engines. I had a tough time mounting my tripod far enough back from the controls, but I took several photographs of gauges, levers, and the banks of hydrogen valves, as well as the broader room. The telephone handset to the forward Control Room hung by its wires and I had a sudden urge to put it to my ear to see if anyone was there. I turned cold at the thought of it touching my skin, and took a photograph of it instead.

It's funny how my mind started playing tricks on me. I swear half a dozen times I thought an air marshal was behind me, moving about, looking at dials and gauges, but no one was ever there when I turned. Maybe heading forward was a good idea, even if I got in the way of detectives.

I hustled up the steps to the central corridor where the cabin doors all stood closed now, and lugged my equipment toward the main, forward lounge. This was where the passengers would have dined and passed the time. The *Tiaga* was large enough that it probably had a mezzanine and promenades that wrapped around the outside of the cabins, against the gondola's windows.

I stopped in the door. The detectives had moved on, because there were only a few people in the airy, ornate room. Three young air marshals in gasmasks scooped up personal possessions from the floor and tossing them into canvas bags. The insurance photographer was just hefting his camera. He met my eyes quickly, nervously. He felt it too. The silence was heavy. He crossed the dance floor toward the forward control room, leaving me with the three air marshals.

I set down my tripod, wanting a picture of this, though it technically wasn't part of Greatmoore's requested photographs. I told myself it was to compare them with the police photographs later. See what had been moved by the air marshals and morticians. Tables and chairs lay scattered everywhere, but some might have been righted or shifted aside. Cushioned benches along the outer walls were swollen with rain water. Most of the slanted windows that followed the curve of the gondola's walls had shattered outward, leaving no glass behind. Books had tumbled from bookshelves.

They'd been through one hell of a storm. Before or after?

I was glad the bodies were gone. The atmosphere of catastrophe was harsh enough and the feeling of being stalked that had started in the storage hold below had not abated a whit. If anything, it was growing worse.

"Find anything interesting?" I called to the air marshals, just to break the silence.

They jerked up as if I'd kicked them, then waved me off in obvious relief. "Make a little noise when you come in, would you?" one called. "We're on edge."

"I'm not going to sleep for a week," said another.

I nodded and clamped my camera down to the tripod so I could take a photograph to starboard, then to port.

Dragging my gear forward once more, following the insurance photographer, I found my shoes squelching on wet carpeting. I passed a white piano, the veneer swollen and buckled. Pain suddenly shot up my calf like an electric shock and I jumped, fearing there was an exposed electric line somewhere in the wet carpet. I hurried on to the forward door of the control car. Feeling all nerves, I made myself stop and take another picture of the lounge, facing sternward. The three air marshals were throwing things indiscriminately into their bags, moving fast. I'd vowed never to break in the face of fear again after the atelier burned when I was twenty-two.

I didn't see acquiescing to Greatmoore as giving in to fear, blackmail was the cost of doing business, but I knew I would never bow before him again.

Sliding my latest photographic plate into my case, I turned to see the insurance photographer lifting a lever in the far-forward steering room. Maybe if I hadn't stopped to take that picture he would have heard me coming, but I caught him red-handed and he knew it.

"What are you doing?" I demanded, striding forward, my tripod and camera forgotten. I was absolutely furious. If the insurance guys were changing things, then they were really out to screw Greatmoore and I'd never get my life back. "What are you doing?" I demanded again, grabbing him by the lapels of his coat and shoving him back. I could see his wide eyes through his gasmask.

"Nothing!" he yelled. "I wasn't doing nothing."

"You moved a lever!" I was bellowing now, shaking him. He crumpled, knees buckling, and I let him fall. "I'm going to take a picture of this room and compare it to the police photographs from earlier. Any control levers or valve handles that've been moved, and I'm calling an inquest on you."

"No, don't," he begged. "They told me too. They told me to get ahead of you and change things. They said the police wouldn't focus much on the levers."

"Idiot." I stood, lowering my hands to my sides. "You think the police didn't capture the controls when they were photographing bodies? Don't touch another thing. In fact, get off this ship."

"But I'm not done," he cried.

He scrambled to his knees beside his tripod, which was still facing forward toward the prow. He looked alone and terrified. I raised my fists again, trying my best to be imposing like I did with difficult models. "Give me the plate you just took."

"What?"

"Give me the plate you just took, and the two before that. Then get off this ship."

He stood slowly, then reluctantly pulled three plates from his case, handing them over.

"These better be the right ones, or I'll call for an inquiry," I said. I glanced down at the edges of the plates. They were Balder plates. Inexpensive pre-mades. Not bad quality, probably better than the police ones, but nothing compared to my homemade ones. I prided myself on making silver-nitrate gelatin plates better than the best commercial ones available.

"I can't leave," he said, muffled through the mask. "I have to take the pictures for the claim."

"Then they can send someone else up!" I shouted right in his face and pointed back toward the lounge. "Get off."

At last he scrambled, grabbing up his tripod, camera still attached, snatching up his photographic plate bag, and hurrying away. I stood and breathed slowly several times, air whistling through the filters on my gasmask. My temper sometimes got the better of me, but this was unacceptable. This was criminal. I hoped the police actually had captured the steering car in their pictures, but he might be right and the police didn't show a single lever. They hired the worst photographers sometimes and used the cheapest equipment.

Then I caught sight of the blood and froze again, my anger melting away. It was everywhere in the steering car. There were a great many sharp corners and edged levers in here, and the dozen or so officers and crew seemed to have fallen on them with expert precision. There was a dried puddle of it beneath the port console. Only one window had blown out up here, though, so water damage was minimal.

Bringing my camera forward, I took several pictures of the equipment, then one of the adjacent navigation room with its maps laid out on the table.

I planned to take a picture of the radio console and its settings when I noticed a ladder and a ceiling hatch yawning open into darkness. I stared up for a long time, listening, wondering who had gone up there, and even turned around quickly once thinking someone had entered the navigation room with me. Then breathing slowly, I climbed the ladder with my camera and stuck my head through.

To say that the interior of the dirigible's hull was immense is not to do it justice. I was alone and insignificant in a vast space that wanted nothing more than to eat me. I felt like I could fall up into it. Distant tension wires *tang*ed softly as they shifted, and a vast hydrogen bag, one of many such lift-cells, groaned slowly as the ship swayed. The air was cold.

I saw no other people, either on catwalks or high service platforms, but frankly there could have been two dozen air marshals up there and I wouldn't see them.

I didn't like the cold feel of it either, which felt more like an oily indifference than a malevolence. I took one picture only, flash held aloft. Maybe it was my imagination, but when the flash flared the surrounding steel and wood to sharp relief, the groaning of the girders and gasbags increased and the feeling of being watched intensified. I dropped back down to the navigation room and pulled the hatch closed against the vast darkness.

I was done. I had to get out of here.

The nape of my neck was crawling as I slid that last plate into my case and folded up my tripod. The sound of my breath through the gasmask, the increased groaning of the ship, the conviction that someone was peering over my shoulder grew to be too much. Like an amateur, I didn't even unclamp the camera from of the tripod top, but threw the whole thing over my shoulder and bolted out to the lounge.

The three air marshals were gone and I was alone.

I crossed the dance floor at a run, leaping down the iron stairs to the hold and its bright exit hatch.

I laughed with utter relief as I reached the opening, as if I'd escaped something suffocating, and dropped down onto the stairs. There were a few air marshals standing below me and I waved joyously. They didn't wave back, and several looked startled. Haze guns swung around and trained on me, and my waving hand sank slowly to my side. Looking around, I saw that the owners and the insurance men no longer stood at the windows.

Clomping down the stairs now, mocking my own timidity, I yanked the gasmask off my head. "Well boys, that was an experience," I called.

Three advanced on the bottom of the stairs, Haze guns still up, and another half-dozen held back, keeping wider guard.

"What?" I said, noticing that those who held back were wearing blue-quartz goggles.

"Who're you?" barked the lead air marshal.

"I'm the cameraman for Mr. Greatmoore. Why? What's happened?"

"The clearing sirens were blown hours ago. Where were you when we ran the sweep?"

"Hours ago? What are you talking about? I was in there half an hour at the most. Did you bother to check steering? I'm not hard to miss, what with the tripod and all." My footsteps slowed as they didn't move or laugh at my joke. "Mind raising those barrels?" I asked.

"Let's see some identification."

I fumbled for my wallet, in my confusion forgetting that I was wearing a mechanic's jumpsuit instead of my normal suitcoat. As he inspected my identification and his companions with specialty goggles watched the open hatch, I looked around. The sun was low in the sky.

"That's not possible," I said, stunned. I felt hot, and the nape of my neck began tingling again. I looked over my shoulder. "Mind if I step into the airman's lounge?" I said.

"C'mon!" He grabbed my upper arm and pulled me along, and though I normally would have shoved him off and told him where to go, I found myself following along meekly, my tripod still over one shoulder and my case of plates banging against my hip. He took me into and then through the lounge to the parking lot where a large tent had been erected.

"Chief!" he yelled. Several air marshals appeared in the door of the tent, followed by the imposing figure of the air marshal chief shoving wide the tent flap. "He came off the ship. Says he's only been in for half an hour."

The chief sharply beckoned me in.

"What is this?" I tried to demand, but it came out weakly. "What's going on?"

"That ship's messed with everyone's minds, is what's happened," he grunted, turning back into the tent.

I followed him into noise and electric lights and a big, wireless aerial set-up in the center of the tent where police radiomen were chattering on microphones. There were reporters hanging about but the chief pointed at them immediately as they began to rush forward.

"Sit! Down!" He turned to me. "Would you like a cup of coffee, Mr. Photographer? No cream to be had here, so you'll have it black and strong as turpentine, as God intended."

"My name's Jack, and that would be lovely," I said, eyes darting, having trouble putting thoughts together. There were a lot of people gathered in the tent, and not all of them had been here earlier. The reporters eyed me hungrily. I set my case on a table and tossed the police gasmask onto beside it, noticing for the first time that it looked burnt and curled at the edges. As the chief came back with a tin cup of coffee, I began to carefully unbolt my camera from the tripod and wrap the brass lens.

"You've been gone for six hours," the chief stated bluntly. "Most of my men got out after the first walk-through, but ten didn't come back with us. We searched and lost five more, and I sounded the evacuate claxon. Now seven of the missing have trickled back out with gaps in their memories and no concept of where the time's gone. You make eight."

"The Harrow?" I said horrified, thinking about the Harrow mappers who had to draw quickly while in transit because they couldn't remember anything afterward.

He nodded. "A bit of the Harrow seems to have come back inside that ship, though how much is a dicey question. We're going to tow it out again and release it into the poisoned lands, but I want my people back first. Harrow Hunters are coming. Belchick and Shadeki should be here by tonight with their heavy, protective gear."

Even I knew Andrea Belchick and Roderick Shadeki from the dailies. "It's that bad?"

"I'm not taking the chance. Tell me what you saw and where you went."

"I didn't see much at all," I kept my voice calmer than I expected I would. "Certainly not enough to warrant six hours. I took photographs in the Lounge, the Control Car, and the Engineering Car. That's it."

"Did you go up inside the hull? Did you climb up to the transverse catwalk and the crew quarters?"

"No. I might have if the ship was more inviting, but I felt like someone was following me at every turn." I shivered.

"*Everyone* felt that. Something's in there, and I've got men stationed with deep-sight goggles below the hatch to make damn sure it doesn't come out."

I stared at him silently as my heart drummed, aware the reporters were trying to listen over the chatter of the radiomen. "I didn't go up," I said when I found my voice again. "I only stuck my head up through the hatch in the Navigation Room, and then only for a minute."

"And that was enough. Everyone who's disappeared or lost time was up inside the hull."

I finished boxing up my camera with numb hands when I noticed a small stack of police photographs sitting on a table to the side. "You developed them already?" I asked.

He pointed to a back corner where a smaller tent had been set up within the tent. "Mobile darkroom. We were trying to figure out where everyone was and who was missing. One of my photographers came back, but not the other. This guy was mostly taking pictures of the bodies on the main deck. My other photographer went up into the hull to the crew quarters."

"May I look?"

He waved his hand. "Go ahead, but they're useless. Almost too blurry to figure out who's who. I fired the man immediately."

"Mr. Greatmoore will want copies anyway for his investigation."

"Then Mr. Greatmoore can request them himself, can't he?" the chief snapped. "He was the first to flee when it became clear people were missing. Him and all the airship executives. Cowards."

"Did the insurance photographer make it out?" Just thinking about him tampering with the levers got me angry again. "He should have come out early."

"I only have a roster of my people. Your people and the insurance people came and went without telling me, so they may all be down safely, or they may still be up inside." He picked up my case of plates and pressed it to my chest. "Develop these. I need to see if you photographed anything useful."

"I didn't take any pictures of your people, except those three young air marshals you left in the lounge to collect people's possessions."

He frowned. "I didn't ask anyone to pick up possessions. We weren't planning to empty the ship until our initial investigation was settled. That's someone else's jurisdiction."

"They were there, and they were gathering people's things. I saw them."

He looked down, frowning, his face growing dark. "Damn it all." He leaned close. "Bring me any photographs of them boys, and don't let on to anyone else that they exist, right? Bring me the negatives too. Everything. If I see so much as a hint of this in the dailies, I'll hold you responsible."

He didn't move his great, craggy face from mine, but I squared up against him and ignored the onion stink on his breath. "No need for threats. I'll get you your photographs, but I'm not developing them in that darkroom over there. That's the way to slop a negative. Let me go back to my studio and get them developed properly, and I'll bring them to the station tomorrow. I swear, I didn't take any pictures of your people other than those three, so there's nothing to develop and show you."

In truth, while I do take great pride in my work, I probably could have developed them in the mobile dark room. But I was thinking about Greatmoore and the blackmail and thinking I wanted to get away from this hanger as quick as humanly possible.

"Tomorrow," he said, still in my face. "Tomorrow morning. Telephone the station first, because we may still be out here."

With that he left the tent, heading in the direction of the hanger. I stared after him. So Greatmoore had run away? Idiot. Running away in front of reporters would only make it worse for him in the dailies. Public opinion was not in his favor, and I doubted any photograph of mine would change that. The competing airship companies were working to prove it was ship failure or crew error and not something endemic to the Harrow.

Several of the reporters sidled up to me as soon as the chief slipped through the tent door. "What's your name?"

I grimaced, not wanting my full name out there. "Jack," I said, running my fingers up through my hair, pushing it back where the gasmask had mashed it down.

"Hell of thing, isn't it? That ship? Must have been terrifying."

"Terrifying?" I knew their questions would try to shape a narrative, but I decided to shape a different one. Not that I wanted to do Great-moore any cheap favors, but anything I could do to help him would loosen the grip he had on me. "Not, it wasn't that frightening at all. Empty, mostly. Your brain gets the better of you in there."

"But you were gone for six hours, man! What did you see?"

I pushed past them. "The morticians had the bodies off by the time I got on, so I didn't see anything." I'd been gone six hours. I couldn't fathom that number. Where had I gone?

"Hey, you lot!" bellowed the chief from the door on the far side of the tent. "Don't bother him." He glared until they backed off, then went for another cup of harsh coffee.

I nodded uncomfortably to the frustrated reporters and made my way around the radiomen to the police photographs. There were more than a dozen, and they were as bad as the chief had implied. Worse, maybe. The broad photograph of the lounge showed thirty or forty well-dressed, blurry bodies lying tangled and tumbled near the starboard window and the waterlogged piano. Several air marshals in gasmasks stood nearby. Odd thing was that they were fairly sharp and clear. Maybe the photographer had his focal length off or something?

I stared closer. Something was really wrong with his camera. Probably a cheap department issue, or maybe his nerves had gotten the best of him and he'd rushed. Too bad for the chief. There was a dark smudge off to the side that looked like a big dog but was probably some air marshal who had moved as the shutter opened. There were several mottled, diagonal lines across the whole photograph.

There were a number of pictures of the pile of bodies, closer but still blurry, that showed faces frozen in a horror. You could make them out, though they were awful. One had been labeled in ink right on the picture with the name 'Gregory Dallbot'. The Harrow Hunter. He looked like he had an enlarged head.

There were pictures of the forward control car where the officers had not just fallen, but in some cases impaled themselves on levers and rods. Engineering looked calmer, with blurry men curled up on the floor. There were several photographs of people laying stretched out on the floors of their cabins as if they were carefully positioned that way.

I set the pictures down, rubbing my eyes, a headache growing. The police photographs were bad, Greatmoore was gone, a Harrow-tainted airship was looming over us all, and I'd lost six hours. I couldn't handle this all at once, so I stowed my equipment in my cabriole and left. I accelerated up the hill, kicking up dust, trying to escape those blurry photographs of frightened people clumped around a piano.

Wind whipped in my face and I couldn't breathe properly. I couldn't see with the sun balanced on the horizon, and I nearly careened into a ditch several times. How had I lost six hours? I'd only stuck my head up through the hatch for a few seconds—long enough to take a picture. I had the picture somewhere in my case. A great picture of empty nothing, right? I got an uneasy feeling. What if I'd taken a picture of *something*?

Logic reasserted itself and I put on sunglasses before I killed myself. The sky on the horizon glowed in brilliant blues and greens, a sure sign that the western arm of the Harrow was stirred up. I was old enough to remember as a child watching the sunsets of pink and rose and gold, but that was before the Harrow stretched so far south.

Back home an hour later, dusk settling over the neighborhoods like a raven's wing, servants helped me out of the car and rolled it into the garage. They quickly got a fire roaring and brought out dinner, not asking any questions. I couldn't eat much, though. My eyes were drawn to the case of photographic plates standing just inside the foyer where I'd uncharacteristically dropped them.

I wanted them gone; I wanted this whole business done. I'd develop them right away and get them to Greatmoore and the chief. Might as well get it over with. I wasn't going to sleep anyway.

I hefted the case, leaving a plate full of food but taking my carafe of whiskey, and went down to my darkroom behind the studio at the back of the house.

I brought out the insurance photographer's plates first, because they were wedged in the front of my case. My headache was no better, throbbing behind my tired eyes, so I was generous in my pour of whiskey. The things I'd seen and experienced today? I'd encountered a bit of the Harrow. I might be infected now. My heart began to pound hard and panic verged as I methodically fixed the negatives and inked the prints. The chief had let me go without protest, but how did he know I was safe? Was anyone? There was no way to be sure except wait a few days. Even then . . .

I hung the pictures up to dry, studying them in the ruddy light. Two were taken in the Steering Car, and were reasonably clear. Good. I'd be able to tell what levers he'd moved by comparing them to my photographs taken later. His third photograph was from the lounge before I got there, showing the starboard side with the piano and capturing one of the air marshals gathering possessions. It seemed a little blurry in the dim light. Mottled even, with more of those blurry, diagonal lines. Probably a bad plate.

I stepped out of the darkroom for a break and to refill my tumbler of whiskey, then touched my toes twice to try and release the tension gripping my shoulders. The sun had set behind the Harrow and the studio windows were dark, but my servants had lit a few electric lamps that I'd recently installed. They were brighter than the old gas-lamps, harsher perhaps, and I didn't normally like them. But now I appreciated their stark glare in my gloomy mood.

My memories of this long day were already receding like the tide, though the fear remained. Throwing back my whiskey and refilling again, I returned with the tumbler to my plates and the task at hand. It seems I'd taken thirteen photographs, a great many for me.

The first was the morning's wide-shot of the *Tiaga* from outside on the hill. It showed excellent detail in the sun. I'd completely forgotten I'd taken it. I had, hadn't I? I'd been late to the gathering. True to form, my camera had produced a stunning work of art. Too bad no one would want to buy a print of the crippled *Tiaga*.

The next one was from the *Tiaga's* hold. I'd been straddling the open hatch, and some nameless mortician had been walking toward me in a protective suit and gasmask. The flash had burned dark streamers around him in an unfortunate halo. I suppose it looked interesting as an artistic effect, but I always strove to avoid gimmicks. The next one, of the empty and ornate loading room, was properly crisp and of my usual quality. Good. It meant there was nothing wrong with my camera. I knocked back my whiskey yet again, my tongue feeling numb.

I guess the three photographs in Engineering were passable. I could clearly see the levers and valves and the numbers on the gauges, but everything showed a faint shimmer of blur and there were the same mottling problems as the insurance photographer's. I returned to his lounge picture. Yes, very similar in faint diagonal lines.

Maybe it wasn't the quality of his plate! Maybe some effect of the Harrow had contaminated the silver nitrate.

What had we all been exposed to in there? What did the Harrow do to you? No one really knew, though scientists had cut up enough unfortunate souls who'd been caught in it. Harrow Hunters said that there were still people trapped there, but they were impossible to communicate with.

So with already fraught nerves, I nearly dropped the first print I developed of the lounge. It showed all of the piled bodies. How? They were sprawled in blurry, familiar contours around the piano. But that wasn't possible! This must be the poor quality police photograph from before. That was the only explanation. The chief had slipped it into my case! The nerve of him, having a joke at my expense. I'd drive right over to the station in the morning and give him a piece of my mind.

But as I hung it up to dry, I knew it wasn't. I saw two of the three air marshals gathering possessions just off to the side. And while the bodies of the deceased were all hopelessly blurred, the two men were my camera's usual, crisp quality.

Hadn't I felt an electric jolt up my leg while stepping right into the midst of all those blurred corpses?

I fixed the second of my two lounge photographs and made the print, and this one I did drop. I had to snatch it back up from the floor before it got ruined.

Next to the three air marshals stood a lanky dog as big as an Irish wolfhound and black as night. It stared directly into my camera with half-lidded eyes. I'd seen a blurred, dog-shape in those police photographs too. This was real. It had been in there with us.

My hands shook as I emptied my whiskey tumbler yet again and stumbled back out of the dark room. My camera still lay nestled in its case by the front door, and I went to it and looked down at the worn leather. How was it capturing these things? Was it really a magical camera, as Edward had always claimed before the fire at the atelier? People had revered his photographs and compositions back then.

The camera was his masterpiece, an accidental invention made from bits of aether and etherea when we were just sixteen. Oh how he'd lorded it over us. It was going to take him to new, artistic heights.

"Will there be anything else, sir?" my manservant asked from an alcove, and I nearly jumped out of my shoes.

"Dembley! You frightened me half to death." I looked down at my empty glass. I was in no shape to drive. "Yes, yes there is something. We'll need to get to Thaddeus Greatmoore's house tonight. Get the car started in about half an hour."

I returned to the darkroom with slow steps, I'd only been delaying the inevitable, and I knew it. I needed to develop the final photograph. I needed to know what I'd seen inside the hull.

Harrow mappers never remember what they've drawn during flights.

So I pulled out the final exposed plate from my case and began to bathe it as the chemicals unexpectedly turned black. My fingers tingled, but there was no stopping this. I had to see.

The developed photo, which I carefully hung up to dry, did not show the vast, open interior of the dirigible that I remembered. I couldn't tell what it showed at first, just a miasma of shapes and blotched lines, until I brought my eyes close. Panicked, I slapped on the bright electric light overhead and stood panting, my hand on my throat, imagining that stalking presence from the ship was hovering over me now. My skin crawled.

I ran and fetched a magnifying glass and brought my eye close to the photograph again. The faint shapes leapt out under the lens and I witnessed the sharp, tiny images of thousands upon thousands of people. Souls in torment. The damned. I could see their pleading eyes and the dark gashes of their howling mouths. Stumbling back, my arm with the magnifying glass sinking to my side, I also recognized that the blurred lines running diagonally across the photograph as the faint outlines of fingers and a hand clamped over the camera's lens. The images of trapped people were caught up in the whorls of the hand's skin.

I fled as fast as I could, heading for my telephone alcove off of the front hall, and rang the air marshal's station. It took three tries and two transfers, but I raised the radiomen in the tent at the *Tiaga's* hanger. Through them I got the chief.

"What the devil is this?" he demanded, his voice crackly over the miles. "I've got the Harrow Hunters here, and we're suiting up to go back in. I'm still missing a bunch of men."

"Chief! That thing isn't just tainted with the Harrow!" I was shouting so he could hear me. "I've developed my photographs. That ship *is* the Harrow. It's all there — inside. Maybe it's an arm of the Harrow, or a seed, but it's the real thing. The damned are all over the inside the hull by the thousands. You've got to get it back in the air and away from your people because it's boiling, I tell you and it's going to boil over!"

"Damn," was all he said, then after a pause, "Right. I know what to do. You bring those photographs over round the station first thing in the morning, you hear me? I want to see what you saw."

Then he hung up and I gently hung the earpiece back into place. I looked up to see several servants and my driver clustered tight in the hall looking terrified.

"Pray to God he listens to me," I said quietly to them. "Pray for us all."

"But what if the Harrow breaks out in Denton?" shrieked my head cook, a robust woman of advanced years.

"It's not just the chief working the derelict," I replied, taking her hand. "Half of the air corps is there, and the Harrow Hunters." I nodded to my driver. "But we'd better play it safe. Rouse everyone, children too, and take them west to Bratton. Spend a day or two over there, and if there's been no word of an outbreak, head on back."

"What about you, sir?"

"I'm heading to Greatmoore's. Leave me the cabriole."

We argued, but he didn't really want to stay with me in the area, so I found myself alone on the dark road, drunk as can be, on the way to Greatmoore's house about twenty minutes out into the knolls. I took my magical camera, Edward's magical camera, which had captured so much.

I was surprised not to crash on the way, and equally surprised when Greatmoore opened the door himself at my second knock. He wore his rumpled clothes from the day and was clearly as drunk as I was, because he embraced me as soon as he saw me.

"Jack."

"Thaddeus." I hugged him tightly back.

"I'm sorry I sent you up into that thing. I thought I'd sent you to your death when you didn't come back out."

"You don't know the half of it."

And so I told him as we sat over glasses of port in his private study, and he looked more and more shaken as he flipped through the photographs.

"The Harrow itself," he said, shaking his head. "Here at last. An ingenious way of getting behind our defenses, eh? Just like the Trojan Horse."

"The Harrow Hunters will handle it, I'm sure."

"Either way, we can't fly over it anymore. God help those people who died on board—they'll have to burn the bodies." He threw up his hands and sagged back into his chair. "That's it, then. It's over, no matter how much my competitors or the insurance men say that it was my fault and not the Harrow, the chief will tell the truth. The age of airships is done."

Greatmoore's entire fortune, his life's work, was built on dirigibles, so I knew he was speaking as much of himself as of the industry.

"No more than the ruins of anything else," I said, and pushed the camera across the desk to him. "Take it. Bring it to the police if you want, I won't deny my part in it."

His lip rose in a quick sneer that faded. "That's your livelihood, Jack. The source of all your stunning photographs. The source of your fame."

"Edward's fame. I killed him for it."

He stared at the closed case. There was no heat in his gaze, or any emotion at all. "You've been too squeamish to look at a dead body since, haven't you? Guilt is heavy."

"Even if I could, you wouldn't let me forget."

"He was a genius, wasn't he?"

"He would say that he was the best of us. You think he knew it could photograph the Harrow?"

"Knowing him, that was probably its original purpose, until he found out how beautifully it could photograph flowers and people and other mundane chaff." Greatmoore abruptly slid the camera back toward me. "Use it for its purpose. I won't blackmail you again, but you've got to promise to fulfill Edward's vision. Investigate the Harrow. Figure it out. Push it back, for all of us."

I reached out my hand. "If you promise to invest in Harrow-armor for the airships. Keep the flights alive."

Instead of taking my hand, he came around the desk and embraced me again, tears streaming down his face. Then he showed me out without saying another word and I drunkenly turned the cabriole and started off down his drive toward the main road.

It was about fifteen minutes later that a fireball blossomed very high in the sky, in roughly the direction of the *Tiaga.* I jerked the car to a stop and climbed out, staring up at the heavens. A boom like thunder swept across me as the flames glowed in vibrant blues and greens before collapsing into reds and raining toward earth. I watched the debris fall until the flames faded back into darkness, wondering if we'd been fast enough.

Had Edward really intended his camera for the Harrow?

Despite Greatmoore's assertions, I had always thought of Edward as a hopeless romantic when he wasn't being an arrogant prick. The Harrow was too much reality for him. I firmly believed his invention was only ever intended to reveal the beauty within the mundane, not pierce the veil of evil. The revelation that the camera could see through The Harrow was not something he would have stumbled across in his lifetime.

Nor would I, if I hadn't been forced up into that ship. I was as hopeless a romantic as he, and I'd killed him. Maybe I deserved the Harrow.

I climbed back into the cabriole and turned around, headed for the *Tiaga*'s airfield an hour away to learn what had happened to the air marshals.

Reinventing the Wheel

He found her in a town deep in the shite-end of the Dakotas (his words, not mine), beyond the endlessly flat prairie of the *other* shite-end of the Dakotas, out where the Earth cracked and broke and fell away into sudden chasms, or rose into unassailable edifices, where the rock crumbled under your feet to toss you into a pit full of rattlers, only to rise up again into the forbidding crags of the Black Hills. Found her already half-pissed on a Tuesday morning, the finest Natural Philosopher in the civilized world ("*and* America," quoth the good Professor. "Which the Royal Academy would recognize if they'd ever take a rest from their incessant rectal self-examination.") Half-pissed, she was, and deeply committed to losing a game of poker that already cost her a voucher for her next royalty cheque, two cast-iron pans, and the shirt off her back.

These, again, his words, and that's like as not the way he'd start this story, if he was here to tell it. It's their story, not mine. But the Professor ain't here, and Wheel-Leg Malloy, well, he's the one you're stuck with. Me, I'd'a left the "q" outta "check," and I'd'a started the story in a different place.

Yep, I figure the best place to start this here tale is where *I* come in, which would be, oh, 'round noon on a hot June day, back in '91, down south of the salt flats east of town. I was taking the weight off in the shade of a big, old buffaloberry bush with every intent of dozing the siesta hours away, which is what I'd'a been doing if it hadn't been for the new Jules Verne novel I'd picked up on my way out of town, and he'd'a been dead by that afternoon. Then nobody'd ever have heard of either of them, nor cared that they hadn't. So, if you was the sort to pay heed to theories of causality and predestination (and all that *shite*), you might say it was Mr. Verne and his fantastical stories that saved Dr. Stephan Cooper's life, and all the rest that that entails.

First I saw of Cooper, he was face-down in the dust, foot caught in a stirrup. Don't know how far that old mare dragged him, and I don't know if it was luck or fate, but she'd lamed herself but good, so when she dragged him to where the only person in ten miles might'a seen him, she done it slow enough that she didn't break his ankle, and even left some skin on his face.

City boy, I thought, as the mare stopped to graze on a patch of bluestem. Come looking for gold and found death instead. Which is proof pudding that even Wheel-Leg Malloy can't be right all the time.

I marked my page, 'cause there's nothing so infuriating as losing your place in a good book, and went to check out the body. Turns out he was still alive (but you knew that already, otherwise you wouldn't be here listening to my regaling and such), but wouldn't be for long. By the look of it, he'd crossed not one but three rattlers, and the skin around the bites was red and weeping. Foot was so swole up I had to cut his boot off. Waste of good leather, that.

Well, I did what I could for him, too late to draw the venom, but I got some water into him. The horse, well, luck again, or maybe fate, but she just had a sharp rock up in one of her hooves, and when I worked that loose, she was able to carry his weight all the way into to town.

First week, we wasn't sure whether he'd live or die. Slept most of the time, and when he didn't, he just talked nonsense. On the one hand, reincarnation, everlasting life, transubstantiation. On the other, perfect machines and elegant equations. One of 'em he'd recite from memory, in a tone of voice that said this wasn't the kind of equation you brought home to meet your mother. Well, takes all sorts, don't it?

Doctor took two of his toes that went bad and a bit of his foot, and the little finger from his right hand, but eventually the fever broke, and we knew he'd pull through.

It were coming up on August 'fore one of the strangers passing through town—man name of Wilson Fern—said he reckoned he might'a seen a girl was a spitting image of the one Cooper was looking for. Fern was a prospector, come out of Providence two years prior, he said, and been hungry nine days out of eight each week, those whole two years. Sold his claim for the price of a ticket home, gambled away half of it the first night, and, well, here he was, and here he stayed. (Ain't that right, Fern?)

Anyway, it were young Wilson Fern said she was the one stamped his deed in the Land Office.

Cooper'd been waving around this old newspaper photogram of a girl in a white dress, fair bit of lace on the sleeves and around the neck, standing next to some kind of contraption of her own design. Reckon her hair'd a been half-way down her back, if it weren't standing straight up from her scalp.

"This was one of her early experiments in magnetism," Cooper told me, when he'd finally regained his faculties. "Not terribly groundbreaking, as the Academy was quick to point out, but she was only fifteen at the time." He'd offered a reward to the man or woman who could help him find his quarry.

Fern put a caveat on his statement, though. "Well, spitting image of that girl's mother, maybe," he said. "Unless that picture's twenty years old."

Which it was, near enough.

Cooper's eyes narrowed. Thrice bitten twice shy, as they say, and it wouldn't be the first person to bear false witness for a handful of silver. "Do you have proof of this, sir?"

"Reckon I might, Professor." Barely in town a month, and half the folk were already calling Cooper that. "Yep, reckon I might have that right here." Fern's grin held a whole lot more teeth than it does now, and he showed them all as he pulled a dust-encrusted piece of paper, folded up and sweat-stained, out of his pocket.

Cooper took it between his fingertips, like he wasn't sure which was more contagious, the dirt or the sweat, but when he unfolded the deed and saw the handwriting and the signature, his smile looked set to compete with young Mr. Fern's here.

"It's her."

What's that, boy?

That was what they call a *rhetorical question*. I heard you just fine the first time. "Who in tarnation *is* she, Malloy?" Well, first of all, them's mighty strong words, Mr. Ward, for a boy ain't had cause to pick up a razor yet. Me? 'Course I cuss like a rabid badger. You earn one cuss word for every gray hair, and I got so many I can clear out a church in five minutes flat and get it struck by lightning to boot.

Second, I'm working up to it, building what you call narrative tension. Storytelling ain't just a regurgitation of the facts. It's putting those facts into an order, telling them with the right flow, the right cadence, the right rhythm to build to an emotional impact. It's character development, and plot, and world-building. And most of all, it's a-weaving all them things together, careful-like, like a spider, and all'a you my precious little flies.

And here you gone and fucked it all up. And what'd you get for it? A face-full of spider webs and one pissed off spider in your hair. Hope you're happy.

Third of all, every man, woman, and child here already knows her name: Calliope Smith, named after either a Greek goddess, or after the most god-awful, cacophonous instrument invented since the bagpipes. Callie Smith, who published the first mathematical proof of the Samsaric Phenomenon. The first woman ever invited to lecture at the Philadelphia Philosophical Society. The inventor of the Reciprocal Wheel.

Or as she's best known: Callie, the Destroyer.

Now, Ol' Coop, he was ready to saddle up and ride for Deadwood soon's he paid Fern his reward money, but while it may be the easiest trail in the Dakotas, that don't make it easy. 'Specially for a man who's already demonstrated an uncanny affinity for falling off cliffs and getting masticated by the local wildlife. Might'a been those exact words I used, or something similar, to prevail upon the good professor that he'd be more like to actually survive long enough to find the object of his desire if he had someone to accompany him. Moreover, I suggested that if he'd give me a couple days to wrap up my local obligations, I had some business up Deadwood way that wouldn't suffer from my attentions sooner rather than later.

And so it came to pass that we departed this here fine metropolis of Fairburn on a Monday, first Monday of the month of September, 1891, and set off for Deadwood. The 7th of September, it was, when we left, at first light. Cooper rode his old mare, and I wheeled along beside him. We traveled at a good pace, stopping only for lunch and dinner, and when we was beset — briefly, mind you — by bandits.

We camped just before dusk, got up with the birds the next morning, and rolled into town before noon. September 8th.

Coop, well, turns out his constitution weren't as recovered as he'd made out 'fore we lit outta Fairburn so I sent him ahead to wet his whistle while I made arrangements for his horse. Half Moon Saloon's as quiet a place as you can hope for, in a place like Deadwood, but by the time the old mare'd been stabled and a boy set to brushing her down, there was a fair racket percolatin' out them doors.

Seems the Half Moon Saloon was where he found Callie Smith, the preeminent natural philosopher of the civilized world and America to boot, no matter she was just a girl, already half-pissed on a Tuesday morning, and deeply committed to losing a game of poker down to her knickers. And the Professor, well, he had somethin' to say about it.

Now, this here part of the story is where I tell you what she looked like. It's where I tell you how beautiful she was. It's where I tell you the color of her eyes, where I describe the fullness of her lips, the shape of her face, the purity of her skin, the swell of her breasts in her unmentionables. These are all *important details* in a modern narrative, because all of those things are clues. They're the clues that tell us how much we're supposed to like her. How much we're supposed to root for her. Beauty means goodness and virtue, and ugliness means wickedness and sin. An *ontological relationship*, as it were, 'twixt a blemish on your face and a stain on your soul.

So maybe I ain't gonna tell you what she looked like, after all.

Thing is, when I rolled through them doors, it weren't her I was worried about, but him. Boy ain't got enough sense not to pet a grizzly, how's he gonna order a beer without losing a few teeth?

I found him standing beside a table turned on its side, cards and chips and well, you wouldn't call it *good* liquor all over the floor, squared off against three less-than-happy gentlemen. He'd put himself betwixt them and this gal he'd been looking for, and she weren't having any of it. Barely five foot naught in her stocking feet, she was (having lost her boots already), but damned if she wasn't fixing to smash a chair over his head.

"Pardon me, ma'am," said I, as I grabbed holt of the closest chair leg. Don't reckon she heard me, 'cause she tried to swing anyhow. Ended up knockin' her own self off her feet and setting her ass on the floor, all sudden-like.

One of the Professor's interlocutors looked up at the sound. His drunken eyes focused on me, and widened. His fist hovered in the air. Didn't lower it, but didn't throw it, neither.

"Wheel-leg Malloy," he said, and the others glanced at him, and then at me.

I nodded my acknowledgement, patted Cooper on the shoulder. "See you met my friend here. Told me he was gonna buy you boys a round," I shook my head at the mess on the floor. I meant the table and the cards and all that, not the gal sittin' in the middle of it, trying to milk the last drops outta the spilt bottle of whiskey. "Boy's about as graceful as a three-legged cow in tap shoes. You should see him on a horse. Go on, Professor, buy these fine gentlemen a drink."

Now, ol' Coop had more'n enough in his purse to stand these boys a few rounds, and settle any outstanding accounts vis-a-vis the poker table, no matter that they wasn't U.S. mint. Lady Liberty or Queen Victoria, gold is gold, no matter which despot grinds you under her heel. And if they maybe exaggerated their winnings a bit, well, that's a hard lesson learned, ain't it?

But there ain't no cure for stupid, and for all his book learnin' the boy didn't have the sense God gave a squirrel. He left that purse out too long, and too open. And that, as they say, is what they call a fatal mistake.

Miss Ellie Porter weren't none too happy when we come by, Callie Smith slung over the Professor's shoulder like a sack of wet laundry. Ellie runs a respectable house, and safe, and she don't brook no shit from nobody, not even yours truly. She allowed as to we could lay her out on a bench on the porch, and she'd take it from there.

Come next morning, Callie were looking none too hale, but that didn't stop her finding her way back to the saloon. We'd given her respectable time to recover before calling on her at the boarding house, but Miss Ellie, she allowed as there were some folk understood "hair of the dog" as meanin' the whole damned canine, from snout to tail. By the time we pushed through those doors, Callie Smith was seated at the bar, nursing her second glass of whiskey.

"Ma'am." I tipped my hat, and she glared at me without recognition.

Cooper was a step behind me. He pushed past, with his hand extended. "Dr. Smith? Dr. Calliope Smith! I say, it *is* you. At last! It is an honor to meet you in person. I'm Dr. Stephan Cooper, of the Royal Academy. We've corresponded, when you were still in Philadelphia. Your work is brilliant. Invaluable, nay, critical!"

Callie watched him warily as she drained her glass. She waved at the bartender.

"My own work is based on your equations. On a *practical application*, as it were. You'll be happy to hear that not all of your work perished in the..." Coop's enthusiasm was starting to falter under Callie's gaze. "...Your landlady was good enough to forward me the surviving pages, when you couldn't be found."

"What have you done?"

Don't reckon Coop noticed her tone, because he perked right up. "I built a machine to travel into the Samsaric realm. Well, designed, really. London's not the sort of place one opens up passageways into other worlds. Bloody regulations, what? As if we're all as reckless as the unfortunate Mr. Faraday. And besides, what are the odds of making the same mistake?"

"Between three and five percent," she said, "depending on whether you're using the reductive method or the expansive, modulo the rigor of your math. I remember your math to be somewhat... elementary."

"You *do* remember me! Brilliant! Obviously, you'll want to check my equations before we build —"

Well, that was as far as he got.

"We? Build? There *is* no we. Other than a few dozen sophomoric and... and... *inappropriate* letters, *I do not know you.* You are going to catch the next train east, and I am going to drink myself stupid so I don't have to think about your damned fool ideas. And if I hear you're building anything with my equations, I'll find you and personally put a bullet between your eyes."

Well, that there was the first time I saw ol' Coop too stunned for words. And if the Wheel-Leg Malloy of July 1893 had had access to Mr. Wells' machine long enough to come back and whisper in my own ear, well, I might'a taken her word as a commission, and laid him out somewheres in the Black Hills where he'd never be found, and her right alongside him. But I ain't got a line on the future better'n anyone else, and such powerful emotions raise a curiosity in me that drive me to distraction. Took the rest of the day, and more'n one bottle of whiskey, but before we carried her back to Ellie Porter's Boarding House, she'd told us enough.

This here is what we in the storytellin' craft call an expository lump. We step away from the characters and the plot, we break the narrative flow, all to explain some piece 'a something that the audience needs to know that is not practical to get across in some other way. And relaying to you the perambulatin' dialog that accompanies six hours of hard drinking, well, that just ain't practical.

Seems ol' Coop, he wasn't the first to think of building a machine to travel into the Samsaric Realm. What kind of natural philosopher would Callie Smith be if she hadn't thought it herself? If she hadn't worked out the equations *for the express purpose* of making that trip? Well, she done it, and she done it right (if she hadn't, the big glass crater in the middle of Philadelphia would'a made the papers, even out here). So she done it, and she went, and she come back with a new mission in life.

Now, here I gotta digress further, because I'm mighty sure that, despite the news hittin' every publication from the lowly *Black Hills Courier* to the *New York Times Roman*, and even — *especially* — the esteemed *Journal of Practical Philosophical Inquiry*, more'n half of you don't read worth a hill o' beans, and ain't never heard of the concept of samsara, nor understand its impact on the world. It's a Hindoo word, meanin' the Wheel of Suffering, or the Wheel of Reincarnation, same thing, far as they're concerned, and it's related to the idea of karma.

For the Hindoos, life is suffering, and the ultimate goal is to escape it. Easy enough, you're thinking. Bullet in the brain'll fix that, or your Aunt Tina's three-week-old beef stew. Not so fast. See, because of reincarnation, when you die, your soul flutters off and gets caught up in the great wheel. This here's where karma comes in. Karma's your balance ledger, with all your good and bad deeds, and the rightness of your life. If you live a good life, doing good for other folks and in general living the life you been given, then next time 'round, you get a better shake. If you live a bad life, if you're evil or inconsiderate or try to subvert the wheel by trying to make a better life for yourself than you been given, well, then next time 'round, you get a worse deal. The goal is to do better and better until you don't have to suffer no more. You escape the wheel of suffering, by either escaping life itself, or becoming one with the world, or becoming part of God, all depending on your flavor of belief.

Now, this here's a truism you can take to the bank: more often than not, religious mysticism don't stand up so good to scientific scrutiny. And when Dr. Callie Smith walked through the door into the realm of the Wheel of Suffering, well, what she saw shook her to the very core, and she swore she would destroy it if it was the last thing she did.

"Sh...shamshara is the biggest scam ever wash," she said. Her eyes was droopin' by then. "Karma my ash. No such thing. It's a machine, a giant, all-encompashing machine, and us all just grisht for the mill. And there's no eshcape. No eshcape."

Now, as much fun as it might seem to talk like a drunk, it's exhausting. So I'm just gonna tell you.

The wheel of suffering ain't a sorting machine. It ain't like that coin-countin' machine like what they got at the First Dakota Savings & Loan down in Rapid City, shuffling the good souls into good lives and bad souls into miserable ones. It's a perpetual motion machine, made to put you back into your place, no matter what you done. Don't matter how good you been, next time 'round, you gonna go through the same shit you always do. Calliope Smith, well, she went and she saw, and she studied the photograms she made while she was there. She did the math and checked it three times to Sunday. And then she started building a bomb.

'*Course*, the first thing she tried was a bomb. Ain't no monkey wrench in the world big enough to break a machine of a size to chew up millions of souls. You could throw the town of Deadwood into the works, and the mountain it sits on, and it wouldn't make no nevermind.

Took her some time to set up, repeated trips with wheelbarrows full of dynamite and nitroglycerine and fuse. She got herself a research grant from the University of Pennsylvania and bamboozled cash from one Mr. Rockefeller, him having a powerful interest in being able to control what kind of next life he might look forward to, and then later a Mr. Frick, whose own particular sins in 1889 looked sure to make his next life a mean and joyless one. I see we got a couple from Jonestown here, they know what I'm talkin' about. Seems she let on that she'd figured a way to rig the machine, let a man choose — or buy — what his future life might hold.

But all that money, it went for explosives, and it was a mighty big bomb she built. But when she rebuilt her portal to see the destruction she had wrought, well, seems that big machine, it just kept grindin' away.

Now, most folks, when they'd lost near all their earthly belongings, blown up not one but two fortunes, and scarce made it out alive, they might'a taken that as a sign, and given up. But Calliope Smith ain't most people. After an analysis of the combined forces of the Philadelphia constabulary and the debt collectors arrayed against her, she determined to relocate. Where to?

Well, that weren't no decision at all. Under the circumstances, the best train was the one that was already startin' to roll out of the station. It meant leavin' all but the most important of her bags — the one containing what she could gather of her books and notes outta the wreckage — on the station platform, but the coppers couldn't do nothing but watch her wave at them as the train clattered away down the track.

Now, here's where chance, or fate, or the hand o' God, or whatever you're wanting to attribute it to, here's where that comes in. The seat Callie Smith found for herself came with a present, left by its previous occupant: a folded-up newspaper that come all the way from Salt Lake, and having traveled east as far as the great island of Manhattan, was now beginning its trip homeward. Callie, she saved it, and after all this was over, it was one of the few things I cared to hold on to, as a keepsake.

Callie, she never did pay much heed to the Indians out west, nor to the white settlers, nor, truth be told, to much of anything that weren't constructed of cogs and gears and coils and pistons, or of the equations defining the principles which them mechanisms was supposed to utilize. She couldn't remember the last time she read anything as lurid and imprecise as a newspaper, but she unfolded it anyway, trying to look like she belonged in that seat, and she couldn't help be struck by the headline:

HEAP A BIG SCARE
Kansas City, Nov. 22. — The cannibals of darkest Africa have rivals in the Messiah-crazed Indians of South Dakota. This information was obtained to-day from Mrs. James A. Finley, wife of ex-Councilman Finley, now postmaster and post trader at Pine Ridge agency. In an interview to-day describing the ghost dance, she said the dances had been in progress for some time. One ghost dance that she saw was participated in by 480 Indians. "They form a circle and begin to dance around and around a tree. They keep going round in one direction until they become so dizzy that they can scarcely stand, then turn and go in the other direction until they swoon from exhaustion, and while they are in a swoon they think they see and talk with the new Christ."

She proceeded to read the article through, and then read it again, trying to sort fact from fantasy. According to the article, the Indians believed that the dance would call forth a new Messiah, who would save the Indians and return North America to a pristine paradise. The ritual, according to Mrs. James A. Finley, involved sacrifice both animal and human, and transubstantiation, not of wine and bread to Christ, but of human flesh to buffalo. Sitting Bull, spiritual leader of the Sioux Indians, led the ghost dance rebellion. The white authorities, on the other hand, simultaneously assured the settlers that there was no cause for alarm, while sending the 7th Cavalry and the 22nd Infantry to quell any insurrection.

"It's all bullshit, if you'll pardon the expression, being of the female persuasion and all." The speaker was, roughly speaking, a gentleman early in his middle years (if his hairline was any indication), dressed in workman's clothes, with a bushy mustache and hands that looked permanently stained with coal dust. He was, she noticed, missing two fingers on his right hand.

"Quite all right, Mr..."

"Harrelson," he said. "Jack."

"In which way, Mr. Harrelson, is this bullshit?"

"All ways. Starting at the top, where the newspaper editors go for shock rather than truth, to make a buck for their corporate overlords, the railroads and mine owners."

"Neither of which are mentioned in this article."

"Of course not. But they're the ones pulling the strings, inciting white workers' fear of Indian massacres to keep them distracted from the working conditions that kill them more surely than any supposed Indian Insurrection. The governors play on these same fears to gin up support for another war, and I don't need to tell you whose pockets get lined by Winchester and Remington and the rest for that. There'll be a massacre soon enough, mark my words, but it won't be whites doing the dying."

"You are a cynical man, Mr. Harrelson."

"I'm a realist. The Indian nations are broken, soon to be ground underfoot by the power of American Capitalism."

"What, then, do the Indians think to gain?"

"Well, that's the other piece of hogwash—"

"Bullshit," Callie corrected.

"Right you are, ma'am. The other piece of bullshit is that the Indians are looking for a messiah, and that what they're looking for looks anything like the Christians' Jesus. Way I had it from a Sioux of my acquaintance, the ghost dance is supposed to bring forth the spirits of their dead, in corporeal form. All of them that ever was. And then they'd have the numbers to drive the white man from this continent."

Harrelson shrugged.

"You don't believe they'll succeed?"

"'Religion is the opiate of the masses,'" Harrelson said. "Ain't an ounce of truth in any of it."

But Callie Smith, well, she'd seen the Great Wheel herself. She'd seen the gears and cogs and broken souls processed and extruded out into the birthing bodies of the most innocent in the world, and her mind filled with equations of resonant frequencies, of feedback loops, of repetitive motions creating nearly infinite waves of energy.

The man was still speaking, she realized.

"You look like you're a thousand miles away," he said.

"Behind every lie is a truth, Mr. Harrelson," she said. "The bigger the lie, the bigger the underlying truth. And that truth, asserted with sufficient force, can change the world."

Harrelson gently patted the case tucked under his seat, which contained enough truth to obliterate the train, as well as the track beneath it. "My position entirely," he said.

But I think that we can all agree that it was Mr. Harrelson's words, and not his explosives, that had more of a lasting effect on the world, this one, and the ones hereafter.

Callie filled a notebook with equations and diagrams and quite a bit of spilled ink by the time she reached Chicago, where she obtained the precision instrumentation she knew she would need, courtesy of a forged letter of credit and a spectacularly explosive bank robbery, courtesy of Mr. Harrelson. Thus armed, she hopped on the next train west. If her calculations were correct, the problem was one of numbers: there simply weren't enough Indians to generate the energy needed to break the barrier between the lands of the quick and the dead. Her equipment would serve to amplify that energy. She'd explain her plan to Sitting Bull, show him the mathematical proof, leavin' out the bit where she'd be feeding the Indian dead into the Wheel of Suffering. And so what if it destroyed all the Indian spirits or led to the wholesale slaughter of the whites in the Americas? It was a small price to pay to break a machine of eternal universal suffering.

She'd bought a horse and a wagon in Rapid City to carry her equipment out to Sitting Bull's camp. That was a cold day, December 15, 1890. The next morning, the newspaper announced that Sitting Bull was dead, and the army moving to disperse the ghost dancers.

She drove that wagon out into the badlands, unhitched it, and pushed it down a ravine. Then she rode to the most notorious town in the Black Hills, walked into the first saloon she saw, and crawled into the bottom of a whiskey bottle, and didn't come out until Coop pulled her out.

Now, ol' Coop, he was conflicted. He didn't have no skin in anyone's game, really, excepting maybe his own, and Callie, well, she was three steps ahead and had already achieved what he'd thought would be his crowning glory. He was sympathetic to the plight of the American Indian, in the abstract, and also to the trials and tribulations of the settlers trying to make a go of it, again, in the abstract. If he'd given it any thought, he'd'a been sympathetic to the coal miners coughing up their lungs for less than subsistence wages, and with the farmers ruined after a bad crop, and anyone else suffering injustice. He weren't a bad sort, just the sort that focuses on what's in front of him. He didn't know any Indians to speak of, nor factory workers, nor coal miners. He'd met settlers, enough to gain a healthy distrust, but none enough to call friend. When it come down to it, there was only one person for hundreds of miles all around that he could relate to: Calliope Smith.

Not that she cared one whit for the boy. Even a blind man could'a seen that. But the more she ignored him, the deeper he fell, and he was sure, damned sure, that he could earn her love.

You can earn damn near anything—gold, land. Friends and trust and respect. Enemies, too, and a sharp blade in the back. But if there ever was a true thing in this world, it's this: the one thing you can't never earn is love.

An object at rest will remain at rest unless some force is applied to it; likewise an object in motion will remain in motion until, yes, Bill, until it meets a force strong enough to stop it. Callie Smith's trajectory had brought her west and had, fittingly, come to a dead stop in Deadwood, and it didn't seem like nothing could move her again. Stephan Cooper didn't seem the type to possess enough force to move a drunk chicken, but there's all manner of force. Some of it's like a bullet, and some of it's like water, soft enough to flow through your fingers but still strong enough to wear a mountain down to a foothill.

Callie eased up on the drinkin' and gave the gamblin' up altogether. One sheet to the wind 'stead of three, as it were, maybe two when they'd argue over the value of a variable, or when enthusiasm had them by the shirttails far into the night. She and Coop'd spend their evenings at the saloon, heads bent over books, over sheets of paper with rapidly proliferating silver-grey markings, equations scribbled and scratched out and overwritten. Drawings and diagrams sketched, glasses and bottles serving as protractors of different arcs.

One night in October, the mist come down from the hills and settled over the streets. Callie and Coop had had a breakthrough in one of the designs — corrugated rubber joints threaded with metal bands to maintain conductivity — and had worked late into the night, with a couple celebratory drinks thrown in. Callie was unstable on her feet, and Cooper, no less unsteady, offered to walk her home.

They'd gone a couple blocks when a figure stepped from the misty shadows. His face was covered, and when he showed his hand, metal glinted in the hazy light of the street-lamp. Footsteps shuffled in the dirt behind them, and, sure enough, there was another masked bandit, pistol drawn.

"Nice and quiet," said the first one, "let's have the gold."

"Spent it all on whiskey," Callie said. "Should have caught us on the way in."

"Not you, the Brit. We seen the kind of cash he carries."

"Are you daft? You think I'd carry that with me?"

Callie laughed. "You want that, you gotta take it up with the guards at the First National. Maybe if you ask real nice, they'll just open up that vault for you."

"Goddamn it, J—"

"Shut up!" the first man barked. "I said no names!"

"Sorry. Shit. But I told you this was bad idea."

The first man was silent for a moment. "New plan, Professor. We take the lady, and tomorrow morning, you get that money for us, or we use her for target practice."

Coop hesitated, decided. "Fine. Where—"

"No," Callie said. "We need that for equipment." And she drew her own gun and pulled the trigger.

Eighteen shots rang out, and when the smoke cleared, Callie stood, unscathed. Cooper, also unscathed, lay in the dirt with his hands over his ears. Of the two would-be highwaymen, there was no sign. No blood, neither.

But an object in motion remains in motion. Gravity takes its toll, 'course, and sooner or later, if nothing else puts a stop to it, it meets the fundament, the Earth, immovable and absolute. Applyin' the metaphor to the human condition, that's death. A broken window, and a splash of blood on a child's bedsheets.

By the time I rolled out of bed and bumped down the stairs into the street, a woman's wail pierced the night, crying out her daughter's name.

Callie and Cooper lit out of Deadwood first thing in the morning.

Law says, a body's got a right to defend himself, and besides, nobody knowed just *whose* gun had fired the fateful bullet. But there's more laws'n a judge has in his books. There's laws governing electric current, and light, and heat, all of which impact all of us every day, and which a judge can rule against till he's blue in the face, for all the good it'll do. Heck, ol' Isaac Newton's got a mess of his own, the first of which we was just talking about. There's another law: that of cold hard cash in the hands of a grieving family, and while the bounty on Callie's head weren't legal in no way, the sort of man would take that commission ain't too concerned with that sort of thing.

Now, I figured with Coop involved, wouldn't take too long 'fore they was both lying dead of gravity poisoning at the bottom of a ravine where their bodies would never be found, or met with some other equally deadly fate of their own devising. But when Callie and Coop run, they run far and fast. New names in each town, always moving on, till they ran into Jack Harrelson and some of his mates, themselves hiding out after a string of successful bombings that took down railroad bridges from San Francisco to Denver, and who were happy enough to trade shelter for an exchange of technology.

Round these parts, weren't one word neither way about the pair. Tom and Laura Tanner, the parents of the dead girl, kept raising the bounty, month after month. Hundred dollars, then two, then five. Don't know where they got the money, but that bounty, it went up to two thousand before it was over, and that's a sum catches the attention of men all over the country.

Now, you may be listening to this here tale and thinking to yourself: *That Wheel-Leg Malloy, he sure can spin a yarn, but he ain't the sort you'd be trusting to manage your electric grid.* Well, who d'you think built these here legs with his own two hands?

Couple years passed. Come May of 1893, the Chicago World Fair promised to be a showcase of new technologies from across the globe, and there weren't no force on Earth gonna keep Wheel-Leg Malloy away.

Well, that was a sight. There were all manner of devices — electrical and mechanical and chemical in nature, even psychical and alchemical, if you looked hard enough — showing off the vast ingenuity of human-kind. Phosphorescent lamps and electrical rails, aerosol sprays and Mr. Ferris's magnificent wheel. There was a 'lectric kitchen, with a stove heated up without coal and a machine to wash your dishes for you. There was polyphase generators and Pabst Blue Ribbon. Even a moving walkway, so's regular folk could feel what it was like to be me, 'cept, course, for the challenge of negotiating a spiral staircase. Truly a marvel to behold.

Most surprising thing for me, though, weren't in the fair proper at all. Seems that ol' huckster, Buffalo Bill, he been denied a concession, but had procured for himself a spot of land just outside the fairgrounds, and no matter what the expo directors thought, the call of the wild frontier ain't let go the imagination of the common man, nor woman neither. I followed the crowd to see what all the hoopla was about, and what do I see? (Apart from a bunch'a aging cowboys and Indians makin' fools a themselves, that is.) I see a pair of women's legs, skirt bunched up 'round her knees, protruding from underneath a massive carousel of sorts. The aforesaid contraption was emitting smoke from places I gathered it weren't supposed to, given its non-carousing state. Crouching next to those legs and handing in tools and parts was a gentleman with whom I'd had some acquaintance: yes, indeed, it was the Professor, Dr. Stephan Cooper, whose metabolic state as a living creature was proof pudding that Wheel-leg Malloy can be wrong twice. Which meant the legs, most like, belonged to none other than the intrepid Callie Smith.

By the time I wheeled through the crowd and negotiated my way past the folks manning the gate, Callie had emerged from beneath the contraption, smeared pretty much all over with soot and grease. Straw stuck to her clothes and hair.

"It's not going to work," she was telling Coop.

He wouldn't hear of it. Better quality ball bearings, he suggested. Oil of greater or lesser viscosity. More dancers. A second carousel. Callie, she just kept shaking her head.

Now, this is probably a good time to describe the carousel. As I said, it was large, a central platform consisting of a circular metal grate that rotated 'round the center, but evenly spaced around the platform were additional mini-platforms that rotated around their own centers. Suspended above these was another layer that spun, chandelier-like, a bit above where a man's upraised hand might get caught in the works. That layer also contained more circular disks that spun at an even greater velocity. A mirror of everything above also moved below the main platform.

Another peculiarity of this carousel was the complete absence of carousel animals. There were no horses, no camels, no unicorns, no giant gilded swans. Instead, there were Indians. Fully articulated mechanical Indians of all sizes and, it appeared, all nations, that, when the machine was in motion, danced, stomping and shuffling in their own circles in what Callie and Coop had calculated as a mathematically precise performance of the very dance that had so terrified the authorities that they ordered a massacre.

Didn't look so scary now, recreated as an amusement ride in the carnival authenticity that was Buffalo Bill's Wild West Show. For as little as a quarter, folks could traverse a passage under the machine, climb a set of stairs, and join the dance in the center of the carousel, where things moved slow. They could move further toward the edge as they so chose, and dance for as long as they liked, at whatever speed they wanted. The machine never stopped, 'cept to change direction every hour, and nobody was ever asked to get off. Some folk reported interesting effects — hair raisin' in the air, a sense of exhilaration and abandonment, strange electrical effects, like the after-image of lighting, colors and halos, and even, sometimes, the ghostly visage of a flesh 'n blood Indian superimposed on a mechanical dancing Indian. But just as these effects became pronounced, the machine would break, the motor burning out, the bearings overheating and the oil catching fire.

"Fair to say you got specifications?" I asked. "Blueprints? Diagrams? Notes? Maybe even a calculation or two?"

The two exchanged glances, and then Callie shrugged. "Can't hurt," she figured, and while Coop took a disagreeable tone, she was the lead researcher on this project.

I spent the next few hours reading. Brilliant stuff, and a lot of it way over my head, in particular those equations derived from Maxwell's *Universal Theory of Analytical Theology* and Callie's own work in the field, both of which were dense and impenetrable. I ultimately had to take the results on faith. On the other hand, when it comes to spinnin' wheels, I have a certain *practical*, as they say, knowledge.

I banged on the machine with my fist. "Ain't gonna work," I said, when Callie extracted herself from its bowels.

"What could *you* know?" Coop said, doing his best to remind the world he was British. "Do you even understand a hundredth of what you just read?"

"Metaphysical alchemists, the two of you. Trying to turn energy into matter, using harmonic frequencies to sporadically amplify the forces enough to exceed a particular threshold to trigger an event. But every time the harmonics approach that threshold, the machine tears itself apart. That the gist of it?"

Callie nodded curtly.

"Problem you got is conversion of energy. Machine's converting too much energy to some other kind than what you're aiming at. Heat. Light. More heat than light, though."

Coop allowed as I was more or less correct. "So we are well and truly buggered," he said.

"If you want to get to heaven, you have to break free of the ground," I said. They both looked at me funny. "Don't matter what materials you use, long as you're restricted by a coefficient of friction of any non-trivial magnitude, you'll burn out before you reach the level of energy you want. You've got to move beyond the strict realm of matter."

"You're saying we have to defeat gravity first."

"You've got to employ energy not just to drive the mechanism, but as part of the mechanism itself." I unbuckled my wheel-pouch and extracted a clump of stones all clinging to each other. I pulled two of them from the mass, broke them away from each other, and turned one of them around.

"Try pushing these together," I said.

Coop reached for them, but Callie was already grinning.

"Broke an axle out in the Badlands a few months back, sand in the bearings, so I thought I'd do some experimenting on reducing the amount of friction in the system. Found these here for sale in the Electricity Building. 'Most powerful magnets in the world,' the sign said. Exaggeration, most like, but they sure do stick mighty good."

Callie's smile disappeared and her brow furrowed into what I'd already learnt meant she was writing equations in her head. "And they repel just as well," she said. "Thank you, Mr. Malloy."

Now, this ain't the sort of redesign that's an overnight fix, but Callie was kind enough to send an invite by telegraph when they was nearing ready for the inaugural run. As good an excuse as any to revisit the World's Fair, so I caught the next train to Chicago. Turns out I weren't alone, though. Telegraph Office wasn't too tight-lipped about who they let know there was a message for Wheel-Leg Malloy from a Miss Calliope Smith, nor where it originated from.

When I arrived, two days and three trains later, Callie was just fixing to start up the machine. She waved me over with a dirty rag.

"Your timing is impeccable, Mr. Malloy," she said, transferring a non-insignificant quantity of black grease from her hands to her shirt.

"First time for everything," I said, tipping my hat. "I assume that the magnets had the desired effects."

"They did, thank you," Coop said. "We'll need to get your Christian name for proper attribution when we present our research."

"Nonsense," I said. "Got all the accolades I need, and some to spare. 'Sides, assuming you succeed and generate, nearly *ex nihilo*, a war party of angry dead Indians plumb in the middle of the Chicago World's Fair, well, I ain't sure I want my name attached to that."

"They're not going to be running around the Expo," Callie said. She gestured at a large, rounded object standing not too far off from the carousel, back and out of the way, covered with a brown, canvas tarp. A wire ran from atop the carousel to a lightning rod protruding from the top of the object. This was, turns out, a reproduction of the very device she'd built in Philadelphia, years back. "They'll be drawn into the Samsaric Portal. The Wheel of Reincarnation calls the dead to it, after all, and we've reinforced that by creating a field of energy which the dead will be inclined toward remaining within. By-product of your own contribution, incidentally, though Dr. Cooper did the hard lifting here, mathematically speaking. By alternating bands of steel and bands of copper in the construction of the disks, and running the disks in opposite directions, we were able to generate a fair bit of electricity, on top of everything else. Not necessary, really, but if you have a surplus, why waste it?"

Now, I'd read her notes, and had a fair idea of her theories, but by my estimation, there weren't no way more'n a couple dozen Indians would be called forth. Manageable-like. If I'd known just how successful the machine would be, chances are better'n even that I'd'a put a few holes in Callie and Coop both, and redesigned the machine with a stick or two of dynamite.

I could go on at length about the sound of the machine as it leapt into motion, the sounds and sights and smells, but it'd be a lie. About as anti-climactic as you'd expect. The generator kicked out some steam, the wheels started turning. The mechanical Indians danced. But it was all in the background. In front of it, cowboys rode bucking broncos, roped calves, shot bottles off a fence. Indians danced and sang, waved tomahawks and shot arrows and re-enacted the Battle of Little Big Horn, with Bill Cody hisself taking the role of General George A. Custer. Nope, weren't until a few children led their parents to the carousel that things became interesting.

At first, it was a general sense of anticipation, emanating in waves from the machine, a sense that *something* was on the verge of happening. That feeling you get in dreams when you're standing atop a cliff, and when you tip off the edge, you'll either fall to your death or be transformed gloriously into an eagle, but you don't know which. Then came the physical sensations: ghostly lights flickering across the faces of the mechanical dancers; the sounds of singing in a dozen, maybe a hundred different languages; the scent of campfires, the ghost of roasted buffalo meat, and deer. More and more folk paid their quarter to dance, and not many seemed willing to stop.

There was a feeling of impending lightning strike, a charge building up. Callie and Coop looked at each other nervously, and her hand found his and gripped it, white-knuckled. This, I reckon, was where it'd all gone to hell before. But the smoke wasn't so much burning oil as it was bonfire, and the screams were less tearing metal and more the cries of warriors rushing into battle.

Space tore. That's about the best way to describe it, no matter that there ain't no way to imagine that. Space tore, and an army flowed out, each wave of ghosts dancing for a spell on the platform, then leaping to the ground as another wave arose, where they sprawled in the dust like they was flesh and blood. Because they were. They picked themselves up, raised their knives and rifles and bows and pistols in triumph, and rushed toward the crowd, which was understandably frozen in terror.

And then they swerved, their feet turning them toward the Samsaric Portal. They slashed through the canvas covering, tearing it away. The portal glowed like the gateway to Hell, if Hell was filled with fields of saffron 'stead of hellfire. The dead didn't hesitate. They stepped in — and disappeared.

Death is a strange attractor, and once the Indian dead realized where they was heading, well, they didn't dawdle about it. They weren't the only ones, though. Realizing they were in no danger from the dead, the crowd — audience and performer alike — crept closer, and were caught up in the motion. Men, women, children, horses, didn't much matter. All of them readied to cast off this shell and throw themselves into the great unknown hereafter. Callie and Coop were not immune, once Callie'd extracted herself from a congratulatory peck on the lips that Coop had clearly mistaken for something else that he'd been wanting for a long time.

With a deep breath, Callie took Coop's hand in her left and mine in her right.

"What'll happen to us?" I asked, knowing already that there wasn't no turning away.

"Too many variables," she said. "Many of them undefined, or imaginary."

We stepped — or rolled — into the rush.

Couple things happened, all at once.

Coop stepped into the field guiding the dead into the portal, and was immediately surrounded by ghosts.

A shot rang out, and Callie's left shoulder blossomed red. She stumbled and let go of Coop's hand.

Coop disappeared in a swirl of ghosts.

Callie tried to reach for him, but her left arm wasn't working. She turned her head toward me, her hand gripping me tight. Then more red bloomed, front and back, leaving a fist-sized hole where her kidney was supposed to be.

"Oh," she said, and tumbled forward into the dust.

Third shot hit me in the leg, shattering one of my axles, and I dropped to one knee. Fourth hit the other, above the wheel, and pneumatic fluids sprayed.

A figure stepped out from behind a fence post, walked toward us with his rifle cocked and trained on my chest. Tom Benteen, outta Fairburn. Good hunter, but bad at cards. Seems he had some debts he was willing to take extreme measures to settle. I seen him on the train, but hadn't put two and two together.

"This ain't between you and me, Malloy," he said. "Don't make this harder'n it already is."

The body at my wheels moved. She was still alive. I knelt down and rolled her over.

"Cooper?" she asked.

"Gone," I said.

"Should have been me," she said.

Tom Benteen had come close, close enough for his shadow to fall across Callie's body.

"Keep your hands where I can see them," he said, "and move away from the girl."

I saw from his shadow that he was circling around so he could see my firearm. Then his shadow merged with others, and was gone, and I didn't need to look up to know what had happened to him. Death don't play favorites. Hell, it was callin' me something fierce, but Callie was lying there, bleeding, her fingers wrapped into my shirtsleeve, and I couldn't just leave her there. I remember thinking: maybe if I balanced her over my back just right, I could crawl in. Wasn't sure I could make it, though. In front of the portal, dead Indians and living folk were piling up whilst more dead Indians and living folk were trying to fight their way out. Meanwhile, the light from the portal had started to pulse and throb, painful-like.

"I can't see," Callie said.

"Everything's jammed up. Indians still trying to get in, but there's a rush of them trying to get out."

"Need to break the connection to the portal," she said. "Can you shoot?"

"They don't call me Wheel-leg for nothing," I said. But I pulled out my Colt and gave it my best. Took a chip outta the portal, but otherwise, no luck.

Now, I ain't fluent in any tongue but English, and you don't have to look too far to find folks'll contest even that. But I got enough words in Lakota and Arapaho to engage in some casual trading. So by shoutin' out the words for "cut" and "rope" while pointing at the cable, I was able to make my intentions understood. One of the warriors scaled the exterior of the portal and took an axe to the cable where it connected into the mechanism. There was a shower of sparks, and the Indian was thrown backward into the roiling crowd. The cable, spittin' sparks like it was particularly angry, snaked through the crowd, searing flesh and filling the air with the scent of its passing.

Suddenly released, the crowd bolted, the quick and the dead both, and neither faster than the other, far as I could see. Bee-line away from the portal. Those jammed up inside the portal fought their way out. Wasn't many of them, considering it must have been a few thousand had gone in. Maybe a couple, three dozen. The carousel was still running, the dancers caught up in whatever they was experiencing — don't know what and never will — and more dead Indians just pouring out, taking to their heels as soon as their feet was on solid ground.

The pulses from within the portal were coming slower now, deeper, but more intense. Each one with enough force to form ripples in the dust.

"Get me inside," Callie said. The portal was maybe twenty feet away. "Quickly."

I figured, with my legs shattered, I'd be lucky to make it to the portal with Callie 'fore it commenced to doing whatever it was fixing to do. Or I could make it twenty feet the other direction. Got the feeling that weren't going to be anywhere near enough. I grabbed her by the collar, and crawled. The portal pulsed again, throwing pebbles into the air and rattling my teeth. Callie screamed, likely from the shattered bones dancing around her body. I reached the threshold of the portal, turned around and dragged her up next to me, and then shifted my weight to push her through.

Then the world inverted.

As any good shot-firer can tell you, the explosive ain't the be-all and end-all of the explosion. By careful control of the materials involved and the spaces and hollows in which the fire is born, the shot-firer can shape the charge to direct the force into the rock he wants to turn to rubble, without bringing the roof down over the heads of the miners.

Sometimes, though, it's just plain luck.

Thinking back, I might have deduced it from the fact that the pulses coming from the portal were creating ripples in the dust spreading out from it, like waves in a pond, but directly in front of the portal? That dust just sat there, the footprints of those who'd come through undisturbed. Wasn't in much of a deducin' mood at the time, though.

When the portal tore itself apart, it shattered outward, leaving two lone figures sitting in the middle of the blast zone.

Callie's eyes were closed, her breath rasping. "Did we make it?" she asked.

I struggled to figure out what to say, but when I looked down, it didn't much matter. Calliope Smith, inventor of the Reciprocal Wheel, the woman whose destiny was to kill Destiny itself, was dead.

Ain't much good can be said for leveling a fair chunk of the Chicago World's Fair, and a co-equal amount of Chicago proper to boot. They say real men don't cry, but truth is, when I looked out at the wreckage of the carousel, strewn with bodies both organic and mechanical, at the destruction beyond, can't say my face wasn't wet. Fact was, weren't much between Buffalo Bill's Wild West Show and Lake Michigan that had escaped injury. The Mines Building was sagging into the Transportation Building. Behind it, the Electricity Building was on fire.

I sat there, rocking and crying, Callie's body in my arms, until someone come and took us away.

Don't suppose it should'a come as a surprise, three months later, when a white baby born to a prominent family in London said her first words months before she should'a been able to talk, and they come out in the Crow language, in full sentences, no less. That was the first one to make the papers. I'm sure there was others, didn't warrant any attention. More poor folks than rich, all over the world.

Don't seem to be any rhyme nor reason, now, where souls are being placed, and while memories ain't coming through in what you might call mint condition, well, memories never were the most reliable thing to begin with. Sure do shake up a few things, though. Ain't quite as easy to justify subjecting the masses to generations of poverty if you know there's a better'n even chance that your next life is going to be one of generational poverty. Inheritance laws follow blood, not souls. No less than the Supreme Court undertook to inform a three-year-old Chinese girl that she was in no way entitled to Leland Stanford's fortune, whatever she chose to call herself.

Seems the Social Contract looks a lot different when all the sides get to have a say, and there's been renewed interest in re-examining the field of Ethics, and in applying that to the general jurisprudence, as it were.

Of those who were on the other side of the portal's threshold when it blew, there's been no sign. Been no shortage of classified adverts propping up the income of newspapers across the globe the last ten years, calling for Buffalo Bill Cody or any of his performers, or those who were known to be at the show that day, to reach out to family and friends. Not a one of 'em's been answered legit, best of my knowledge. No different for Coop. I figure all them souls've been destroyed, chewed up by the Great Wheel, turned into the energy that destroyed the sorting mechanism. There's plenty disagree with me. They've gone to God, some say, or reached Nirvana. Maybe the damage done left them unfit for humanity, and they've been put in an animal body. Maybe that last one ain't so far-fetched. Heard tell of a raccoon in Denver as is working on a novel. In French.

Did see Callie, though, earlier this year when I was out East. She was a nine-year-old black boy, giving a lecture at Yale on the mathematical theories underlying Post-Rupture Theophysical Cartography. Went way over my head, but then, she always did.

Author's note: Article text condensed from the *Salt Lake Herald*, Sunday, November 23, 1890 (Twenty-first Year, Number 147, p. 1) - *Heap A Big Scare*.

ABOUT THE AUTHORS

James Chambers is the Bram Stoker Award-winning author of the original graphic novel *Kolchak the Night Stalker: The Forgotten Lore of Edgar Allan Poe* as well as the Lovecraftian novella collection, *The Engines of Sacrifice*, described in a *Publisher's Weekly* starred-review as "...chillingly evocative...." He has also written the story collection *Resurrection House* and the dark, urban fantasy novella, *Three Chords of Chaos*. His tales of crime, fantasy, horror, pulp, science fiction, steampunk, and more have appeared in numerous anthologies and magazines. He has edited and written numerous comic books including *Leonard Nimoy's Primortals*, *Gene Roddenberry's Lost Universe*, *Isaac Asimov's I*Bots*, the graphic novel adaptation of *From Dusk Till Dawn*, and the critically acclaimed "The Revenant" in *Shadow House*. His website is www.jameschambersonline.com.

Jeff Young is a bookseller first and a writer second – although he wouldn't mind a reversal of fortune.

He is an award winning author who has contributed to the anthologies: *Writers of the Future V.26*, *Afterpunk*, *In an Iron Cage: The Magic of Steampunk*, *Clockwork Chaos*, *Gaslight and*

Grimm, By Any Means, Best Laid Plans, Dogs of War, Man and Machine, If We Had Known, Fantastic Futures 13, The Society for the Preservation of C.J. Henderson, TV Gods & TV Gods: Summer Programming. Jeff's own fiction is collected in *Spirit Seeker* and TOI *Special Edition 2 – Diversiforms.* He has also edited the *Drunken Comic Book Monkey* line, *TV Gods* and *TV Gods –Summer Programming.* He has led the Watch the Skies SF&F Discussion Group of Camp Hill and Harrisburg for seventeen years. Jeff is also the proprietor of Helm Haven, the online Etsy and Ebay shops, costuming resources for Renaissance and Steampunk.

David Sherman is the author or co-author of some three dozen books, most of which are about Marines in combat. He has written about US Marines in Vietnam (the *Night Fighters*series and three other novels), and the *DemonTech* series about Marines in a fantasy world. The 18th Race trilogy is military science fiction. Other than military, he wrote a non-conventional vampire novel, *The Hunt*, and a mystery, *Dead Man's Chest.* He has also released a collection of short fiction and non-fiction from early in his writing career, *Sherman's Shorts; the Beginnings.* With Dan Cragg he wrote the popular *Starfist* series and its spin off series, *Starfist: Force Recon* — all about Marines in the Twenty-fifth Century.; and a Star Wars novel, *Jedi Trial.* His books have been translated into Czech, Polish, German, and Japanese. He lives in sunny South Florida, where he doesn't have to worry about hypothermia or snow-shoveling-induced heart attacks. He invites readers to visit his website, novelier.com.

Jody Lynn Nye lists her main career activity as 'spoiling cats.' When not engaged upon this worthy occupation, she writes fantasy and science fiction books and short stories. Since 1987 she has published over 50 books and more than 165 short stories.

Her latest books are *Rhythm of the Imperium* (Baen Books), the third in her humorous military SF series; *Moon Beam* (Baen Books), a young adult science fiction novel with Dr. Travis S. Taylor, and *Daring* (Cat and Dragon Press), a collection of her young adult science fiction and fantasy stories.

Over the last twenty-five or so years, Jody has taught in numerous writing workshops and participated on hundreds of panels covering the subjects of writing and being published at science-fiction conventions. She has also spoken in schools and libraries around the north and northwest suburbs. In 2007 she taught fantasy writing at Columbia College Chicago. In 2017, she became a judge for the Writers of the Future contest, the largest speculative fiction writing contest in the world. She also runs the two-day writers workshop at DragonCon, and reviews fiction for *Galaxy's Edge* Magazine.

Jody lives in the northwest suburbs of Chicago, with her husband Bill Fawcett, a writer, game designer, military historian and book packager, and a black cat, Jeremy.

Her websites are www.jodynye.com and mythadventures.net. She is on Facebook as Jody Lynn Nye and Twitter @JodyLynnNye.

L. Jagi Lamplighter is the author of the YA fantasy series: *The Books of Unexpected Enlightenment*. She is also the author of the *Prospero's Daughter* series: *Prospero Lost, Prospero In Hell,* and *Prospero Regained*. She has a brand-new short story collection, *In the Lamplight,* out through eSpec Books. She has published numerous articles on Japanese animation and appears in several short story anthologies, including *Best Of Dreams Of Decadence, No Longer Dreams, Coliseum Morpheuon, Bad-Ass Faeries* Anthologies (where she is also an assistant editor) and the Science Fiction Book Club's *Don't Open This Book.* Her website is: http://www.ljagilamplighter.com/ Her blog is at: http://arhyalon.livejournal.com/ On Twitter: @lampwright4

Award-winning author and editor **Danielle Ackley-McPhail** has worked both sides of the publishing industry for longer than she cares to admit. In 2014 she joined forces with husband Mike McPhail and friend Greg Schauer to form her own publishing house, eSpec Books (www.especbooks.com). Her published works include six novels, *Yesterday's Dreams, Tomorrow's Memories, Today's Promise, The Halfling's Court, The Redcaps' Queen,* and *Baba Ali and the Clockwork Djinn,* written with Day Al-Mohamed. She is also the author of the solo collections *A Legacy of Stars, Consigned to the Sea, Flash in the Can,* and *Transcendence,* the non-fiction writers' guide, *The Literary Handyman,* and is the senior editor of the *Bad-Ass Faeries* anthology series, *Gaslight & Grimm, Dragon's Lure,* and *In an Iron Cage.* Her short stories are included in numerous other anthologies and collections. Danielle lives in New Jersey with husband and fellow writer, Mike McPhail and three extremely spoiled cats. She can be found on Facebook and Twitter. To learn more about her work, visit www.sidhenadaire.com.

David Lee Summers is the author of eleven novels and numerous short stories and poems. His most recent novels are the global steampunk adventure, *Owl Riders,* and a horror novel set an astronomical observatory, *The Astronomer's Crypt.* His short stories have appeared in such magazines and anthologies as *Cemetery Dance, Realms of Fantasy, Straight Outta Tombstone,* and *Gaslight & Grimm.* He's one of the editors of *Maximum Velocity: The Best of the Full-Throttle Space Tales* from WordFire Press. He's been nominated for the Science Fiction Poetry Association's Rhysling and Dwarf Stars Awards.

When he's not writing, David operates telescopes at Kitt Peak National Observatory. http://www.davidleesummers.com.

Gail Z. Martin writes epic fantasy, urban fantasy and steampunk for Solaris Books, Orbit Books, and Falstaff Books. Series include *Darkhurst, the Chronicles Of The Necromancer, the Fallen Kings Cycle, the Ascendant Kingdoms Saga, the Assassins of Landria* and *Deadly Curiosities.* Newest titles include *Scourge, Trifles & Folly2,* and *Assassin's Honor.*

Larry N. Martin is the author of the new sci-fi adventure novel *Salvage Rat.* He is the co-author (with Gail Z. Martin) of the *Spells, Salt, and Steel/New Templars* series; the Steampunk series *Iron & Blood*; and a collection of short stories and novellas: *The Storm & Fury Adventures* set in the *Iron & Blood* universe. He is also the co-author of the upcoming *Wasteland Marshals* series and the *Cauldron/Secret Council* series.

Michelle D. Sonnier writes dark urban fantasy, steampunk, and anything else that lets her combine the weird and the fantastic in unexpected ways. She even writes horror, although it took her a long time to admit that since she prefers the existential scare over blood and gore. She's published short stories in a variety of print and online venues, and has upcoming projects with eSpec Books and Otter Libris. You can find her on Facebook (Michelle D. Sonnier, The Writer) or at www.michelledsonnier.com. She lives in Maryland with her husband, son, and a variable number of cats. The Clockwork Witch is her first full-length novel.

Jeffrey Lyman is an engineer in the New York City area. His work has appeared in *Sails and Sorcery, Trouble on the Water,* and in *The Defending the Future* anthology series, including the *Best of Defending The*

Future. He was co-editor of *No Longer Dreams* and the *Bad-Ass Faeries* anthology series. He is a 2004 graduate of the Odyssey Writing School and was a winner of the Writers of the Future Award.

Much to his embarrassment, **Bernie Mojzes** has outlived Lord Byron, Percy Shelley, Janice Joplin and the Red Baron, without even once having been shot down over Morlancourt Ridge. Having failed to achieve a glorious martyrdom, he has instead turned his hand to the penning of paltry prose (a rather wretched example of which you currently hold in your hands), in the pathetic hope that he shall here find the notoriety that has thus far proven elusive. His work has appeared in a number of anthologies and magazines, including *Bad-Ass Faeries II* and *III, Gaslight & Grimm, Betwixt Magazine, Daily Science Fiction,* and *What Lies Beneath.* In his copious free time, he published and co-edited *Unlikely Story* (www.unlikely-story.com) and the ever-timely *Clowns: The Unlikely Coulrophobia Remix,* as well as editing *The Flesh Made Word* for Circlet Press.

Should Pity or perhaps a Perverse Curiosity move you to seek him out, he can be found at http://www.kappamaki.com.

Greg Schauer (editor) has been a bookseller since 1979 as the owner of Between Books in Claymont, Delaware. He has also helped produce concerts by local and national bands at the Arden Gild Hall in Arden Delaware, one of the country's oldest continuously run secular utopian art colonies, for more than a decade. In 2014 he teamed up with Danielle Ackley-McPhail and her husband Mike McPhail to form eSpec Books. He has previously worked on *Stories in Between: Between Books 30th Anniversary Anthology* with W.H. Horner and Jeanne Benzel and *Steam-powered Tales of Awesomeness Vol 1* by Brian Thomas and Ray Witte and *With Great Power* with John L. French. He is editor or co-editor on *The Society for the Preservation of CJ Henderson, The Die Is Cast,* and *The Awakened Modern.* He can be contacted at gschauer@betweenbooks.com.

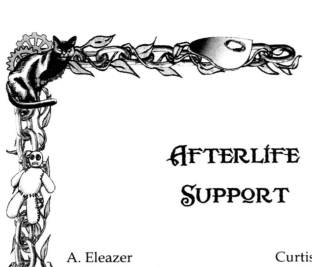

Afterlife
Support

A. Eleazer
Aidan Schneider
Alla Lake
Allison Kaese
Amanda S.
Amy Matosky
Andrew Topperwien
Ann Stolinsky
Ann Wiewall
Anthony R. Cardno
Ashli Tingle
Barbara Silcox
Beth McNeal
Brendan Lonehawk
Bruce E. Coulson
Carl and Barbara Kesner
Carol Gyzander
Catherine Gross-Colten
Cathy Franchett
Cato Vandrare
Chad Bowden
Cheyenne Cody
Chris Cooper
Christopher J. Burke
Cindy Matera
Connie Brunkow
Craig Hackl

Curtis & Maryrita
    SteinhourYew
Dagmar Baumann
Dale A Russell
Dave Hermann
David Mortman
DavidZurek
Derek Devereaux Smith
Donald J. Bingle
D-Rock
Elaine Tindil-Rohr
Eric Hendrickson
Erik T Johnson
Erin Hudgins
Gail Z. Martin
    & Larry N. Martin
Gavran
Gina DeSimone
GMarkC
H Lynnea Johnson
Isaac 'Will It Work'
    Dansicker
Jacalyn Boggs
    AKA Lady Ozma
Jakub Narębski
Jasen Stengel
Jean Marie Ward

Jen Myers
Jenn Whitworth
Jennifer L. Pierce
Jeremy Reppy
John Green
Joseph R. Kennedy
Judy Lynn
Judy Waidlich
Karen Herkes
Katherine Long
Katherine Malloy
Kelvin Ortega
Kevin P Menard
Kumie Wise
Lark Cunningham
Linda Pierce
Lisa Hawkridge
Lorraine J. Anderson
Louise McCulloch
Margaret St. John
Maria V. Arnold
Mark Carter
Mark J. Featherston
Mary M. Spila
Max Kaehn
Michael D. Blanchard
Michael Fedrowitz
Mishee Kearney
Moria Trent
Myranda Summers
Nanci Moy & David Bean
Nathan Turner
Nellie
Nigel Goddard
Paul May
Paul Ryan

PJ Kimbell
Quentin Lancelot Fagan
R.J.H.
Ralf "Sandfox" Sandfuchs
Revek
Richard P Clark
RKBookman
Robert Claney
Ross Hathaway
Sam Tomaino
Scott Elson
Scott Schaper
ShadowCub
Sheryl R. Hayes
Stephen Ballentine
Susan Simko
Tasha Turner
thatraja
Tim DuBois
Tomas Burgos-Caez
Tory Shade
Tracie Lucas
Tracy 'Rayhne' Fretwell
V. Hartman DiSanto
Y. H. Lee

CPSIA information can be obtained
at www.ICGtesting.com
Printed in the USA
FFOW03n1842120518
46540612-48540FF